Rubies Fall

REBECCA M. GIBSON

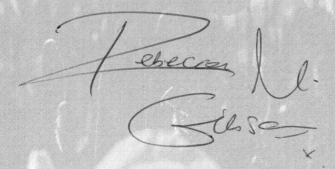

CRUSHING HEARTS AND BLACK BUTTERFLY
PUBLISHING

Editing by CLS Editing
Cover design by Covers by Christian
Book design by Designs2Media

Published by Crushing Hearts and Black Butterfly Publishing, LLC

ISBN 13: 978-1539876809
ISBN: 1539876802

Whilst this novel is set during the First World War, all battles and specific events written about are entirely fictitious. Any relation to real events or people is completely coincidental.

"My friend, you would not tell with such high zest
To children ardent for some desperate glory,
The old lie; Dulce et Decorum est
Pro patria mori."
Wilfred Owen, 1918

England, 28th March 1896

Pain shot through Annabel's body. Her hands tightened on her protruding stomach as the baby squirmed inside her, desperate to break free. She clutched herself tighter, willing the child to stay still and safe.

The next pain came even stronger, and she cried out involuntarily. She told herself she was fine, but a gleam of sweat beaded out across her forehead, betraying her.

"Annabel." Theodore's anxious voice came from the doorway. "Is it time?"

She nodded, there was no use denying it further. Her head felt heavy on her neck. As pain engulfed her once more, she leant against him. The baby was so early. Theodore was sure to grow suspicious. Instead, he wrapped a protective arm around her shoulders and steered her in the direction of their bed chamber.

It seemed to take forever to get there. Annabel was out of breath and exhausted. She didn't know how she would manage the next few hours.

Fear gripped her more intensely than any pain ever could. She didn't want it to happen like this. Not without the one person who it would mean the most to. A single tear trickled down her cheek at the stolen moment.

When Annabel was settled amongst the pillows, Theodore smoothed her dark blonde hair back from her face, kissing her forehead. Concern lined his flawlessly handsome features, making his chocolate eyes gleam even darker.

"Patsy," Annabel whispered, placing a hand on his cheek. "You can't be in here. You don't need to see this. Please, get me Patsy."

Theodore nodded, running from the room. His suit tails hit the doorframe with a thwack as he turned down the corridor. He was meant to be going to a dinner tonight, but Annabel felt sure he'd spend the night pacing his office instead.

Patsy rushed in not ten minutes later, still wearing her hat from her own evening plans.

"How do you feel?" she asked, her cheeks flushed.

Annabel looked at her with fury, and Patsy laughed.

"Not a good question I see." She chuckled as she slid the hat pins from her hair and balanced the elaborate hat on the bedpost. She whipped off her gloves, tossing them onto the table by the window with a flourish. Patsy had improved at an alarming rate over the last few months in the manor. Her knowledge and confidence soared. As she was now only sixteen, they had managed to attribute her age to why she had only just emerged in society. She appeared as if she had never known another kind of life.

Patsy took Annabel's slippery hand just as she let out a long wail. As the pain within her subsided, the sound of a distant hansom cab approaching the manor could be heard. The midwife it housed would be there in record time, chasing the large amount of money the delivery would yield.

As the situation fully sunk in, Patsy's features darkened. Annabel felt sure she was reliving the last birth she had witnessed. The memories flooded Annabel's mind as well until she was blinded by them. With a nervous jerk of Annabel's heart, the baby moved slowly towards its freedom.

As the light of a new day crept its way into the room, Annabel finally collapsed back against the pillows. The room was deadly silent for a few excruciating seconds before it was filled with the sweetest cry she had ever heard. Annabel's heart melted.

"W-what is it?" Patsy whispered to the midwife. She seemed to be speaking from behind a veil. Her voice, filled with so much emotion, sounded just like the old Patsy. The Patsy with fiery hair and ragged clothes. The new version of her was as far removed from that girl as possible.

Annabel's smile split right across her face as the baby was brought into view.

"You have a healthy little boy."

Annabel took the infant to her breast for the first time, wrapping her arms around his tiny body. More love swelled inside her than she even knew was possible. He was exquisite. She stroked a trembling finger along his cheek, watching his features crease with the effort of his first breaths.

They had made this.

Their love had created beauty in the form of new life.

She hugged her son closer, relishing the complexities of every little thing about him. When he opened his eyes some minutes later, they were the exact same shade of blue as Annabel's.

"What's his name?"

A slight pause of anticipation permeated the room whilst Annabel checked to see if the name fit. The first name she had been forced to choose. Every first born son in her family had the same name, and she didn't want to draw attention to her newborn child by breaking the tradition. The next one was more daring. Perfect, much like him.

"Grayson Daniel Brogan, but we'll call him Daniel."

Patsy breathed out a laugh.

"Welcome to the world, Daniel."

Part One

Chapter One

28th March 1914

The room was swathed in darkness, hiding a young man slouched over a cluttered desk. His furiously scratching pen was the only sound in the otherwise silent space. Occasionally, he looked up, unseeing. Crumpling the piece of paper he had been writing on, he tossed it behind him in the general direction of the fireplace. The fire inside had died out hours ago.

Ink was splattered across his face from when the nib of his pen had snapped, sending up a spray of the sticky substance. Deep in thought, he had paused only long enough to pick up another pen and toss the first over his shoulder, where it had speared the dark wood floor. He hadn't bothered to wipe his face.

A few pencil sketches, made on expensive paper, were plastered on the walls behind him—all portraits of people going about their daily lives. There were delivery men stacking crates onto carts, farmers wiping brows or riding horses, and more than a few of his best friend Genevieve.

The young man behind the desk paused for a few seconds to scrawl his name along the bottom of the page with a practised flourish. Gray Brogan. A name which graced the gossip columns almost daily. The name that was due to inherit one of the largest fortunes in the world. He was richer than the king, and society couldn't get enough of him.

The nickname had first been uttered by his aunt Patsy, who flat out refused to call him Daniel like his mother did. Gray liked his shortened name. His given name, Grayson, always made him think of his stiff, pretentious grandfather. Daniel, his middle name, was too common in his opinion. Gray somehow seemed more mysterious. As an aspiring artist and poet, he thought he needed that air of mystery.

Looking up briefly at the sound of the door opening, he saw Genevieve enter, wearing a long pink gown that trailed along the floor behind her.

"You look nice," he muttered, bending back over his work.

"Thanks. You don't."

He looked up again and frowned.

"What's wrong with me?"

"You're covered in ink. Your mother's going to kill you."

"What time is it?"

He pulled a gold watch out of his waistcoat pocket and shot to his feet. "Shit!"

He ran his hands through his hair and dashed towards his room, hoping not to be spotted by anyone on the way. Genevieve's tinkling laugh could be heard just before the door clicked shut.

His valet was waiting for him as soon as he entered. Gray washed quickly from the sink in the corner of his dressing room, combing his hair back with pomade so it stayed in a careful side parting. His valet helped him pull on a crisp white shirt and waistcoat, followed by a black, perfectly fitted suit. He just had his matching bow tie knotted around his neck when the door opened and his mother walked in. His valet bowed his head and silently exited the room.

"You look stunning, Mother, as always."

She smiled, and her eyes—the exact same shade of blue as his—crinkled slightly as she reached up to straighten his tie. "Thank you, Daniel. You look very handsome yourself, like always." She placed a tender kiss on his cheek. "Apart from the ink."

She winked at him, and he spun around, squinting into the full-length mirror behind him.

"I can't see any ink."

Annabel took a carefully folded handkerchief from one of his many drawers. Wetting it slightly, she dabbed at his face until the handkerchief came away blackened, but her son's face was finally clean.

"What will we do with you?" she sighed, smiling again. Annabel let her fingers linger on his cheek for a few seconds after she had finished cleaning it, a wistful expression on her face.

"My little boy is all grown up. Eighteen already and so handsome."

"Oh, Mother, must you be like this? I won't have sadness on my birthday. We should be jolly."

His mother laughed under her breath. "If my son commands it, then it shall be done. Come on then. Escort your old mother down to dinner, will you?"

Gray lifted his arm, bent slightly at the elbow, allowing Annabel to link hers into it.

When Gray entered the ballroom some hours later, every pair of eyes glanced his way. The females with desire, and the males with envy. Walking into the middle of the room alongside Genevieve, he put his hand lightly on her tiny waist, just as the orchestra began to play. He immediately swept her around the floor in a perfect waltz. The first dance was always reserved for his best friend—a well-acknowledged fact to all in attendance.

Their limbs moved gracefully, with an ease that any professional dancer would have killed for. Their steps were flawless, perfectly in sync at all times. They looked stunning together, although, their features held just enough similarity to remind everyone of their family connection—even if no one quite knew exactly how they were related.

Gray's blond hair shone gold beneath the lights, contrasting perfectly with Genevieve's mahogany shade a foot below him. His suit tails whipped back and forth as they turned, entrancing the audience, whilst Genevieve's pink dress swept the floor with the gentle swoosh of expensive fabric. Her delicate fingers around Gray's long ones looked elegant enough for royalty. Everyone in attendance stayed clear of the dance floor as Gray and Genevieve danced, knowing full well they could never match their level of perfection.

Lady Annabel and Lord Theodore Brogan, only slightly less skilled than their son and niece, joined them at the beginning of the second song. Gray's uncle Victor and aunt Patricia Rockwell were next. Their ungraceful step and stumbling feet reassured the other guests, who flooded onto the dance floor in abundance. Multi-coloured skirts covered the polished marble as their wearers swapped partners and sipped champagne. The air of celebration infected everybody's mood for the better.

Gray spent the evening eating too much cake, drinking too much champagne, and dancing so much his feet burned in his leather shoes. He waltzed his way well into the morning, removing first his jacket and next his waistcoat, before rolling his sleeves up past his elbows as the dancing grew faster and their feet grew clumsier.

As the sun started to rise, having shared a few kisses with the man they had all come to see, the young women left. Gray and Genevieve stumbled up the stairs when the ballroom was finally empty, falling over often.

"Shh." Gray laughed. "We'll wake Mother and Father."

They both found this incredibly funny and fled into Gray's rooms as fast as their drunken feet could carry them.

Removing his shoes, Gray skidded along the hardwood floor in his socks, his shins slamming into the side of the copper bath tub. He swore, rubbing the hurt area. Genevieve laughed, ducking behind the wall into his bedroom as Gray lobbed a shoe in her direction.

He threw on the first pair of pyjamas he found, missing the leg hole several times and buttoning them up completely wrong. Walking over to his large sleigh bed, he found Genevieve curled under his black satin sheets and the fur throw pulled up over her head. Gray laughed, jumping on the bed until she knocked out his knees. He fought his way under the covers, fashioning them over their heads to form something of a den where they talked in drunken slurs until well after sunrise.

Chapter Two

Gray woke up to his mother gently shaking his shoulder. He groaned, pulling the blankets higher. Light flooded into the room as Annabel ripped open the curtains, earning another loud groan.

"Mother," Gray exclaimed. A sharp pain pounded in his head as the sunlight shot through the thin skin of his eyelids. He rolled closer to Genevieve, who was evidently in the same delicate state, having retreated farther under the covers as well. Having her there felt strange—almost like they were five years old again and had fallen asleep whilst building forts.

"Morning," she croaked.

"Afternoon, I think," he whispered back, wincing because all sound seemed to be causing him pain.

"Come on, you two." Gray's mother laughed. "I know you're awake."

"Only because you woke us up, Mother," Gray muttered.

"Yes, well, it's half two in the afternoon, my love. You need to eat, and most importantly, you need water. Judging by the noise you made on your way to bed this morning, you drank far too much last night."

She peeled back the covers, brushing the messed up hair off

his face. The pomade still clung to its strands, making it fall back into place easily.

"I can drink as much as I like on my birthday."

Gray's mother laughed as Genevieve sat up slowly, jostling the mattress. Plumping the pillows beneath her head, she downed the water Annabel handed to her in one gulp. Gray followed suit not long after, falling back into his previous position as soon as he had finished. He didn't want to admit it, but the water had helped a lot. Annabel bent forwards and kissed them both on the cheek. She smelled of a flowery perfume and rustled slightly when she moved. Gray found everything about her reassuringly familiar. Her long hair tickled his face where it had been styled to fall over her left shoulder.

"I'll leave you both to get dressed, but you have to be down for tea, Daniel."

He made a low sound of acknowledgement but otherwise didn't move.

"You can join us, Jen, if you like," said Annabel. "Bring Billy, I don't want you to leave him on his own again."

"Yes, Anna." Genevieve nodded, her mouth now full of toast. "I'll ask Papa." She sprayed crumbs as she spoke, her usual decorum absent in the comfort of her best friend's room.

As soon as Annabel left, Genevieve got a mischievous twinkle in her eyes, and she threw her toast at Gray. It hit him in the face, leaving a streak of butter on his cheek.

"That's for the shoe last night."

"It doesn't count if I don't even remember it," he muttered into the pillow, but his mouth curled into a small smile. "I feel terrible."

"So do I. We were incredibly drunk."

"Was a jolly good laugh, though."

"I think we blew their minds, Gray."

Genevieve buttered another slice of toast from the silver tray, holding it out for Gray, who propped himself up on his elbows and began to eat.

They ate every last piece of food, finding they were rather hungrier than they had thought, whilst trying unsuccessfully to patch up the holes in their memories.

Genevieve decided it was best to visit her papa, invite him to tea, and help him pick out an appropriate outfit. Gray eventually rolled out of bed, making it downstairs in a grey day suit and black tie. As he walked into the family parlour with a well-loved book in one hand, a butler placed a large black coffee in his other.

His nose buried in the book, he sipped at the bitter liquid as he sat down, letting the warmth flood into his sore muscles and bring him slowly back to life. Another butler brought in a tray of small sandwiches shortly after, and Gray placed his book down on the side table beside his father.

"I wish you wouldn't read that book, Daniel," Theodore said.

Gray shifted in his seat. "What's wrong with it? It's a good book."

"I don't doubt it, son, but—"

"You just have an issue with Wilde."

"I don't have an *issue* with Wilde. I just don't think he is an appropriate role model for my son."

"Well, I like him, and isn't that all that counts?"

"Why isn't he appropriate, Uncle Teddy?" Genevieve asked as she entered with her father and seated herself on Gray's other side.

"I don't agree with his lifestyle. He was imprisoned you know, Daniel."

"Really?" asked Genevieve. She had never taken much interest in literature so was completely oblivious, although, she loved a juicy tale.

Gray smiled at her eager expression. "Yes, gross indecency—" he paused for effect. "—with other men. Two years' hard labour."

Genevieve let out a low whistle, and Theodore chuckled as he turned the page of a newspaper resting on his knee.

"I think that's enough of this conversation. We needn't talk about prison when none of you are ever heading there. I've been blessed with a beautiful family."

Gray pretended to be sick into his coffee cup, and they all laughed. Although Gray's mother, who was seated by the window, looked down with a sadness in her eyes Gray couldn't place. He thought she was probably worried about his future. She was always worried.

"Anyway," Annabel stated, reassembling her face within the blink of an eye. She had gone from vulnerable back to just Mother in the space of a second. "You have your whole life ahead of you. Let's not dwell on illegal pursuits and abnormalities. I'm sure you have hundreds of good stories from last night, and it looks like Jen's itching to tell me all about them."

Genevieve needed no further encouragement. She was off in a stream of words as if they had been building up all day, ready to burst forth at the exact right moment. Her father, Billy, laughed at her enthusiasm, eyes twinkling at the evident joy on her face. Her food went forgotten, still without a single bite missing long after everybody else had finished. They learnt of the newly engaged woman with the ruffled dress, suggesting she was hiding the real reason for her shotgun wedding. Annabel glanced down again, and Gray wondered, not for the first time, whether this had been the reason for his own parent's quick nuptials as well. The dates never quite added up, no matter how he tried to work them out.

There were more stories of ghastly dresses, necklines Genevieve considered far too low, and men she thought too forward. There were couples named and shamed as creeping off into abandoned corners of the house and even the particularly vivid retelling of a heated argument that had taken place just after Annabel and Theodore had gone up to bed. Gray listened to this story eagerly, laughing when the small event was blown completely out of proportion and thinking that his friend could be a phenomenal novelist if she would only take an interest in the art.

The day ended in the smallest parlour with Gray curled in a comfortable armchair, nursing a small tumbler of whisky in his hand. As he headed up to bed a few minutes later, his father called after him, a hopeful twinkle in his dark eyes.

"Daniel, you are coming hunting tomorrow, aren't you?"

Gray nodded. "Of course, why not?"

His father smiled and stood to clap him on the shoulder. "Sweet dreams, my son. Get plenty of rest. You will need all your energy to outride me."

Gray laughed. "All right, Father. Whatever you say."

The next morning, Gray's valet helped him into a pair of cream jodhpurs and a brown tweed jacket. Gray splashed his face with water to wake himself up, grabbing a slice of toast from the tray by his bed. As he made his way downstairs, he hit his riding crop rhythmically against the brown leather of his boots.

"Morning, Daniel."

"Morning, Father."

"Have you eaten?"

Gray held up his half-finished piece of toast, taking another bite.

"Jolly good. Are you ready then?"

"Mhmm."

Teddy handed his son a long rifle. Gray took it, stuffing the rest of the toast into his mouth to free up his hands.

"I know it's not strictly hunting season, but I just fancied it, you know?"

Gray nodded again, trying to swallow the large amount of bread in his mouth.

"And heck, if I can't organise a hunt when I ruddy well please what is the point of all this power?"

"Your modesty astounds me, Father."

Teddy laughed.

"So long as it doesn't rain on us," Gray continued. "Will there even be any animals worth shooting?"

"I hope so. They have to earn their keep on my land somehow." Teddy laughed again as he saw Gray roll his eyes sarcastically.

Two magnificent horses stood waiting for them in the drive, Billy holding onto their reins. Gray and Teddy offered him a quick greeting before jumping onto their steeds and kicking them into a trot. Gray pulled on the reins steering out of the manicured grounds and into the wild meadow lands beyond. The meadow was lined with a light sprinkling of trees where the wildlife tended to live.

"I'll race you to the stream, old man," he shouted.

His father laughed, a smile splitting across his handsome face as they broke into a gallop.

The wind whipped into Gray's face, removing any traces of sleep still left in him and filling him with exaltation. He laughed almost manically as his father caught up to him, splashing into the stream just a second before his son.

"Old man, you say?"

Without pausing to laugh along with him, Gray pointed the rifle at his father. His grin revealed all his sparkling teeth.

"Daniel, what are you doing?"

Teddy tried to sound humorous, but the shock of Gray's move was evident in his voice.

Gray pulled the trigger.

The bullet flew an inch to the left of Teddy's face, straight between the eyes of a grazing deer a few hundred yards behind him. Gray boomed out a laugh.

"Got him."

"You very nearly got me."

"I had it all under control, Father. I promise. The wind was blowing the wrong way for the shot to have gone anywhere near you, had I been slightly out."

"Well, now that's reassuring. What if you had been more than *slightly* out?"

"Then we wouldn't be having this conversation. As it happens, I wasn't. Thus, we have got ourselves a deer in the first fifteen minutes. A record I would say."

"You're a damn near perfect shot, son. God help the Germans if this blasted war ever breaks out. Well done, but don't do that again. I value my head much more than having a deer for dinner."

"I wouldn't have missed, Father, I'm damn near perfect." He laughed, riding over to where the deer's lifeless body had hit the ground, its deep scarlet blood oozing into the ground.

When they returned later that day, their cheeks flushed with laughter, it was to find Genevieve stood on the driveway, tapping her foot.

"I thought you'd never come back. I've been bored stiff."

"We shot three deer, Jen. All through the head."

"Oh, brilliant," she said with a straight face, making Gray smile. "You have killed some animals, now onto what we are going to do with the rest of our day."

Genevieve took Gray's hand, walking him upstairs and into his room where she had laid out a fresh suit, hat, and coat.

"I'll wait for you outside whilst you make yourself smell more human."

Gray swiped her arm playfully, and she laughed.

"You know I love you, but the smell of horse isn't something I'm particularly fond of on anyone that isn't my papa, and even then it's no perfume."

He washed and dressed as quickly as he could whilst Genevieve conversed with him through the closed door.

"What's the occasion?" he asked when he was deemed suitable for the outside world.

"Do we need an occasion? How about because we are young, filthy rich, and in desperate need of a way to spend our millions."

"You mean my millions?"

"If you're going to get technical, it's your parents' millions, but there we are."

"All right, so what's the plan?"

"We're going into town to eat some lunch, get hideously drunk, and make a real spectacle of ourselves."

Gray laughed, holding out his arm for her to take. "Sounds perfect."

Chapter Three

Oblivious to the growing torment sweeping the rest of the country, Gray spent his time as he had always spent it. By day, he remained holed up in his writing room, the curtains closed and a pen in his hand. By night, he attended a barrage of parties and dinners with Genevieve, keeping himself firmly at the top of the social calendar. He was so busy with the pace of his opulent life that, when the country was officially declared in a state of war, Gray did little more than just raise his head.

His father now worked for the war committee, so the sight of important looking men with their shiny black shoes clomping anxiously along the marble foyer, became as much a part of the house's routine as waking up in the morning.

Steadily, the young men in the house enlisted, either one by one or sometimes in large groups, to fight alongside their pals on the front. Before they knew it, the household was almost entirely run by women and the men deemed too unfit or old to fight.

Every other person Gray saw was wearing khaki. They strutted along the streets, bearing wide grins of pride and pretty girls on their arms. They laughed as they joked of heroism and gallantry. Throughout the streets, posters of soldiers and union jacks were pasted on every wall and notice board. The air of excitement that flooded the town was so thick, one could almost reach out and grasp it.

Despite the many distractions in Gray's life, it wasn't long before the brewing war reached even him, hunched over the desk in his gloomy office. The war slowly infiltrated the words of his poetry whilst more and more of the sketches pinned to his wall were of the young men in their uniforms or of women waving them off. One particularly striking image, done in soft pencil strokes, depicted a young woman with a union jack clasped in her hand. She was waving it like a handkerchief as her sweetheart marched away from her.

Scared of his powerful father and of him pulling the wealth from beneath their feet, the suited men who visited the house every day tried to pay no mind to Gray when he walked past them in his civilian clothes. Yet, he saw the way they looked at him. People were polite at first, but they turned scornful in their stares. Their eyes grew cold and distant as they moved past him silently. He was young, fit, and strong—perfect for the war.

"Why don't you become an officer, lad?" one of the gentlemen asked as he stood with Theodore in the entrance hall.

Gray had been dragged into the conversation as he'd tried to make his way into town. He looked at the floor, shuffling his feet. His father clapped him on the shoulder.

"I think he would be better placed working for the war with me. Wouldn't you, son?"

"Well, I—"

"He is the perfect breed for an officer, Brogan. You must see that."

"We have plenty of young men for the jobs in France. I think my son needs to be here, working with me."

"Father I think I'd like—"

"I'm sure your father knows what's best for you, young sir. You will be a fine man if you turn out like him."

Gray's heart sank. He loved his father and respected him more than anyone else, but he didn't want to become him. He dreaded boardrooms and stuffy men in black suits. Gray wanted to write and draw, not listen to politics or business. However, that wasn't an easy opinion to convey, especially not now. In spite of this, he just nodded slightly, smiling a tight smile as the men continued to talk about him as if he were a particularly well-bred racehorse. Genevieve didn't have this problem. She wasn't expected to work or go to war. She could sit and write all she pleased if she was so inclined.

As the weeks progressed, the seeds of doubt that had been planted inside him were growing into a fierce desire to help. He used to be looked at with reverence when he walked through the town, but now people averted their gaze, whispering about him behind their gloved hands in much more sinister tones. The town's people were beginning to despise him. They thought him arrogant, above them in some way. His father could let the working-class men die for their country but wasn't willing to sacrifice his own son. Gray heard them saying these things as he went into shops and tea rooms. He heard them scoff as he came out with wrapped parcels in elaborate packaging and ribbons.

Eventually, Gray even started to disgust himself.

Did he think himself superior?

What right did he have to take up an office job, earning sickening amounts of money, when other men were giving their lives for a few shillings?

He'd seen the papers as he drank his morning coffee, the pages and pages of names. As he'd set the paper down, he noticed the black ink had rubbed off on his fingers, the last legacy of the fallen.

Chapter Four

The rally took place two months after the country's monumental announcement. Gray, a patriotic poster staring at him from his dressing room wall, wore a brown suit and a pair of supple leather shoes to make his way into the town on foot. He carried a varnished walking cane with a silver lion's head on the top, not because he needed it, but because he thought it made him look somewhat regal. The lion would surely prove he was patriotic. He twirled it in his hand as he walked, feeling the sun's warm touch on his back, the exercise lifting his spirits. The folded poster tickled his thigh as it rested in his pocket.

He arrived in town a little early so decided to visit the park on his way. He had brought a small leather sketchbook and figured he could attempt a drawing or two while he waited. As he entered the park, he wondered for a moment, as he had on many an occasion, what he would find if he went for a long walk in the woods beside it. The dense gathering of trees seemed to stretch out indefinitely.

He was expressly forbidden to enter them, and he knew his mother would find out somehow should he risk it. People were always watching him in some form or other. He wouldn't even get away with sitting just inside the tree line, a sketchbook resting against his knee. Instead, he settled on drawing the way the sun shone through the paper thin leaves from a distance. The earthy scent of the setting filled his nose, making him smile softly while he worked.

As the lines of pencil slowly formed into a complete image, he could hear the distant sound of a celebration. The sounds were not dissimilar to those played when the first soldiers had signed up, marching off in their smart uniforms with rifles resting on their shoulders. There were bugles playing, louder and louder as they grew closer. Soon, cheering joined the music, and the noise grew more intense as people became infected by the merriment.

Gray set down his pencil and blew on the picture to remove any stray residue that might smudge the drawing. He smiled as he saw the image lit up by the afternoon sun. He rose to his feet, putting his hat back on his head and whistling ever so slightly out of tune as he continued towards the town centre. The walk was not a long one, so he didn't even make it to the end of the song before he was stepping on the smooth cobbles of town. As he rounded the corner by his favourite little tea room and strolled into the centre, he saw a red, white, and blue draped podium had been erected directly in front of the town hall.

A magnificent line of men stood on top of the stage, all dressed in freshly pressed red uniforms with gleaming golden buttons. Gray's eyes ran over them appreciatively, seeing how the outfits flattered each of the men perfectly. It made them look strong, handsome, and brave all at the same time. Imagining his own body dressed as such, his smile grew to almost painful extremes. Remembering himself, he snapped back to his surroundings.

An audience had already gathered in the streets as a higher ranked soldier got up onto the podium, to deafening cheers, and addressed them. He introduced himself as Major Corvin. The major looked just past middle age and had a fleshy build as if used to three good meals every day. He talked with a booming, upper-class voice, captivating the crowd with a clever air of directing his speech to each man personally. It seemed they were recruiting more men for the war, and he made it sound phenomenal.

Squeezing to the front as if he were in a trance, Gray found himself cheering at the major's words with everyone else. The crowd members, recognising him instantly, parted without thought. Fixing his gaze directly on Gray, the major's moustachioed mouth turned up into a menacing grin. He had found the perfect specimen.

"You!" he bellowed, pointing directly at him. "Have you enlisted?"

"N-n-no," Gray stuttered, surprised by being called out in front of everyone.

The major frowned, looking both furious and disappointed at the same time. Beneath it, there was a sparkle in his eyes. Gray was playing right into his hungry hands.

"Why not, lad? Do you not care about your country?"

Gray's stupefied mouth seemed unable to form words. His lips moved soundlessly as they grappled for the correct utterance.

"Come up here."

Gray hesitated for a moment, looking around at every pair of eyes now fixed on him. He blushed as he walked up to the podium where the major clapped him on the back like an old friend. He possessed a surprising amount of strength, making Gray stumble.

"By your attire, young man, I would hazard a guess that you are the famous Mister Brogan?"

Gray nodded to a loud cheer from the audience and several

wolf whistles. The rules of decorum that imprisoned the twentieth century had fallen down within the air of celebration. Employing his usual charm, Gray grinned. Captivating a crowd was something he could do in his sleep. His handsome face enthralled them as he dipped his hat forwards ever so slightly.

"Good day, ladies," he crooned to general titters of nervous laughter.

"I see you are already popular with the women, but will you become popular with your king? Will you fight with us and serve our country, or will you shame us and stay darning socks with the females?"

The crowd booed, responding exactly as the major wanted. They were in the palm of his hand.

"Do you think yourself too good for your king?" He paused for effect, looking around at the crowd as if he were performing in a theatre.

Gray said nothing. His heart was in his mouth. The crowd stared at him, each holding their breath for his response. One could have heard a pin drop.

Somewhere in the distance, a dog barked in a frenzied, wild sound that shattered the silence. It seemed to rile the crowd, which shifted with a rustle of material and an intake of breath.

"Come on, Brogan. You scared?" someone yelled out.

"The big house has turned you weak," another cried.

"Are you a coward, boy? Don't be a chicken."

Gray turned a significant shade of red. A light sheen of moisture broke out across his face. He felt another bead of sweat trickle down between his shoulder blades, and prayed for a breath of wind to alleviate the stifling atmosphere he found himself in.

"What kind of shot are you, my lad?"

Gray jumped as the major directed the question to him. He stood beside him, his hand still resting on Gray's arm. He reassembled his face, smiling at the chance to please this tough looking man.

"Damn near perfect, Major."

The crowd practically screamed with glee. The hostile atmosphere shattered back into celebration. Gray jumped as the major shoved a form into his hand immediately. His name and details were already written in a neat hand at the top. This had clearly been prepared in advance, in the hope of this exact eventuality. Gray knew his opportunity to prove himself, outside the grand manors and parlours his family owned throughout the country, had opened up. This was his chance to make his family proud. Without waiting for proof of his age to be presented, the major held out a pen.

"But…you've written my age wrong, sir. I'm eighteen. Not nineteen."

The major smiled. "I thought you'd want to see action, son. You want to be in France, don't you? What's one little white lie?"

Gray smiled and took the pen. With a shaky hand, and the jeers from the crowd still fresh in his mind, he positioned his pen at the bottom of the form. Taking a deep breath, he signed his name—the elaborate signature glistened on the page for a while as the sun hit the wet ink.

The accompanying cheer was so loud that Gray was forced back a step. Their hands were raised, their handkerchiefs now waving at him. There were squeals of delight from the women and shouts from the men. They surged forwards, helping him down from the podium with an almost desperate need to touch some part of him as he passed through the crowd. He felt like a hero already.

The problem of his future seemed to have been solved in an instant. The hours of doubt, of wondering whether to enlist or not, and the moments he had stood dumb on the podium, seemed to him like a waste of precious time. The only option clear to him now was to serve. To fight for his family, his king, and his country. To protect the language with which his idols all wrote. He would be a part of the great, rich history of England.

Cheered on by his example, the other young men in attendance pushed forwards to form a long line into the town hall. Friends smiled at each other, heckling in good humour until they stood in the line with them. None of their ages were checked either. The army just took their word as gospel.

For the men, this was not only their chance to serve their country, this was their chance to serve beside Gray Brogan—and they were desperate.

The major winked at him, not even worried he was signing over someone a year too young to fight.

Gray was pushed over to the town hall as well. Although, he didn't have to wait in line. The inside had been transformed by the army. A trestle table had been erected in the entrance, behind which three khaki-clad men sat in readiness with a stack of enlistment forms. Inside the hall, there were scales for weighing people all around the room. More uniform wearing men strolled around with measuring tapes and clipboards, nodding as they noted down a figure. Gray averted his eyes from the other men, lined up in front of more tables all in various stages of undress, dependent on what the particular station they were at was testing.

Despite him enlisting with the others, Gray's much higher social status had not gone unnoticed, and thus he was ushered into a small office where a doctor with a long white coat thrown over his grey shirt sat behind a much more substantial desk.

"Ah, Brogan isn't it? I was told you would be coming. We set up this room just for you. Don't want the officers mixing with the other folk now, do we?"

"Oh, I am not enlisting as an officer, Doctor. I'm going to be a private. I want to prove myself there first."

"Nonsense, boy. You're richer than the bleeding king. You can't be mucking around with the farmers and shop workers."

"Well, you see, I don't have any army experience. So I thought—"

"Neither have most of the officers we have over there now, and they're all doing a mighty fine job, if you ask me. That's what we have training for."

The doctor had come over to him and was eyeing him up like a slab of steak. This made Gray's blood boil. Who did this man think he was to speak to Grayson Daniel Brogan like he was a naughty schoolboy?

"I think you've forgotten your place, Doctor," he snapped.

The doctor took a step backwards, nearly colliding with his desk. His mouth started to move as if he meant to speak, but no words were audible.

"I shall do as I bloody well please with my life. I am, as you put it, richer than the bleeding king. Why should I become an officer when someone much more in need of the money and better equipped to the job can take my place? We are fighting for a cause far greater than you or I, and I shan't like the responsibility of mucking the whole thing up. I shall be a private, and if my skills prove me more suited to officer standing out on the front, then so be it. Until then, can we just get this ruddy examination over with so I can get back to my life?"

"Oh, um, yes. Yes, of course, Gra— Mister Brogan. Can you please stand behind this line and read out the letters on the wall?"

Within the next few minutes, he was measured, weighed, and prodded—his cheeks flaring bright red as he stood in nothing more than his underwear. He tried to remain aloof in front of the doctor but couldn't help removing his clothes in a series of awkward, clumsy movements when he needed to and replacing them in much the same manner. He passed all the tests with ease. A picture of perfect physical ability, he was the kind of soldier they desperately needed.

The important looking men, sporting stripes on their arms and medals on their chests, tried again to get him to sign up as an officer. Gray ignored them, as he filled out yet more paperwork and collected his pack, containing all the items the government thought he would need. He winced when he was given the khaki uniform. The clothes were standard issue and not tailored. The heavy boots wouldn't fit at all. He looked at them with poorly hidden disgust, vowing to order a better pair before he was sent away for training. He'd be done for if he ruined his feet before even getting to France. He would set his tailor on the uniform at once. Thinking of all the things he could buy to put in his new pack made his smile re-emerge as he loaded his arms with the trappings of his new life.

Some of the people he met in the town hall, and even through the streets of the town, argued his insistence to enter the war as a private. Some of them applauded his decision. However, everyone was shocked. The subject was only left alone when he stated he would join as a private or not at all. A Brogan serving as a private was better than a Brogan not serving.

Returning home many hours later, and with some fairly

substantial bills charged to his family accounts, he was positively giddy with excitement and full of optimism at the heights the decision would surely raise him to. Just to wear that uniform—once it had been tailored—and to be amongst the line of soldiers with gleaming buttons seemed like an extremely bright future indeed.

Chapter Five

Nobody was in the house that day for Gray to tell of his new-found profession. His father was in London and wasn't due back until the evening. His mother was out with his aunt, taking tea or some other frivolity.

Rushing upstairs, he instructed his valet to leave the pack in his dressing room. As each of his new possessions arrived at the house within the next hour, he packed them carefully. His valet tried to assist, bringing the parcels to his room and automatically attempting to put them away.

"Blake, no. I wish to sort them out myself."

"But why, sir? This is my job."

Gray smiled at the man, so similar in age to himself.

"Because this is my venture, my foray into the real world. I must do everything myself."

The valet laughed, leaning carefully against a chest of mahogany draws and folding his arms across his chest. "Then our roles have somewhat reversed, sir."

"Don't go getting ideas," Gray said with laughter in his voice. He knew he shouldn't talk to the staff, but he and Blake had gotten on since they were children. Back then, Blake's father had prepared his tiny suits every morning.

"Whilst you're here, you can fetch my leather folder from my office. Make sure you put plenty of paper inside it. I plan to draw and write everything I see."

The valet laughed again, but he knew his place and quickly gathered the requested items. Once Gray had received them, he placed them at the top of his pack, securing the fastenings with a triumphant smile.

"This—" he gestured to his pack as he stood up "—is to be the turning point of my life." He grinned, and proceeded to dash downstairs, a significant bounce to his step. "Pour me some brandy, Blake, would you? Have it ready in the main parlour. This day calls for celebration," he called over his shoulder.

His valet chuckled and hurried down the corridor in the opposite direction, where he would be racing down the servant's stairs so he could arrive in the parlour before his master.

Gray paced up and down the parlour with his glass pressed into his hand, but he hardly drank a drop. He tried sitting down. He even picked up a book and thumbed through to the last page he had read. However, after going over the same line at least ten times, he set the book back down and practically jumped out of his seat. His mother's clicking footsteps in the foyer were a welcome relief.

"Mother," he exclaimed as he ran from the room and almost collided with her.

"Daniel, what are you doing? Are you all right?"

"Yes, yes. How is Aunt Patsy?"

She looked into his face with a quizzical expression. "F-fine. Thank you, Daniel. The children are doing well too. Little Rupert has taken up drawing. I promised Patsy I would tell you that. I thought perhaps you could give him a little help. He does so look up to you."

As she spoke, she delicately removed her gloves and hat, handing them to a silent maid beside her. Once she was unburdened by the items, Gray threw his arms around her waist like he was still a child.

"I have had a marvellous day, Mother."

She patted his head, running her fingers through his golden hair. "Come on. Let's get into the parlour, and you can tell me all about it over a nice cup of tea."

The maid beside her, a new girl to the former one who had gone to put away the hat, curtsied and scurried off to make the beverage.

Annabel had a smile on her lips, probably noticing the excited flush in her son's cheeks or the grin splitting across his face. She put her arm through his, and together, they sat by the window in the exact seats, it was rumoured, Gray's mother and father had had their first unchaperoned conversation.

"I wanted to wait until Father came home. I wanted to have Jen here too, but everybody's out, and I can't hold it in anymore."

His mother leant forwards in her chair and clasped her son's hands in her own. She was relishing Gray's enthusiasm and was desperate to find out what had made him so happy.

"I've enlisted," he blurted out, his fingers fidgeting within his mother's.

"Enlisted in what, love?"

"The war, of course, Mother." Gray looked into his mother's face, expecting to see the same joy he felt mirrored on her feminine features, but it had suddenly gone pale.

"The—the war?"

"Yes, Mother. Are you all right? I've joined up as a private. They tried to convince me to go officer, but how poetic to be just one of the men fighting for his country."

His mother continued to look at him with a stupefied expression on her beautiful face.

"Say something, Mother. Isn't it brilliant? It's the beginning of my life!"

"You're a fool, Daniel Brogan," she whispered. "A bloody fool."

"W-what?"

"This isn't some party with your friends that you can leave whenever you get bored. This is war. People die at war, Daniel."

"Oh, would you stop worrying about me for one minute? Must you smother me my entire life? What makes me so much more special than every other man dying for his country?"

"You're my son."

"Every man in that newspaper is someone's son, Mother. Don't you get that? What do I tell my own sons in five, ten, twenty years' time, if I'm the only man who didn't do what was right?"

"We have spoken about this before. You are not useless here. You have money, power, and influence. You can help far more from here than you ever could in Flanders or France."

Frustrated, Gray threw his arms in the air, accidentally knocking over the fresh tray of tea a maid had placed on the table not five minutes earlier. The china crashed onto the floor as the hot liquid leapt onto his shoes, soaking into the rugs and up the hem of his trousers. They both jumped at the sound.

The gold tray spun on the floor for several seconds before it finally came to rest a few feet away. Gray tried to apologise, stuttering out meaningless words as the maids and butlers hurried to try to clear the worst of the mess. Annabel had turned her face to the wall, and Gray could only see her expensively clad back. Her long neck was bent down as her face rested in her right hand. A stray lock of dark blonde hair had escaped its fastening and was now resting upon her shoulder.

"You do not understand the love a mother feels towards her children, but the love I feel for you is far, far greater. I made a promise to myself before you were born that you would never come in harm's way, that I would protect you so you never had to see hardship. I won't go back on that promise."

Although he couldn't see her face, Gray imagined it to be buried in sadness. The kind she only wore when she thought no-one could see. When she was thinking about something locked in her mind—something she would never talk about.

"I'm sorry, Mother," he whispered as he walked over to her. He placed a hand lightly on her shoulder and kissed the top of her head. "We all have to make sacrifices for the war effort."

Unable to think of anything further to say, Gray walked out of the room, stepping on his heels to remove his tea-soaked shoes as he did so. He left them where they fell without breaking his step, knowing one of the staff would find them in a matter of seconds and have them back, polished and perfect, in his room by the morning.

Heading straight to his office when he got upstairs, Gray closed the curtains with a harsh, angry movement so the room was once more thrown into darkness. He dumped himself into a chair and banged his fist against the table. He didn't understand. He'd thought everyone would be so pleased.

As he always did in such times, he took up his pen in frustration, piercing the page on his first attempt at getting out his muddled thoughts. Scrunching up the paper and throwing it over his shoulder, he started on a new drawing. Without paying attention, he had drawn himself standing on the podium, the crowd a sea of expectant heads. The pen made the picture harsh, more real than if he had drawn it in pencil. Looking at the image, those same feelings of triumph came back into his system. He pictured his pack, sitting in the middle of his dressing room, and he smiled to himself.

A few hours passed before the raised voices started to filter down the corridor, growing closer towards Gray.

"Annabel you're being ridiculous. Of course, he wanted to sign up. All the men his age have already gone to the front. He probably feels he has been left behind. I know I would have done the same thing at his age. He wants to help his country. That's an admirable trait in any man."

"He's only eighteen. He can't be sent away can he?"

The echo of his father's shoes indicated he had moved back down the corridor, closer to his wife.

"I will talk to him, Annabel, and see what I can do, but he's already enlisted, I think he's made his decision."

The doorknob turned just a few seconds later, and his father's form came through the doorway. His mother stood behind him but quickly continued past to her own room. Theodore closed the door.

"Your mother told me. How are you feeling?" He walked towards his son slowly and then perched on the desk beside him.

"I was feeling great. I felt more complete than I ever have before. Everyone was screaming and cheering me on, and it was phenomenal. I was making everyone in the town proud. I thought I would make Mother proud too, but it seems that's not possible."

"Daniel, you don't have to make your mother proud. We are both proud of you already."

"But are you not pleased I have signed up? I don't want to be that rich boy who was too cowardly to fight for his country like everybody else."

His father just smiled knowingly, nodding his head as if deep in thought.

"I can get you a job at home. You can work with me or in a training camp. You can still be a part of the war without going to France."

"No, I want to be one of the men. A private. Please do not argue with me, Father. I want to prove to everyone, to you, that I can stand on my own. Growing up in such fortunate circumstances I've had opportunities no-one else can even dream of, and I am grateful for it. I promise I am. Yet, I can't sit here whilst people in the town are dying for me. I can't just sit in this manor house. it's wrong."

His father didn't argue any further. He seemed to have come into the room without any drive to convince him to stay at home. He must have known Gray had made up his mind. Arguing would only make him leave on bitter terms. He could never forgive himself for that. They sat together for a while, discussing the happenings of the day— Gray growing more and more excited as he spoke. Neither one of them wanted to face Annabel until they strictly had to. They only left the darkened room when a uniformed butler entered to announce dinner.

They found Annabel in the parlour, staring at the tea stain that stood out against the rugs, despite the scrubbing it had undergone since Gray had been upstairs. She held a book, the same book Gray had tried to read earlier, in her hands. She didn't look like she was reading it either. As they walked in, she looked up.

"I'm going to the front, Mother. Sorry if that upsets you, truly, but I must go play my part. I couldn't live with myself if I stayed behind."

The book fell out of his mother's hand, landing on the floor with a dull thud. His father retrieved it and touched his wife's hand gently. The look of despair in Annabel's face grew more agonised with every passing second.

Gray shuffled his feet. "I've been to France before. I can speak the language fluently. Besides, Father said I'm a near perfect shot."

"That you are, my boy." Theodore left his wife's side and clapped Gray's shoulder, full of pride.

"But…but no, Daniel. Just no." Annabel spoke up, her voice strained. "When would you… No."

"I leave in a little under a week. We're catching the train on Monday at noon. Mother, are you all right?" Gray knelt down on the floor, taking the older woman's hand.

She looked into his face deeply. "Why would you do this?"

Gray looked down, ashamed. "I… I thought maybe you would be proud."

His father sat down on a chair behind him. "We are, son. Just shocked is all."

"My baby boy," Annabel said, touching Gray's cheek. "You're not old enough to fight."

"I'm eighteen, Mother, and I've been declared of perfect fitness. I'm ready for this."

"But why now?"

His grin reappeared as he remembered the triumphant afternoon he had experienced. "I was at the rally, Mother, and it's as if this is what I am meant to do with my life. As if God himself has picked me for this exact purpose. I can't let down my king and country. I just can't."

"Sweetheart, it isn't going to be glamorous."

"But…but it'll be over before Christmas anyway, and then I will be home. Everybody's saying it."

He was starting to feel guilty, ashamed of his quick decision and how it was affecting his family. His father was proud, but he could tell his mother was beside herself.

"Annabel," his father attempted, "Daniel's a brilliant shot. No-one will get within one hundred yards of him. He will do his country proud. I'm certain of it. Besides, once you've enlisted, you can't get out of it I'm afraid."

A tear slid down the woman's face, and Gray reached for her, folding himself into her comforting embrace whilst tears clouded his eyes as well.

"What is the point of you being the most powerful man in the country if you can't exempt your own son?" she whispered over Gray's shoulder.

"We both know I could, Annabel, but it isn't what he wants. Don't… Don't say what I see in your eyes. This is his decision."

She rubbed Gray's back, clinging to him that much tighter and rocking him gently as she had done when he was a child.

"You need to tell Genevieve. Teddy, call for her, will you?"

Gray heard his footfalls fade away as his father exited the room. The mother and son sat in their own world, each hyper aware of the other's love now they knew they would be separated for the first time in a matter of days. They broke away from each other when they heard the lighter step of Genevieve's feet. Turning, Gray caught sight of her face. She was livid.

She had been in the town all day and must have already heard the rumours about Gray enlisting. Teddy's appearance at her door would have just confirmed them.

Her pale skin had turned bright red. She ran straight up to him, slapping her small hand against his cheek so hard that Gray's face whipped to the side, his cheek burning. He flexed his jaw, reaching a hand up to touch the sore spot in disbelief.

"You're an idiot, Grayson. An absolute idiot."

She reached around him, in contrast to her previous action, and squeezed him to her as tightly as she could. He hugged her back with equal strength before she ran from the room without looking back.

He made to follow her, but his father laid a hand on his shoulder, holding him steady.

"Jen will be fine. I promise. Just worry about yourself." He patted his son's cheek, offering him a hug before following Genevieve out the door. Although, his destination was the dining room where their dinner was turning steadily cold.

"Mother."

Annabel, having stood up, wrapped her arms around Gray. He let go of a few tears as her reassuring scent filled his nostrils, the feel of her expensive clothes resting against his cheek. She soothed him gently before taking his face in both of her hands and looking up into his eyes.

"I love you, sweetheart."

"I love you too, Mother," he sniffled.

"Don't do anything stupid, please. I couldn't bear to lose you."

She stood on her tiptoes to kiss him on the forehead, lingering for a second to keep the memory of her only child close to her heart.

The three Brogans ate in stony silence that night. Unable to bear this new awkwardness amongst his family members, Gray fled to his room as soon as he was able. He lay in bed, surrounded by the inky blackness of night. His pack, waiting for him next door, seemed to burn a hole through the wall. He could see it sitting there in his mind's eye.

"You awake?" came a whispered voice just past midnight.

"Yes."

"I stand by my former analysis. You're an idiot, Grayson."

Genevieve climbed, still fully clothed, into bed beside Gray. Her warmth was so comforting his eyes misted over and a lump formed in his throat.

"Don't call me Grayson," he said, trying desperately to return to their usual joking manner.

Her small hand came up to his cheek. "I love you. Don't ever forget that."

"I love you too, Jen. Always have, always will."

"All right, let's not get strange. Just don't let me be alone here for too long, I'm going to be bored out of my mind. Not to mention you've never spent a single day without me in your life."

Gray gave out a breathy laugh whilst a weight seemed to drop into his stomach from the thought of actually being away from her comforting presence.

"I'll miss you."

"That goes without saying, Grayson."

"Stop calling me Grayson. My grandfather's an arse, and you know it. I don't even know why Mother named me after him. She hasn't spoken to him in years. The last time he stayed here, Mother took me to Paris, remember?"

"Oh, the worries of the rich. Fancy having your mother take you to Paris? The hardship of it is almost unbearable. Oliver Twist could have been based on your life."

Gray laughed again and pulled her to him, placing a kiss on the top of her head.

"I really will miss you, Jen."

"You'll forget about me soon enough. You're going to be saving the world."

"Forget about you? I couldn't, even if I wanted to, and you know it."

Genevieve laughed. "Oh, it's all too true."

"I'm scared."

The phrase came from nowhere, piercing the night like a knife. He hadn't thought of fear until that moment. A long silence followed his confession as they soaked it up.

"I'm not going to tell you what you want to hear. I don't think it will be all right, but I think you're strong. I think you'll come back."

Gray admired Jen's honesty, as well as her other many loveable traits, and he held her even tighter as his eyelids finally grew heavy.

"Please don't die."

He heard Genevieve's whispered words just before he fell off into the all-encompassing darkness of sleep.

Chapter Six

Gray found his newly tailored uniform folded neatly in his dressing room the morning after he had enlisted, along with a brand new pair of boots that looked like they would, not only fit his feet perfectly, but also protect him from whatever elements he was likely to face. Once he'd pulled the grey shirt over his head, tucking it into his khaki trousers, he wound the thick wool puttees around the lower half of his legs. He felt they drew the eye down to his new boots, highlighting their beauty. He stood in front of the mirror to place the cap on his head and grinned at himself when he saw the effect.

He looked glorious. He had brushed back his hair, but he could still see it slightly from the side. His blue eyes sparkled, contrasting with the dark uniform. As a final touch, he thought necessary for his first appearance as Private Brogan, he took up the cane he had carried the day before and strutted down the stairs.

His mother cried, but an intense pride radiated off his father as he sat at the breakfast table with a newspaper open in front of him. Annabel stood with a rustle of skirts and kissed Gray on the cheek before brushing past him, out into the grounds.

"She'll come around, son. You'll see."

She didn't.

She tried to appear happy, but Gray could see the effort behind her every smile and gesture. She was desperate for him to stay, yet the more she wanted to hold onto his final days, the faster they disappeared.

Gray's last few days at home passed in an almost giddy excitement. His adventure, as he saw it, loomed ever closer, making his mind sharply aware of everything about his home. He noticed the way Genevieve's eyes lit up just before she started to speak, the way his mother's flowery perfume hung in the air of every room, and the perfect daily workings of the house he had grown up in. Regardless of his new, hyper-aware state, the days slipped past him like a breath of wind in the night.

Monday morning arrived too soon. As he woke on that final day, Gray, in his nervous state, thought even the birds were singing more cautiously that morning. They chirped from the distant trees of the forest which unknowingly held so much of Gray's past.

Looking dejected and saddened as he waited for the motorcar to take him into town, he shuffled his feet in the marble entrance hall. His freshly pressed and tailored khaki uniform stood out amongst his polished surroundings.

From a distance, he looked just like any soldier. Another young man heading into the great unknown. However, up close, his eyes were bloodshot with the effort of not crying. His mother stood at his left and his father to his right. A few feet behind him, not visible from the driveway, stood his best friend and sister in everything bar blood. He looked at the young girl often, fear in his eyes as he took a step towards the shining car.

His mother wiped her face with a lace handkerchief, tears

streaming down her cheeks whilst his father just stood with his eyes squinting in an attempt to not show emotion. Unable to stand the tension any longer, Gray threw his arms around his mother, holding her so tight it must have hurt. He kissed Genevieve, nodded his head in his father's direction, and bent to retrieve his pack. Gray gave a final look into his mother's flawless face and left the safety of Hoddington Manor behind.

As he slid into the back of the car, the supple leather seat creaking with his weight, he heard footsteps approach. When Gray turned his face, he noticed his father's upper body leaning over the door and into the car. Theodore seized his son's shoulder, grasping him in a fierce hug. When he let him go just a few seconds later, both men's eyes were red with suppressed tears.

"Look after yourself and come home to us."

Gray nodded, unable to say anything past the lump clogging his throat.

"I love you, son."

"I...I love you, Father," Gray managed to choke out.

The words were barely audible, but Theodore had heard them. He smiled, retreating from the car before joining Annabel and Genevieve in the grand entrance. He raised his hand in a final farewell.

*

The first thing Gray noticed upon arriving in the town square was the sheer magnitude of people. Every type of person imaginable seemed to be there. Both rich and poor were united in the joy and honour of their war. Men just like Gray stood with uncertainty by the town hall in their khaki uniforms, awaiting instruction. Ribbons and flags adorned the houses and shops as far as the eye could see.

The atmosphere was rife with merriment and every face wore a large smile. The cheers already piercing the air grew ear-splitting in pitch as Gray appeared in his luxurious vehicle. His driver had a forlorn expression as he dipped his hat towards him for what could be the final time. Gray gave a weak smile back and made his way over to the podium where he stood awkwardly for a few minutes, unsure what he was supposed to do.

"Brogan," Major Corvin boomed, striding over to him. The decorative pistol in its leather holster thumped against his leg.

"You came back, good lad. You're doing your king and country proud."

Gray nodded, still unable to shake the lump in his throat. He was leaving home for the first time. This moment was huge, yet he hadn't even taken the time to let it sink in.

He was ushered over to a small group of men—all similar in age to Gray—where he was told to wait until they were ready to leave. He stood on the outskirts of the little group until one man turned to face him.

"Hello. Brogan, ain't it?"

"Y-yes. It's Gray, actually. Gray Brogan. How do you do?"

Gray held out his hand with what he realised was a well-practised, stiff gesture and tried to fit in with the men around him by attempting a more slouched posture. The two men shook hands as Gray ran his eyes over his new companion's physique. He was a scruffy looking man, the same age as Gray with messy hair that looked as though it hadn't seen a comb for weeks. Large ears poked out of his mop, giving him a slightly mousy appearance. His face was rather handsome and inset with pale eyes whilst his body was tall but incredibly thin and angular. He beamed with excitement, and his smile was infectious. Gray grinned back at him, drunk off the jovial atmosphere radiating from their audience.

"I'm migh'y fine, Gray. Name's Arthur Michaels."

He had a thick Cornish accent which was humorous and warm at the same time. It filled Gray with his former enthusiasm and a new sense of positivity about his unknown future. Perhaps he had made the right decision after all.

The major approached them not ten minutes later, separating them into pairs and pulling them into a neat line. Gray was instantly partnered with Arthur.

"Exciting, ain't it?" Arthur whispered, slinging his pack over his shoulder. "We'll be 'eroes by Christmas!"

The bugles started up again, alongside the sound of drums and cheers from what looked like every woman and girl in the entire town. The soldiers in their red jackets were at the front of the procession, and the new recruits followed behind.

Several roses landed at Gray's feet as he walked. He looked up and winked with all his usual charm, beaming at the finely dressed women who had thrown them. The new soldiers were all ready to march out of town in what was shaping up to be a spectacular and flashy fashion. The cheers were wild with excitement. Sweethearts grabbed hold of their men, kissing them deeply as they marched past.

"Gray!"

He didn't hear the first time his name was uttered.

"Grayson, you fool, look at me."

"Genevieve."

"Gray. Don't leave me like this, please."

"But you said— Jen, I'll make you proud. I promise."

"You don't have to go to war to make me proud, you idiot." She'd broken through to the front of the crowd and was walking beside him. "It's selfish and cruel. What if you get killed?"

Gray reached out his hand, taking hers. "Then I'll die with honour. What have I got here?"

"Me."

Gray's face fell slightly. "I know, Jen. I love you, and I'll miss you. I really will. You're my best friend. My sister really."

She gave him a tiny smile. "But you're still going to leave me here on my own? What will I do without you? I can't come and fight. I'm a woman."

"I'll be home by Christmas. That's not so long."

Genevieve dived for him, throwing her arms around his waist and burying her head in his chest. He stumbled back. Trying to keep moving forwards with the line of men, he planted a kiss on top of her dark hair and hugged her as tightly as he could in that position. Holding her, he realised how much he really would miss her. He'd grown up with her, and she was in every memory he had. They understood each other better than anyone else in the world. That sort of friendship never came around twice.

"It won't be over by Christmas. You and I both know that."

Gray pulled back. Cradling her face between his palms he kissed both her cheeks. "I'll miss you."

"You better, you bastard."

Genevieve's words made Gray laugh. He knew there was no malice behind them. Genevieve kissed him swiftly on the mouth, smiling a little as she stepped out of his reach. When she was back amongst the onlookers she waved. Gray kept moving until she was nothing more than another hat in the crowd.

The music was loud and fast paced as the men marched around the bend and out of town. The cheers were deafening, causing a thrill to course through his veins. The cheering was for him. Not because he could dance gracefully or look good in a suit, but because they thought he was brave and honourable. A real man. He looked back one last time and thought he could just make out his mother's dark blonde hair bobbing through the tightly packed figures. He waved but couldn't be sure it was her, so he kept moving forwards with the other men, into what was sure to be a magnificent part of their country's future.

They moved in a stumbling imitation of a real march until they reached the town's small train station. A train was waiting for them, the steam billowing in the clear, breezeless day.

Gray climbed into a carriage behind Arthur just before the whistle blew. Other men hung out the windows whilst women and children, who had followed the soldier's procession, stood on the platform waving. Still close to the open window, tiny bits of soot from the engine speckled the shoulders of Gray's clean uniform, as the train pulled away from the station with a lurch. He sat down in the lumpy seat, watching the crowd through the window. He ran his gaze over every single thing he could see, trying to hold onto it all in his mind. As the platform grew more distant, he closed his eyes and breathed out slowly, offering his own silent goodbye to home.

Chapter Seven

They arrived at the training camp just after dark. Looking at it for the first time, Gray got his first insight into just how unglamorous the war was going to be.

Several barracks, nothing more than long wooden huts, ran down one-half of the space. Fields occupied the other side, churned up by the multitude of feet that had traversed the space in the past few months. Apparatuses of an unknown use were scattered around the base. A large green tent in the middle seemed the most popular place to be. The intoxicating smell of food radiated from the open entrance, along with the sound of men laughing and singing.

As in the town square that morning, the atmosphere from the tent was electric. Despite the darkness and the tattered appearance of the place in general, there was an air of excited anticipation, making all the men drunk on their own excitement.

They didn't stop in the tent but were marched over to the farthest barrack—a long, thin room full of bunk beds with scratchy khaki blankets. Gray was becoming sick of the colour already. Arthur pushed him to the side, laughing as he vaulted onto the top bunk.

Major Corvin came striding in within a few minutes, picking

out people whose buttons were too dull or whose boots weren't properly shined—leaving them no time to settle in. Their first lesson was standing to attention. A few of the more nervous men couldn't seem to get a handle on it, which resulted in much shouting from the formerly good-natured man. He riled them up something fierce. Assumed too late to begin training properly, the men were given leave to head over to the canteen, where they slurped stew and beer. Gray and Arthur sat for a while on their own, looking around nervously.

"I'm dreadfully scared," Gray muttered. "I've never been away from home before."

"It ain't leavin' home I'm scared of. I don't know wha' I'm doin'. Say I'm crap?"

"You won't be. Have you handled a rifle before?"

"'Course, I'm a farm boy. Bet you've 'unted a lot up in the big 'ouse. I 'eard you say you was damn near perfect at shootin'"

Gray laughed. "Yes, so Father tells me anyway." He took another large mouthful of the sour tasting beer.

"This ain't exactly no manor 'ouse, is it?" Arthur asked with humour in his voice.

Gray laughed again, shaking his head. "I want to prove myself, though. I don't want to be defined by my family. I want to show people I can make it on my own, you know?"

"Yes, sure do. Me father's going to struggle wi'out me though. All the men are gone fightin'. He's got to do it all on his own now, an' tha's a lot a work."

"There isn't really anything I'm leaving behind, apart from my family, of course."

"Wha' family you got? It's jus' Father an' me at my house."

"Standard issue mother, father, and sister. Well, she's my

cousin really, or at least that's what I'm told. But both Mother and Father are only children, so I don't get how. She is my mother's best friend's, brother's, adopted daughter, so I don't think we are actually related at all. But there you go. I live with my grandparents as well. Or at least, it's their house, but they are hardly ever there. They had their own apartment in the house made when Mother married Father, so we only really see them for big parties and such."

Arthur let out a low whistle. "Tha's far too complicated for me."

Gray chuckled. "Yes, it is rather."

"You got a lady waitin'?"

Gray shook his head. "Mother and Father want me to marry, but there isn't a girl I really like in that way. What about you?"

"I were sweet on a girl, bu' her dad didn' like me. Said I wa' too poor, so guess tha's why I'm 'ere. Perhaps she'll take me serious now."

They looked into their pints, reflecting on the pasts they had left behind. Gray was startled out of his reverie when he was thrown forwards, his pint spilling across the table. He leapt up, looking around for something to mop it up with.

"Dreadfully sorry, old chap. You all right?"

Gray looked up at a man with tightly curled hair and green eyes that seemed to hold him in place for several minutes. His face was charming.

"I said, are you all right, old chap?"

Gray started. "Yes, yes, I'm fine."

"It's so tightly packed in here, I couldn't see my feet. Sorry about your beer. I'll fetch you another."

"No, it tasted vile anyway. You did me a favour by spilling it."

The man laughed, holding out his hand. "Charlie Grimsby."

"Oh, my name's Gray, and this is Arthur…erm…Michaels, I think."

"Nice to meet you."

"You don't happen to have a light, do you? I'm desperate for a smoke. I've got some matches back at the barracks, but I'll be damned if I can find it in the dark. I only arrived a couple of hours ago."

"What number you in?" Arthur asked.

"Four."

"Tha's ours. We'll help you find it if you want."

"All right then. I can't stomach any more of that beer anyway." Charlie smiled, revealing a set of perfectly straight teeth. A dimple appeared in one of his cheeks.

"You got a sweetheart back home?" Charlie asked them to break the ice as they walked outside, the fresh country air cool on their faces.

Gray's cheeks reddened, although he wasn't quite sure why. "Why does everyone want to know that?" he asked, avoiding a direct answer.

Charlie laughed. "I have no idea. Everyone seems to have one. I thought it was like a rite of passage or something. I don't understand it."

"No, I don't have one. Just two parents and a sister who I don't know how I'm going to live without." Gray found it much easier to refer to Genevieve as his sister, to avoid his earlier complicated explanation to Arthur.

"That special is she?"

Gray nodded, smiling. "She sure is. Best girl in the world. No man will ever be good enough for her."

"Little sister or big sister?"

"Big sister. She's only a year older, though, so we grew up together." He didn't want to give too much of himself away. He was trying not to rely on his former persona as the suave rich boy.

"What about you?" he asked to switch the attention back onto Charlie.

"Mother and four sisters. Surrounded by women my entire life."

They had arrived at their barracks much faster and easier than they had imagined and stood awkwardly outside for a moment. Arthur took the initiative to go inside first.

"Thank you, chaps. Are you busy tonight? I was going to head back to the canteen, but I'm tired of answering their questions. Did you want to stay here and have a smoke whilst it's quiet?"

Despite the fatigue in Gray's body, he was oddly drawn to Charlie's request and nodded, removing his hat and taking a tentative seat on the edge of his bunk. Charlie sat on the bed beside Gray's.

"That your bunk? How did we not meet before?" Gray couldn't believe someone so vibrant had passed his notice.

"No idea, old chap. We were all too excited to look around us I think." Charlie bent down and rooted through his new pack for a few minutes, pulling out his great coat and several other items in his search before finally coming up with a small box of matches.

"Everything always falls to the bottom, don't you find, old chap?"

Gray laughed as he accepted a cigarette from him, leaning in slightly so Charlie could light it. "Why do you keep calling me old chap? I'm eighteen." He exhaled slowly.

"Habit, I guess. My father used to say it a lot as well, apparently. I've been around women far too long. I apologise if I'm a bit rusty talking to my own sex."

Charlie leant back against his pillow just as Arthur appeared over the side of his own bunk, now wearing a tattered day jacket in place of his khaki tunic, and accepted the smoke Charlie held out for him. Arthur lit it awkwardly from the end of Gray's whilst trying to hold himself on his bed. The overall effect looked rather comic. Once their brief spell of hilarity had ended, they each lay in their separate beds, smoking in silence for a minute or two.

"It's an odd business, this war, isn't it?" Charlie whispered eventually.

"How do you mean?"

"Well, it's supposed to be a very noble affair to die for one's country. But the way I see it, you're dead either way, so how do you know it was noble? I'd rather stay alive. That seems the most fulfilling course of action to me."

"But you're protectin' all the folks in England from Hun and makin' a better place for 'em."

"Yes, I suppose you're right, but I still think it's a pointless war. Surely, the politicians could sort it out without slaughtering half the country. Their propaganda doesn't fool me either. I don't expect to come home by Christmas... Or at all, to be honest."

A cold fear crept into Gray's stomach. "That's awfully sombre, Charlie."

"Why'd ya enlist then?" Arthur asked.

"Landlord told Mother if I didn't, he would end the contract on the house. He said I had a duty to my country, and he wouldn't have cowards living on his property. It isn't like we live there for free. I work ruddy hard to help Mother get the rent in on time."

Shame slid through Gray's blood, reddening his cheeks. "Who...who's your landlord?" He knew that his grandfather owned the majority of the houses in town.

"Lord Hoddington," Charlie said the familiar name with disgust. "Awfully pretentious, stuffy man. He's gotten quite fat now as well, and it serves him right I say. He was going to kick us out completely when Father died. I was only four at the time, so it was eighteen years ago now. Lady Brogan, his daughter, had just returned from that kidnapping business. Well, that's what I think happened. Mother says it was all rather hushed up. But anyway Lady Brogan managed to convince her father to let us keep the house.

"Apparently, she said she would pay the rent from her own allowance, but he wouldn't have that. So we still had to pay. Mother became a seamstress for it. He upped the rent and all, to try to force us out, I reckon. I had to stop school and work at the same shop as my mother.

"I worked out front, at the counter, so I had to speak to the women. You know, convince them to buy dresses, and gloves, and such. My sisters all started sewing with Mother as soon as they could hold the needle straight. Lord Hoddington says times have changed now, though, and all the young men must fight for their country. Don't see him volunteering that pretty boy grandson of his, though."

Gray's cheeks were burning. Arthur hit him on the head from his position above him.

"Hey, don't you live in the big 'ouse, Gray? You are a bit of a pretty boy."

Charlie gasped, sitting bolt upright and turning as red as a tomato in three seconds flat. His eyes were as wide as saucers.

"You're not Gray Brogan, are you? I thought you looked familiar. I'm awfully sorry, old chap, I didn't mean it... Please don't tell your grandfather. What...what do I have to do? I swear I didn't mean it. Mother always said I'd talk us into ruin. Please, please don't tell your grandfather. I'll do anything."

Gray's palms were sweating in his embarrassment.

"Of course I won't tell him! He is stuffy, pretentious, and fat. He's horrible to Mother and gives her such nasty looks when they're together. I may tell her that Grandfather is kicking out your mother, though—"

"Please don't, old chap. Don't say a word of this whole business."

"All right, don't worry, and please stop looking at me like that. I'm so desperate to get away from being the rich, pretty boy. I'd hoped you wouldn't even find out."

"Sorry, Gray. I didn't mean to spill the beans."

"Everyone stop apologising!"

He threw himself back against the pillows, angry that he was once more just that kid from the big house with everyone tiptoeing around him as though they might say something that would offend him. He wanted to be offended. He wanted people to just be normal like Jen always was.

"Shouldn't you be an officer then, old chap?"

"No, I didn't want to be. I'm not good at leading people, and as I said, I don't want handouts. I want to climb up because I deserve it, not because I can afford it."

"Fair enough." Charlie exhaled again, having lit a second cigarette off the butt of his first one. As the smoke appeared in the air, it took the shape of a ring.

Gray smiled and tried to make one of his own but failed. Both

Charlie and Arthur laughed at his feeble attempt and thus spent the next hour trying to teach him the trick—to eventual, partial success.

"You're still not as good as me, old chap, but you'll do."

They leant back against Gray's thin pillow laughing, all three of them now squeezed into the one narrow bed. They each lit another cigarette, totally at ease with each other's company. Gray cast aside his worries, thinking this had been a jolly good idea after all.

Chapter Eight

They lay together like that until they could no longer keep their eyes open. They stood to hurriedly get into their pyjamas and slip beneath their own scratchy sheets. The bed above Gray dipped as Arthur jumped onto it, the springs groaning every time he rolled over—which was frequently. Despite that, Charlie's gentle snoring to his left eventually soothed Gray into unconsciousness.

No sooner had they gone to sleep, the rest of their platoon fell through the door. Drunk from their late celebrations, they laughed and joked with the three "pansies" in bed, who were rubbing the sleep out of their eyes.

A pillow was thrown in Gray's direction, hitting him square in the face. He groaned, throwing it back. This quickly escalated out of control into a full pillow fight, each man pretending to be the fierce soldier they wanted to be. Lights out had been at ten, so nobody really knew who they were hitting in the darkness. Feathers flew around the room and drunken bodies stumbled, hitting the floor with a thud. Laughter rang out at their childish game. The sun was on the cusp of rising when they eventually fell back into their beds, exhausted beyond belief.

Minutes later, they were startled awake by the major banging a stick against each of the bed posts and shouting for them to get up.

"Did you not hear the bell? You'll all be blown to pieces in France. This is not a holiday. Outside in five minutes. Your lieutenant is waiting."

They all scrambled out of bed, eager to please on their first day and disappointed that they had seemingly already upset their commander. Fumbling with their unfamiliar new clothes and stiff boots, they ran out of the barracks, unsure what to do or where to go.

"Attention," the major shouted.

They immediately stood up straight, arms at their sides.

"Turnabout, quick march!"

They tried their best to march, each following the man in front and altogether looking rather shoddy, until they ended up in a small paved yard in front of a stone building where the officer's rooms were located.

A tall, strong looking officer stood waiting for them, his hands clasped smartly behind his back. As they drew closer, they noticed he was in his late thirties, only just within the age limit. His uniform fit him perfectly, his boots and buttons shining in the early morning sun. They all lined up in front of him, and he appraised them critically, taking in their tired eyes and youthful faces with what appeared to be a mixture of emotions. Looking down to their ill-fitting uniforms, he drew in a breath and exhaled it slowly.

"Mere children," he muttered, no-one but Gray seemed to hear him.

They fidgeted for a few seconds as the lieutenant paced in front of them, looking into their faces. He seemed to linger on Gray for a fraction longer. A crease formed between his eyebrows.

"Why did you enlist?" he asked, his voice low and smooth.

"Um...seemed like a good idea, sir. Help my country and learn...learn to live without my family."

The lieutenant's eyes darkened, the crease deepening. He resumed his walk, his heavy boots clomping on the stone.

"Seemed like a good idea." He turned to face his men. "Seemed like a good idea? Well, that level of passion will get you far, private. What's your name?"

"Brogan, sir."

"Private Brogan."

The men laughed a little, unsure whether they should.

"Luckily for you, Brogan, you have me to instil some fight in you. To turn you from boys into men and from farmers into soldiers. You do exactly as I say, and listen to everything I tell you, you will succeed. You disobey me in any way, and you will fail. Understood?"

"Yes, sir," they all chanted with gusto.

"I will be your platoon commander now and at the front. If you don't listen to me out there, you'll wind up dead. So use this as good practise, men, and we'll get along just fine."

"What's your name, sir?" Arthur called out from beside Gray.

"Ah, well, that is important. Isn't it, Private? My name's Lieutenant Prince."

Chapter Nine

Gray observed the lieutenant for as long as he dared. Something about him was incredibly familiar. He reminded Gray of himself, and strangely, of Genevieve. The other new recruits kept their heads down, listening to this new authority figure intently, desperate to please but willing themselves not to stand out. Charlie took Gray's elbow.

"He looks an awful lot like you, old chap."

Gray looked up at Prince, studying him again. They did seem to have a rather uncanny resemblance.

"You're almost identical, Gray, except for the age…and the eyes."

"Rougher than your pretty boy face as well," Arthur chipped in, earning him a whack from Gray as Charlie hung his head slightly.

This caused a general titter of laughs throughout the platoon to which Prince, who had been trying to talk about the actualities of war, became aware.

"I didn't think what I was saying was all that funny. Care to share the joke?"

He was searching the group for the instigator. Charlie coughed, alerting him to their location. Gray looked at Charlie scornfully.

"Sir, if you please, it was me," Charlie chirped up, confidently. "I was just saying how very alike you and Gray here look."

"Well, I'm sure it is frightful. However, none of us can appreciate his good looks if he is dead in a shell hole having neglected to take heed of my lessons. Please try to listen. There will be plenty of time for humour when the war's been won."

After warning them on many a gruesome detail of the front he finished his talk with, what seemed to be, a well-rehearsed speech regarding their commitment to the army. His heart didn't appear into it. The part after the speech was much harder, though, as it was a series of exercises to test their fitness.

They ran, jumped, did press-ups, and then sit-ups. The list was never ending. By lunchtime, Gray was exhausted and in desperate need of coffee.

Gray's eyes felt dry with his tiredness, having had next to no sleep the day before. His ears throbbed after having the major shout at him the entire time they had been working, although his fleshy middle made it apparent he most certainly was not prepared to get down and do twenty.

That night, they came straight back from the canteen after their meal and collapsed into bed, aching and falling asleep almost before their heads hit the pillow. He didn't have a spare second until the following evening when he finally found time to write his first letter home. The sound of Charlie's snoring was already evident beside him.

My dear mother and father,

I hope you are not too angry with me for leaving you. I apologise for not writing immediately, but we have been awfully busy with training. Our lieutenant works us really hard, though he always works with us, which makes the men like him. I feel we have gotten very lucky!

I have met some nice lads here. Arthur, Charlie, and I have become quite inseparable.

We are heading to France in just a few short days. They are rushing us through training for some big push, but I will write as often as I can. Try not to worry about me, Mother. We are in safe hands here with Lieutenant Prince, and there is no doubt this war will be over before it has begun. I doubt we will really see much action at all. I attach a rather dashing photograph of myself taken yesterday in my soldier get up.

Sending all my love,

Private Grayson D. Brogan

Gray folded the letter into its envelope then pulled the covers up to his chin. The bed above him creaked as Arthur tried to find a comfortable position on the thin mattress.

The next day was even harder than the ones before—it marked the first day of many where they practised digging. Led out to a muddy field, just on the outskirts of the camp, they lined up with a heavy shovel in their hands. The major shouted instructions at them the entire time. Lieutenant Prince, who was also in the line, sweat dripping down between his shoulder blades, was evidently growing ever more annoyed at the major but was powerless to say anything. The deep crease had reappeared between his brows, and he often ran his hand over his closely cropped blond hair, the small scattering of grey hinting the lieutenant had lived a less than easy life.

In the afternoon, following a quick lunch which Major Corvin considered a waste of time, they returned to their half-dug trench and found a line of targets directly across from them. An air of excitement flew through the men as they were presented with a standard issue rifle.

"Calm down, men. Youthful excitement does not compliment a deadly weapon."

The jovial sounds died down immediately. Everyone shifted slightly in their embarrassment.

"We are not setting you loose with the bullets just yet. We have a war to fight and Hun to shoot. First, we will learn to fix bayonets."

Gray found this task arduous. He couldn't ever seem to get the blade in the top of his rifle fast enough. Others, like Charlie, got it instantly.

"Well done, Grimsby. Perfect timing. Come on, Brogan, we don't have all day! Your friend here would have stabbed an entire platoon by now."

"I'm trying, sir."

"Not hard enough. Again, fix bayonets."

There were a lot of things Gray wanted to say, but he bit them back. As he had told countless people in the past, he had to remember his place now.

Following the failed bayonet training, the men were told to clean their guns thoroughly and taught a brief theory of the weapons. Once that had been completed, they were each told to crouch down inside their trench for the lesson they had all been looking forward to the most.

Resting his finger on the trigger, Gray took a deep breath and focused on the target. With only five bullets per soldier permitted, he was determined they should all find the bull's eye.

Gray was, as his father had said, a near perfect shot.

The bullet flew from the barrel with a crack, forcing the gun back into Gray's shoulder. Expecting the kick, he controlled it well. He watched the piece of metal glide through the air, the wood at the centre of the target splintering with the shot.

Gray prepared his gun again to fire, resting it back in place for his second shot. He was so intent on his task, he didn't notice everyone else had stopped shooting to watch him, mouths agape in shock.

Arthur chuckled and tapped Gray on the shoulder. He jumped, startled from his thoughts.

"Perfect shot indeed."

Arthur whistled for effect, and the other men laughed with him. They now eyed the targets, all mostly un-hit, with trepidation. None of them would be able to hit the bull's eye, and they knew it.

Having worked on a farm, Arthur was second to Gray when it came to shooting. However, Charlie couldn't seem to grasp the concept at all. Gray and Arthur, knowing they didn't really need the practise, spent most of the day helping Charlie master the proper hold and aim and giving him the rest of their bullets for practise.

Unable to explain the proper hold of the gun, Gray stood behind him, his hands resting over Charlie's as someone would do to a child when teaching them to write. Arthur was at his front, making sure the barrel was pointing at the target whilst obviously remaining out of the line of fire. Arthur's eyesight was incredible. His eyes contained an unparalleled alertness as they gazed out into their faux no-man's-land. He could still see the mark, even when it was lashing down with rain, as it was for most of the day.

Having taught Charlie, they decided on a competition to see how fast they could raise and cock their guns in readiness for an imaginary attack. Their rifles resting on the edge of the roughly dug trench, they were soon laughing—giddy on their own success. Of course, Major Corvin didn't approve of them helping each other or the fact they seemed to be enjoying themselves, even if they were the best rifleman in the platoon by late-afternoon.

Striding over to them, with a fierce expression, he gave them all a lecture on taking the job seriously.

"You will not be laughing when it's real targets at the end of your barrels."

Despite the lecture, the three men were too young and filled with the idea of their own immortality.

"Fill your trench and give me ten laps of the field," Corvin ordered. "Now!"

His voice rose to a shout before sinking back down into a mutter as he talked to himself about their disrespect of authority. Rain dripped off his large nose into his thick moustache.

Prince, who had been helping another man in the shallow trench, climbed out. Leaning into the major, he spoke softly as if hoping the platoon wouldn't hear him disagreeing with someone of much higher authority than him.

"Major, they're the best shots we have, you can't remove them from training. I am leading this platoon. I shall decide what tasks they are set."

"Who is of higher rank, Prince, a major or a lieutenant?"

He was now right in Prince's face. They could see spit flying from his mouth, the moustache jiggling almost comically. The major turned to face the three men in the trench.

"Now," he screamed.

One of Prince's fists balled up tightly, the other ran over his head as he paced back up and down the line, helping his men with their aim. Gray, Charlie, and Arthur each climbed out, placing the large pile of earth back into their trench and put their rifles on top of the smooth surface once it was finished.

"No," the major screamed. "Hold your rifles above your heads. That ought to teach you something about respect."

Grumbling, all traces of their former good mood gone, they picked up their rifles and began to run. Charlie and Arthur's ill-fitting boots sloshed, sending mud spraying upwards to splatter their already dirty uniforms. Sweat ran down over their skin without the free hands to remove their tunics. Midway through the second lap, Arthur's foot got stuck, his boot and sock remaining rooted in the dirt as he fell forwards. Gray stopped immediately, helping his new friend to his feet as Charlie unstuck the boot for him. The major ran up behind them, clouting them each on the head so their hats also fell in the mud.

"Get moving. Michaels, that includes you."

"Me boot, sir."

"I don't care. Move."

So Arthur was forced to run with his left foot bare, limping at the height difference between feet. Gray heard heavier running footfalls and a shovel being thrown to the ground.

"Major, I won't stand for this." Prince still spoke quietly. Only the three running soldiers could hear this disagreement with the Major. "This is my platoon. Being here isn't even your job. You shouldn't be helping with training. You should be in an office. Arthur, come back and put that boot on. You'll be of no use in France if you sever your foot now."

Arthur stopped running. Lowering his rifle, he went back over to Prince who handed him his now unstuck boot. The major glared at them, a vein pulsing in his head.

"Prince, back in that trench."

"No. Punishment is one thing, sir, but deliberate abuse and bullying are quite another. Brogan, Grimsby, come back here."

Gray's arms were on fire. He dropped the rifle immediately to his side, breathing heavily.

The major was now purple.

"This is deliberate disobedience of a higher ranking officer, Prince. You'll all be court-martialled. Mark my words."

Lieutenant Prince put his voice to a whisper. Only Gray, standing right next to him, could make out what he was saying. Although he didn't think he was supposed to.

"You're already leading these men to slaughter, at least let them keep their last traces of humour while you do."

"How dare you talk to me like that? It's court-martial for the lot of you. You can't talk your way out of it."

"And how will that go down back home, Major? If you don't mind me asking?" piped up Gray.

The major spluttered. "What?"

"Well, my father plays an active role in the war office, does he not? He's one of the highest investors in the war, if my understanding is correct. Not to mention my grandfather, Lord Hoddington, holds the lease to your house I believe. In fact, my father's pretty much the most powerful man in the country, right beside your king. You kill me, and you're very well kissing your own arse goodbye...sir."

The major was now so angry his eyes were bloodshot and the vein throbbed so violently it looked ready to explode. He stuttered for a few minutes and then turned on his heel, striding back over to the officer's buildings. He had been outsmarted, and he hated it.

"Good show, old chap," laughed Charlie. "I can see the upper class in you now."

"More than just a pretty face." Arthur was also laughing.

They glanced at Prince, who looked slightly dumbfounded. He was holding a battered silver pocket watch in his hand, but from the angle he held it, Gray couldn't decipher the portrait tucked in the lid.

"Sir, are you all right?"

"Yes, yes. Hodd…um, Brogan. Go…go back to the platoon. I'll be there in a minute."

The three privates looked at each other, confused, but they shrugged it off, moving back along to the refilled trench. Looking over his shoulder, Gray saw the lieutenant watching him intently, the same dumbfounded expression on his face. It looked as if he'd seen a ghost.

They saw no more of the major that day or the next, only catching a brief glimpse of him driving a motorcar out of the camp towards the end of the week. The platoon cheered him out, thrilled that he was no longer around. Prince gave them all a brief telling off, saying once more that they must respect the higher ranks, but the talk lacked conviction. His own mouth twisted up at the corners, indicating he would like to be cheering along with them.

Chapter Ten

The next day started with more bayonet training. The men were tasked to line up and then run at dummies stuffed with straw—stabbing, twisting, and pulling out the blade as quickly as possible. Gray was less adept with this side of combat. He did not see how he would need to know this. Surely, he would just be able to shoot them from a distance? He didn't want to see the person he was killing up close.

"Brogan," Prince often called. "Get your bayonet out quickly. Come on, your opponent won't hesitate. It's him or you. Stab, twist, pull."

Thus they were taught to dehumanise the Germans completely, thinking of them as just monsters to be stopped and not soldiers much like themselves—just on the opposing team.

Following this exercise, there was more digging practise to be done, as well as a four-hour march through the hills. Once again, they did not finish until well after dark, eating and showering in an exhausted daze then catching an hour to write letters or meet up with friends, before they all collapsed into bed wearily.

Arthur, Charlie, and Gray had become a highly skilled team. Charlie was excellent with the bayonet, Arthur's eyesight was incomparable, and Gray was a perfect shot—not that they ever got to use the guns. Following that first practise, they hadn't seen another one. The other men who were less adept with the weapon were becoming quite anxious. The next time they would shoot would be the marksman's test.

"What if I fail it?" Charlie asked one night at dinner, stirring his spoon around the lumpy stew without bringing it up to his mouth. "Mum and my sisters will be kicked out of the house. We'll have nowhere to live."

"You won't fail, Charlie."

"Nah, an' you got the Brogan's on your side now, Charl."

He nodded, still looking down into his bowl.

"I won't let my grandfather kick you out. He likes me more than he likes my mother, so if he will listen to her he'll certainly listen to me."

"Certainly, pretty boy," Arthur echoed, attempting to mock Gray's upper-class intonation.

Gray elbowed him in the ribs, making all three of them laugh.

"We'll be invited over to yours when this war's over, righ'?"

"Yes, I will have a special dinner. My valet can organise rooms for you both as well. Name me your favourite dish, and I will have it served."

"Excellent." Charlie quickly perked up, joining Arthur to decide upon their favourite foods and arguing when they each came out with completely different tastes.

"The cooks will serve more than one thing. You can each have your own favourite."

Gray couldn't help grinning as his two friends looked at him in disbelief.

"What's your favourite, old chap?"

"Venison, I think, or pheasant with roasted potatoes."

"Ain't never had pheasant before. I had deer twice."

"They live in that meadow, don't they? Thought only the owners could hunt— Oh, but I guess you are the owner. If I could have anything, I'd have beef pies with so much gravy the pastry couldn't hold it in. I always bought a pie on the way home from work on a Saturday, just after I got paid. But the baker never put enough in, and it was half empty most of the time."

"I'd 'ave…"

Arthur thought for a moment, one hand on his chin for dramatic effect. "Big cakes like you see in the window of tha' fancy place, an' spuds with crispy skins, an' fat chicken legs still on the bones."

"You could have anything in the world, Arthur, and you go for chicken legs?" Gray laughed.

"Yeah, why not? I like 'em."

"All right, but they will be fine dining chicken legs."

"So long as they still juicy an' fat. Will there be maids an' butlers an' things?"

"Yes, lots of them. Especially if I make it apparent you are special guests of my own invitation."

"I'll pencil it into my diary, old chap. The exact day the war is finished, we will celebrate at the big house. Mother will never believe it when I tell her."

"She can come too if you like? And your sisters. Your father as well, Arthur."

"Oh, dunno 'bout him. He's very… Well, we're both not suitable for the big 'ouse, really."

"Nonsense. You are my friend which makes you more than suitable."

"Bu' fathers a bit…simple."

"So what? I suppose you would say my uncle Billy is simple as well, but he is the nicest, kindest man I have ever met. He's worth a thousand scholars any day. Hello, sir. Are you joining us?"

Gray had just noticed Lieutenant Prince standing behind Charlie with a wistful smile on his face as if he too knew Billy.

"Oh… No, no. I dine with the other officers. I was just passing through. Good night. Get plenty of rest mind we have another march tomorrow."

Looking slightly distracted, as if lost in some memory, he continued through the tent towards the officers' buildings.

"I think he's a little strange, old chap. A brilliant officer, but just slightly… I don't know. It's almost as if he knows something that he isn't telling us."

"What do you mean?" Gray asked.

Charlie leant across the table. "I don't really know what I mean, but that pocket watch he was looking at when you mentioned Lord Hoddington… Well, I wasn't going to tell you. I shouldn't really." He put a large spoonful of stew in his mouth, chewing slowly as if regretting bringing it up and hoping they would move on.

"Go on," Arthur probed.

He leant as far over the table as he could so as not to miss the gossip. In his haste, he knocked the edge of his bowl, sending it spinning across the surface. Gray caught it just before it dumped its contents all over him. Charlie swallowed loudly, looking at Gray out the corner of his eye.

"It's nothing, really. Forget it. I'm just being foolish. Just think he's got secrets is all."

"Well, let's figure them out," Arthur whispered.

"Like Sherlock Holmes or something," Gray said. "I don't think it's a good idea, though. He is our lieutenant after all."

"Spoilsport," Arthur muttered.

Gray elbowed him again and thus resumed their jovial manner, quickly putting their officer to the back of their minds. For now, at least.

The rest of their training seemed to pass in a blur of long days filled with bayonets, marching, and digging. The only break in this tough routine was the odd session of gun cleaning or loading. However, they were never allowed to fire them. Gray, Arthur, and Charlie remained together, feeding off each other's strengths and improving on their weaknesses as a team. Despite the bond the three of them shared, they couldn't seem to inspire any friendships with the rest of the platoon, who only communicated to them when it was strictly necessary to complete a team exercise. Gray thought Prince observed him more than the other soldiers. The thought seemed to be shared by the men, earning Gray the nickname 'pretty boy'.

On the final day, a slight air of nerves rippled through the men at being presented with a loaded rifle for only the second time. In the moderate comfort of the officer's courtyard they each lined up in front of the targets for the marksman's test that could send them all back to their hometowns were they not considered a good enough shot. Charlie, Gray, and Arthur went last. The rest of the men remained behind to watch them as if they were observing a show and desperate to pick up tips from the best shots they had.

Gray hit the centre of the target with every bullet. He wasn't even a millimetre out. Arthur followed suit with only a slightly worse result. Charlie missed the target completely with the first few bullets, his nerves making him panic.

"Breathe, Charlie," Gray muttered from beside him.

Charlie's hands steadied somewhat towards the end, enabling him to just scrape the pass mark, although, Gray was under the impression the person counting on the target had fixed the results of more than a few of the men. He had definitely seen at least one bullet that had soared about three feet from the target. Regardless, they were all passed as fit and ready for action, making up the numbers overseas. He felt a little queasy thinking about it. The war had all been rather abstract until then.

Chapter Eleven

None of the men slept well on the eve of their departure. They awoke from their brief sleep jittery with both excitement and nerves. Strapping themselves into their uniforms, they quickly realised that their equipment was a lot heavier than they had anticipated it being once it was properly assembled.

The first pangs of fear entered Gray's body as they approached the boat that would take them to France. He had no idea how he would run with the equipment weighing him down so badly, or how he would fair should he need to bayonet someone. He had still not mastered that particular task. He didn't feel as if he was ready yet. The training had all seemed so light-hearted, yet he was starting to doubt war would really be like that. However, he was still eager, and the rest of the platoon's enthusiasm rallied him on.

The trip across the channel was choppy, the boat swaying to and fro with the rough weather. The ship's deck was lined with soldiers wearing their heavy greatcoats, leaning over the side to empty their last English breakfast into the sea. Gray was among them, face mirroring his name, and hair sticking to his sweaty forehead. Arthur was running back into the ship to fetch water for the men to drink in between heaves, his stomach having grown tough with years of eating stale bread and mouldy cheese.

Their arrival in France was nowhere near as triumphant as they had all imagined. Their legs wobbled as they attempted to walk on the muddy ground. Second Lieutenant Welsh was waiting for them when they docked, introducing himself as Prince's subordinate and their platoon leader should something happen to Prince. Following this awkward introduction, Prince fell into step beside the lower ranking officer. They were ordered to get into formation, as they had been taught, and march towards their new home.

The march was long. Their packs dug into their already aching bodies whilst their stomachs still churned. Some men tried to begin a song, but it wasn't picked up. None of the men had the energy for singing. As they shuffled onwards, a sound like thunder seemed to draw nearer. The horizon lit up every few minutes as bombardments took place out on the front line. Even this close, it still seemed too distant to be scary. It brought on images of lightning storms for Gray, who had always sat up late into the night to watch them flash across the darkened sky.

As they made it into the first town, the reality of their situation truly sank in.

They passed by what looked like an old hall, now abandoned and surrounded by ruined houses that had been blown apart by some past explosion. The wounded spilt out of the doors. There were too many of them to fit inside.

The few who could walk were being escorted towards the boat that had ferried across their replacements. Gray saw men with missing limbs, and heads with pieces of skull missing. Eyes, stomachs, and faces had been bandaged clumsily with thick field dressings or ripped up clothing. There were so many wounded that blood ran down into the drains at the side of the cobbled road. Even that, the vilest of all liquids, was afraid there. Gray looked at the shell fire in the distance, no longer seeing the childish joy of a storm but the adult fear of death.

Some of the weaker stomached men bent over, throwing up into the tall grass beside the path leading closer to the horrors they were now all too aware of. Despite it all, what scared Gray the most was the look in the wounded men's eyes. Their faces were sickeningly young, yet their eyes seemed aged beyond belief, having seen too much horror for their meagre years. A distance sat in their expressions, as if they had ceased to care about anything. As if they no longer resided in their own skin.

Sobered by the reality they had enlisted into the platoon kept moving.

Without realising it, Gray had grabbed hold of Arthur's hand, a look of panic etched on his face. As he squeezed the warm fingers, Arthur squeezed back—both of them feeding off the warm touch of another person so they wouldn't feel so alone or so afraid. Gray hated to admit it, even to himself, but he would have loved to fold himself into his mother's safe embrace one last time, hating himself for not saying goodbye properly in the naïve belief that he couldn't die.

They reached their destination about three hours later, flinching every time a shell thundered down onto the not so distant horizon. The second town looked a little friendlier than the first. Evidence of bombardment still haunted the area, but it was not as extensive. In its dilapidation, the town seemed to mock the former beauty it had known.

To complete the image, a water fountain stood in the centre, moss creeping along its surface like a disease. On either side of the fountain was a bar—or estaminet as the locals called it. The flickering orange of candles illuminated the windows in front of them—the electricity in such a place had surely been blown apart months ago. Laughter radiated out of the buildings obscenely—a sound that didn't seem to fit into such a lifeless place.

"Right, lads," Second Lieutenant Welsh called wearing a wide grin. "There's one bar for officers, one for privates. Don't get them muddled up. You have to work your way up the ranks if you wish to drink with the officers. The estaminet here does the best fried potatoes I've ever tasted so I doubt you'll mourn for long."

Laughter bubbled up among the men.

Welsh continued after a small pause. "This is where you'll be stationed when you're behind the lines resting. For now, at least, until we move up the line."

Gray, accustomed to all the luxuries life had to offer, couldn't help wondering what the trenches were like if this was their rest. Not quite the idyllic picture of Parisian day trips he had imagined for his time off.

Welsh next showed them to a camp approximately a mile away, telling them they would have the evening off to recuperate after their journey. However, the next day they would begin their combat training anew.

Charlie, Arthur, and Gray made their way into the town hesitantly, taking a seat by the window of the crowded estaminet. Condensation ran down the glass from the breath of the crowd, and the air was thick with the smell of beer and frying oil coming from somewhere out the back. They ordered their own refreshments and surveyed the soldiers who had all clearly seen action.

Their uniforms were stained with mud, or at least that's what Gray told himself the stains were, although blood seemed the more logical conclusion. There were small cuts on their callused hands, and although they were all smiling and soaking up the joy of their leave, they possessed the same vacant look in their eyes from seeing too much too young.

Watching them all closer Gray noticed one soldier sat in the corner. He stood out amongst the crowd of identically dressed men because he was the only man on his own. Huddled in the shadows, his knees were brought up to his chest as he nursed a beer between two violently trembling hands. He shook so much that the liquid occasionally sloshed over the side of the cup, making dark spots on his khaki trousers. His eyes were wild with unseen horrors, his hat missing, and his hair standing up in a mass of different directions. He looked mad.

More than once, Gray saw a soldier try to approach him and reach out a hand to touch his shoulder, but the man jumped at the feel, looking around in fear. He was too lost in his own mind to see the others around him trying to help.

Gray turned away, afraid to look at the man any longer, afraid of what he had seen to make his mind rebel against him like that.

Their potatoes arrived surprisingly fast and shining with grease. It spotted the newspaper they were wrapped in and stuck to their fingers, so they left prints on their glasses when they raised the watered down beer to their lips. Arthur positively beamed at the sight whilst Gray couldn't help but remember the roast potatoes back at home with a sense of deep longing as he chewed the stodgy sustenance absentmindedly.

The rest of the evening went by quickly as Arthur joked with some of the other soldiers, drawing Charlie and Gray into his easy conversation. Filled with laughter and too much beer, they stumbled back to the camp late, crashing down into their billet side by side, their great coats spread over them like blankets for extra warmth.

Their first full day in France dawned still in half darkness, the clouds so thick they stopped the light of the sun penetrating to the wet ground below. The men were all feeling fuzzy from their long day and late night. The rain pounding off their backs as they made their way into the canteen tent diminished their moods even further. Lieutenant Prince and Second Lieutenant Welsh had them digging all the first day. They called it good practise, although, Gray didn't see how. Surely the trenches had already been dug.

By night, they were all plastered in mud and thoroughly miserable. They found their way back into town regardless. Their uniforms hung off them, so soaked with rain the thick material was heavy against their young limbs.

Back at the camp, a large metal container had been set up on the grass and filled with water. Steam rose from the soapy surface as they all gathered around it. They needed to wash, but Gray couldn't see how there would be enough time to empty and refill the tub for all of them in one night. There were no taps in the camp. Not unless someone had figured out how to run a pipe into the middle of a field. Why had they not prepared several tubs? He looked around but couldn't see where they kept the screens to give them all privacy either. The other men didn't seem to be having these thoughts. They stripped off their clothes immediately and without reservation, each shouting out their own crude jokes.

Stripping off as quickly as he could, he jumped into the bath first, causing the water to splash over the sides, much to the aggravation of the men still waiting, already undressed, happy in their own grimy skin.

Once they were clean, Arthur, Charlie, and Gray went back to their tent in silence, too tired to think about another late night.

They each climbed into the relative warmth of their narrow beds, listening to the shells explode on the horizon.

Gray took this opportunity to write home. He had received letters from his mother and Genevieve, with Jen's being much less angry than he had anticipated. His mother had been positively beside herself with worry, making Gray feel guilty about how he had left her so suddenly. He hated his mother being upset, they had always been incredibly close and her opinion mattered to him more than any other. Sat under his thin blanket he composed the most upbeat letter he could think of. Although he couldn't tell her where he was or what he was doing, he could at least reassure her that he was happy.

"Your writin's nice," Arthur stated, their beds so close together he could read over Gray's shoulder easily. Arthur had written a scribbled note in a very messy hand, the letters all jumbled up together, as if fighting for prime position on the page.

"Me father, 'e can't read, but he'll have someone read it out to him," Arthur continued, nodding towards his own letter.

"He can't read?" Gray was shocked. He thought everyone could read now.

"No, couldn't afford school when 'e was a lad. Tha' was jus' for the posh totty like you." He grinned at Gray. "Me grandpa believed all a man needed to know was 'ow to farm 'is land. Leave the learnin' to the scholars an' businessmen."

"Then how come you can read?"

"Law ain't it? Dad made me go to school kickin' and screaming."

"I liked learning."

"Yeah, 'cuz you probably had a private tutor, lad."

They laughed.

"Yes, I did actually."

"What'd you learn? French, Latin, and the waltz?"

Gray laughed again at his accuracy. "Yes, and mighty useful they have all become, Arthur. Are we, or are we not, living in France now? You may need my fluent French skills one day."

"Gray, you say you didn't want to be an officer because you wanted to earn it right? Well, blimey, you already have, old chap. You're a perfect shot and fluent in French. You're mad. No wonder Major Corvin had such an issue with you."

"Charl, if he'd gone officer he wouldn't be 'ere for teasin' now, would he? Come on, pretty boy, teach me some French I can use on the ladies."

Charlie snorted at Arthur's request. "You'd need more than French to woo the ladies, Arthur."

Charlie received a pillow to his head in penance for the comment. His pencil snapped as it ricocheted down onto the letter he was writing. Charlie swore and started to sharpen it with the knife from inside his uniform. Despite it all, he was smiling as he worked.

Thus, they spent that evening with Gray teaching them as many funny French phrases as he could remember from his teenage wanderings in Paris and Bordeaux. He had been to Paris countless times with his mother and Jen. Not to mention the French tutor he had seen from the age of four.

As he spoke, gesturing with his hands as he did so, which was as much part of the foreign language as the words themselves, his letter to his mother lay open on his blanket. The leather folder holding a thick ream of paper, was knocked off the bed as he laughed at Arthur's terrible pronunciation, still so thick with his farmer's accent that Gray couldn't understand a word.

"Did you do this, old chap?" Charlie interrupted. He had bent to pick up the folder and was now flicking through the sketches Gray had composed during the previous days of basic training.

Gray blushed, making a lunge for the drawings, but Charlie held them out of his reach.

"No, they're really good. Oh, can I keep this one?"

He had come across a drawing of himself, his curly hair wildly blowing in the wind as he stood to attention. The picture had been sketched the day before they had all had their hair cut short to fit in with army regulations. Gray blushed even darker as Charlie picked up a few more drawings of himself, one of him running at the straw-stuffed dummy and spearing it with his bayonet. Almost a parody of fierceness seemed to be on his youthful features.

"You must have done all these from memory," he muttered, almost to himself.

"Yes, I like to write poetry, my dream I suppose. Drawing the images I see helps me keep them in my mind for longer so I can write about them later. I've not been alone long enough to write, though. I'm no artist."

"Not an artist?" Arthur piped up, catching sight of his own portrait squinting out into the distance, his rifle resting on his shoulder. "They're bloody fantastic!"

They giggled their way through a few pictures of Major Corvin, his face screwed up in a most ugly manner as he shouted orders at them, and one he had drawn as he waited for Charlie and Arthur to wash, depicting the men lining up for the bath, not even trying to cover themselves. The picture was not obscene, it simply showed the awkwardness he had felt at that moment.

"Well, you made me look a right side more manly than I am," Arthur said, looking at the picture closely. "I think I look taller as well."

Charlie laughed. "Like hell you do."

Still blushing rather fiercely, Gray managed to snatch the pictures back from Charlie, handing him the one he had liked of himself and bestowing the same gift on Arthur. He hovered his eyes for a fraction of a second longer over the likenesses of his mother and his best friend as they had looked on his birthday, laughing.

He, Arthur, and Charlie admired the tender moment, acknowledging the love expressed through his pencil and onto the page to depict his two favourite women. He could have had a picture taken of them, of course, but there was something much more alive about their drawing. He always found they were much more real than in one of the many posed pictures around the manor.

"Your sister and mother I assume?" Arthur asked.

When Gray nodded he continued.

"Both very fine looking women."

"What does your father look like then? Or do you not get along with him?"

Gray slipped out another picture, showing them his father sitting regally in a chair in the formal parlour. Theodore had agreed to sit for the portrait a few months earlier when he'd found himself looking at a full day with nothing planned. An extremely rare occurrence for him. Gray remembered how his father had found it all rather funny but had still been pleased with the result. Gray had even drawn the laughter in the man's eyes.

"You can certainly see why you turned out so dashing," Charlie said. "He doesn't look like you, though. You must have gotten all your traits from your mother."

Gray felt a lovely warm feeling spread through him at the compliments from the two men that already meant so much to him, as they lay side by side, listening to the light rain patter onto the roof of their khaki tent.

Combat training week passed all too quickly. The gratitude he had felt for not going straight to the front quickly faded as he realised there was only one night standing between himself and those shells on the horizon. He wondered absentmindedly how much it would hurt if one landed on him or whether it would be over so fast he wouldn't even notice. He hoped for the latter, although he obviously hoped even more that he would never have to find out at all.

As they packed up their things once more, Gray folded up the sketch of his mother and Genevieve, placing it carefully into the breast pocket directly over his heart for luck.

The men were all jittery with nerves and excitement, eager to see what war was really like. They sang songs for a long stretch of the march, each one becoming filthier as they became more and more comfortable with each other. The end stretch, however, they did in silence. There were only the sounds of their heavy boots squelching through the mud and their mess tins clanging against their packs as they took in the increasingly desolate sights around them.

As they grew closer to the line, they saw that the trees had been uprooted. Holes littered the fields at the sides of the road where shells had overshot their mark. Wounded, defeated looking soldiers trudged in the opposite direction towards their rest billets, looking half asleep. Gray saw more than one pair of frantic eyes, the men shrinking reflexively at the sound of each shell, making them appear old despite their young years. He caught the gaze of one man as he passed, but looked away quickly, too scared by the detached, haunted look he found there.

"It's kind of exciting now ain't it? We're here. In France," Arthur said beside him. "I mean, it's shockin', but it's where the action is, you know? It's like we're really part of it now."

Gray nodded. "Yes," he muttered, not thoroughly convinced.

Chapter Twelve

They reached the trenches around lunch time, although, there was no lunch to speak of. Their first night was to be spent on the front line. There had been a big push and countless casualties, and Prince had said they needed the men much more than they needed further training. Thus, they continued through the reserve and communication trenches until finally reaching the firing trench. The air around them was thick with a sense of despair, and the shellfire was deafening in Gray's ears.

The smell of rotting flesh hit them all for the first time as they trod clumsily over the duck boards. Gray jumped, pressing himself into the wall as he saw a rat as big as a cat scurry along past their feet.

"Brogan," Welsh shouted. "Keep it moving. Get down from the firestep, Richards, you idiot! Never look over the top unless ordered to, you hear me? Jesus Christ, you won't last five minutes."

Richards, a spotty, scrawny fellow who looked far too young to be nineteen, stuttered an apology. He pulled his cap low over his eyes and scurried forwards, crouched so much he was almost on all fours.

Mud splattered and exhausted, they reached the main part of the trench, only to find their accommodation had no beds or bathrooms. Gray wasn't sure what he had expected, but this wasn't it.

A small line of latrines was pointed out to them farther up the line. In the way of sleeping arrangements, other men simply leant against their packs as a makeshift pillow. As he watched, a rat crawled over one man who didn't even seem to notice.

Gray felt sick—immediately realising how thoroughly mortal he really was. He wanted to draw or write the image in front of him and send it back home for the optimistic men still enlisting, but he knew the war office would never allow it. It would never even get past the censoring process.

The platoon was joining a company who had been in France since the war had commenced. A few of the soldiers looked up as the new recruits entered, but none of them introduced themselves. They had all seen too much death to want any close alliances anymore. Welsh, having been there before, had no need to observe his desolate surroundings. He ducked inside a dugout to his right, and did not appear again for hours. Gray had an absurd image of a rabbit scurrying into its burrow.

As the sun slowly set over the muddy battlefield, the men were each served a ladle full of watery stew, the cook looking utterly depressed as he slopped it into the soldier's battered mess tins. His apron was filthy, his hands even more so. The new recruits shuffled their feet in the dirt, looking around anxiously as they waited in line. The veterans just stood, flinching ever so slightly at the shell fire overhead as if it were a nervous tick they couldn't shake. As Gray sat down with his bowl, Lieutenant Prince approached him. Gray stood to attention, removing his cap.

"Sit down, boy. You don't need to do that every time I walk past."

Gray did as ordered, lowering himself gingerly down onto the driest spot of the ground he could see. He jumped back up as a rat squealed beneath him.

"Still not used to them, eh?"

Gray shook his head.

"It will get easier I promise. You won't even notice the rats after a while." At the sight of Gray's wide eyes, he chuckled. His voice was very pleasant.

"I...I suppose I will, sir," he stuttered.

"I don't doubt it. They all look scared at first." Prince paused for a while, making a show of looking around him at the other men. "The company are all saying we look like twins, but of course, that's impossible given the age gap. More like father and son. I know they said it back in England too, but I was always too busy to introduce myself properly." He laughed, taking a large mouthful of his own stew. He chewed quickly and swallowed, looking as if he had eaten watery stew every day of his life.

"Never heard the name Brogan before though. Sounds posh to me."

"Yes, sir. I'm afraid it is. I was named after my grandfather, as is standard tradition, I think. I'm heir to the largest fortune in England, apparently."

Prince raised his eyebrows, letting out a low but in tune whistle that alluded to a good ear for music. "Then why are you not an officer? Took me years to climb the ranks, but you'd get in within seconds."

"I wanted to prove I could make it on my own. Everyone thinks fortune is all you ever need, but I find it rather claustrophobic, to be honest. I thought it would be awfully poetic to be poor."

Prince let out a disbelieving laugh through his nose—his

mouth once more full of stew. "Were your mother and father happy to let you leave?"

"They— I didn't tell them I was enlisting. Just sort of did it. Didn't even know I would do it myself when I'd left the manor. I just wanted to see what the rally was like, see the uniforms and listen to the music. I'd been thinking about enlisting for a while, though, just always in the abstract. Major Corvin can give a right good speech, though. I'll give him that at least."

"Yes, about all he's good for, mind. So you didn't even say goodbye to your parents? That's cold, Brogan."

Gray felt that icy feeling of guilt flood through him again.

"I did. Mother was upset, though. She worries too much. I am so close to her, and I couldn't bear to upset her, but I couldn't very well sit at home and let my fellow men die for me. Could I?"

Prince smiled again. His hazel eyes had brightened significantly, although Gray didn't know why.

"She's probably a lot stronger than she looks. It would do you good not to worry about her as well, I think. I'm sure you will make a fine soldier. The rich do usually have the luck."

Finishing his stew with a loud slurp, he stood up to patrol the trench, checking on the other men as he went. Gray watched him go, noticing a slight limp in his otherwise strong stride. He wondered how he had gotten it and whether it had been a war injury or something that had happened earlier in his life.

"What was that about?" Arthur asked, plonking himself down—uncaring where he landed or what in.

"Just wanted to check that I really wasn't his illegitimate child, I think."

Charlie sat down at his other side, almost choking on his stew as he laughed.

"That'd be an awkward first day at the front wouldn't it?" he laughed.

Just as a smile rose on Gray's lips, a whistle started up from the distance, getting louder as it raced closer. The men who had clearly been there a while immediately dived to the side, holding their hands over their shaven heads. An explosion ripped through the air, not seconds later, showering the entire trench with earth and shrapnel. One man cried out as a piece of the shell lodged in his thigh. A spurt of crimson blood leapt out of the wound and onto his muddy fingers.

"Jones!" someone screamed and a soldier wearing a stretcher bearer's armband, that must once have been white, bustled up to him.

From then on, every slight noise made Gray, along with every other man in the company, flinch. He fit in with them well, bonding silently in their shared fear.

To distract himself from the horror, he flicked his gaze between the men, sliding a blank piece of paper from his folder. The page creased at the edges as his fingers clenched around it.

Gray silently pleaded with the sun not to set. If anything could make his situation worse, it was darkness. However, the sun could not be bargained with.

As the night drew on, the men all tried to find places to rest their feet, keeping them out of the shallow water lining the bottom of the trench. Arthur, Charlie, and Gray leant against each other, finding warmth and reassurance from their familiar bodies. The whistle of the shells flying through the light rain meant none of them managed to drop off the edge into sleep that first night.

Just as the light was cresting the horizon, the clouds receding enough to give them a brief break from the torrential rain, they heard the sound of heavy boots clomping against the wooden duckboards. The men looked up to see Second Lieutenant Welsh strolling towards them. At the sight, all the new recruits got slowly to their feet, a half-hearted attempt at acknowledging the officer's higher rank.

"At ease," he ordered.

The men sat back down or leant against the side of the trench.

"We have just been instructed that, at six hundred hours tomorrow morning, we will be launching an attack on the German line. Please be ready, and may God be with you all." He saluted, walking past them so he could instruct the others farther down the line.

Lieutenant Prince came up behind him. "Men, for some of you, this will be your first time over the top. I'm sorry to present you with this order so soon, but it is why we are here. Try not to panic. I will be leading you as I have done thus far and will continue to do for as long as I am kept alive. There have been a number of heavy attacks in the past few weeks, and we have been assured the German line is weakened and their wire obliterated. Practise fitting your bayonets, make sure your gun is clean, and keep your wits about you. Ammo must be easily reachable and stocked up. Rum rations will be distributed to everybody tonight."

Gray turned cold. He had only been there a day. How could they go over the top already? His father had told him some of the soldiers that had been at the front since the start still hadn't been over. He looked at both Arthur and Charlie, who were as fearful as he was. Charlie was clenching his jaw as if close to tears.

Gray slipped down to the floor, pulling out a piece of paper from his pack. He had to write to his family. His hands trembled with fear, and he had to rewrite the same letter four times so that his words portrayed an image of confidence.

Arthur, because of his excellent eyesight, was placed on sentry duty that night. Charlie and Gray thus had to sit in the mud huddled up together for reassurance. The fear seemed to turn Charlie's insides to liquid. He jumped up often, running down to the latrines—a popular destination that night.

On one of those occasions Lieutenant Prince, noticing that Gray was alone, sat down beside him.

"How are you feeling, Brogan?"

"Gray, sir. Please call me Gray."

"All right, Gray. How are you feeling?"

"Not so good, sir." He smiled tightly up at the officer, who squeezed his shoulder.

"The other men find solace in their families. You said you were close to your mother. You got a picture of her? That helps the others."

"Yes, sir. Right here." He pulled out the drawing he had folded in his breast pocket. "That's Genevieve. Jen's my sister. Well, I don't know what she is to me really, but Uncle Billy raised her in our house. Mother tried to pitch in as best she could, so she's a sister in my eyes, and that's all that counts. That...that's Mother. Sir, are you all right?"

The officer was looking at the picture with a dumbfound expression, just as he had been looking at his pocket watch back when Gray had shouted at Major Corvin. Prince reached over, taking the picture out of Gray's hands as if he didn't even realise he was doing it.

"Hmm?" he said, startling out of his reverie. "Yes, quite all right, Gray. What...what did you say your mother's name was?"

"Oh, Annabel, sir. Lady Annabel Brogan, formerly Hoddington. Did you know her, sir?"

"Yes." He sounded far away, looking back up at Gray as if studying him. "Yes, I think I might have a…a long time ago, though. How many years separate you and your sister?"

"Only one, sir. That's why we're so close, I reckon."

Prince was lost in thought again for several moments before he gave another tight smile in Gray's general direction and walked off, ducking into the dugout he shared with Welsh.

Another sleepless night stretched in front of the men in the trench. The bombardment was heavy throughout the night as it tried to rip apart what was left of the enemy wire. Knowing they would be directly under them in a matter of hours, the sound of the shells took on a new terror for the soldiers. The explosions vibrated the ground the men sat on, shaking their bones and occasionally hitting within centimetres of severe damage.

Approaching five in the morning, Prince walked down the trench, shaking the few lucky men who had achieved sleep into consciousness. Arthur was released from sentry duty only a few minutes before they were due to go over the top. Standing together once more the three friends each made sure their barrels were clean, using desperate, twitching fingers, and tried to force down a rushed meal. Following this, they stood behind a row of wooden ladders lining the trench wall. Prince and Welsh patrolled the line of men, their faces confident but their eyes wild.

"Company listen," bellowed Prince with a clear authority. If he was scared, he hid it well. "Your mission is to reach the German trench. You are to take out every machine gun post you come across, pushing the Hun back behind their lines. Do not stop. Do not come back. You keep moving forwards, no matter what. You stop, you become a sitting duck. You return, and you will be court-martialled. Put your head down. Think of yourself, your king, and your country. We mustn't run. Keep the line steady at all times and walk with the dignity of true British men."

Gray swallowed, his tongue sticking to the roof of his mouth with the movement. Prince seemed to look only at him when he uttered his next words.

"Good luck."

"Two minutes," Welsh shouted, checking everyone's guns as he walked. "Fix bayonets!"

A swooshing sound filled the air as blades were drawn, followed by a dull click as the men fixed them into the top of their rifles. Gray, his hands shaking, felt warm fingers on his as Charlie helped him with the blade. He gave Charlie a small smile before looking at Arthur at his other side. Gray squeezed his new friend's shoulders, drinking in their features in a desperate plea for them to both live.

He noticed Arthur squint slightly as he looked through the trench's loophole, which was directly in front of Gray.

"One minute," Prince shouted, climbing onto the ladder beside Welsh. "May king and country bless you all."

He placed a long whistle between his teeth. The air was so still that Gray heard the click as the metal touched the enamel. Prince held his pocket watch in the hand not already holding the ladder. Gray took a deep shuddering breath, and Arthur lunged forwards.

"Get down," he screamed, pushing Gray so hard that he fell, taking out Charlie's legs as he crashed to the ground. Several other men, their legs unstable in their fear, also fell. The clatter of guns falling and mess tins clanking together drowned out the shot ringing out across no-man's-land. Arthur's body fell to the floor last. A warm trickle of sticky liquid landed on Gray's neck as

Arthur's head rested on his shoulder. The second it had taken to push Gray from the line of fire had cost him his life.

Everything went fuzzy as Gray lay in a daze beneath Arthur's lifeless form. Gray felt a hand grab the top of his pack just as the whistle blew and everyone dived forwards, stepping over the dead man and his grieving companions. Gray didn't look back. He didn't have time to think as he scrambled over the top to the sound of a lone bugle harmonising their slaughter.

The machine guns started up at once. Their attack had been expected.

A frenzy of screaming battle cries met the bullets. The ladder was rough under his hands as he climbed. At the top, Gray saw nothing but a blur of derelict land, illuminated by flashes of explosions as he stumbled through the gap in their wire, scratching every part of exposed skin. His uniform caught and tore in several places. Once through, he flattened as he'd been instructed to do, working on instinct and waiting with the rest of the men for the second whistle. When the high-pitched sound pierced the chaotic air, he heaved himself back to his feet and stumbled forwards, falling often in the upturned dirt. He held his rifle out in front of him, ready to fire, and tuned into the authoritative sound of Prince's voice.

"Keep the line steady. Steady on the left. Richards, don't stop! I said steady on the left. Not so fast. Come on, close up the line. Steady."

Men screamed and disappeared from Gray's view before they had even risen off their knees. He whirled around as something warm splashed his cheek.

"Keep going forwards, Gray," Prince shouted amidst the chaos.

Men screamed out in pain, lost in panic, their eyes wild with fear.

Prince's voice, still chanting his orders to keep the line steady, remained a constant in Gray's sensitive ears, pulling him along. Gray's feet caught. He fell, his mouth filling with mud. He was pulled back up, squelching in something with the next step. He cried out in horror when he looked down, seeing his boots painted the deep red of blood. Prince's voice dragged him onwards.

Bullets whizzed past his head like frenzied insects. Wounded people grabbed at his legs. His rifle hung down by his side, useless in the madness.

Suddenly, he was in the air—thrown upwards by an explosion.

Gray landed on his back, the wind knocked out of him. He struggled for breath, trying with all his might to stand. He wanted to find Charlie, he hadn't seen him since they'd gone over the top. He got to his feet just as shrapnel flew through the air, scratching his hands and face. A loud bang echoed across the horizon, and a flash lit up Gray's vision, just before everything went black.

Chapter Thirteen

Gray didn't know how much time had passed before consciousness caught up with him again. He tried to open his eyes but didn't seem able. Something heavy was pressing onto him. His mouth and nose were filled with mud. Panic coursed through his body as he realised he was trapped beneath the earth.

He kicked out his limbs, desperately clawing at the dirt as he attempted to reach the air. Blood pounded in his head whilst his lungs burned. Reflexively, he tried to suck in the mud in a desperate bid for breath. He choked, his throat trying to extract the intruding substance from his system. Finally, after the longest few seconds of his life, his hand shot through into the cold air.

He lunged towards it, throwing up a pool of black vomit and coughing as his throat cleared before rasping in as many deep breaths as he could. The earth was grainy on his tongue, but the refreshing air raced down into his starving body. He tore the earth from his legs, his fingers brushing over warm pieces of a stranger's flesh, dislodged from their owner in the explosion. He heaved again, throwing up once more. The smell of meat clung to him as he wiped his mouth.

A bullet whizzed past him. He flattened onto his stomach. The sound of machine guns stuttered in the distance. The sudden movements caused pain to shoot through the back of his head, and his vision blurred. Lifting slightly, he looked around for cover whilst he figured out his position. He didn't know if he was facing the German or British lines. Everything looked so similar—just a stretch of barren wasteland. Corpses littered the churned up mud, some wriggling like maggots, not quite dead. His ears were filled with a high pitched ringing, gently punctuated by the soft moans of the wounded. Many were screaming for their mothers.

He crawled slowly forward, as flat to the ground as he could get and still tasting the gritty mud and human flesh on his tongue. His eyes stung with unshed tears whilst every breath he drew made a horrible rasping sound, searing his throat and lungs with pain. Reaching a deep shell hole he fell into it grateful for this small protection. He wondered just how many people this explosion had killed. Sliding down the earth, he saw at least three men, each in the khaki uniform of the British lines. His heart soared, he was all right.

When he hit the bottom, he faced the men, quickly realising two of them were dead. His eyes flicked over their forms, noticing how they were both missing limbs—their faces so covered in dirt and blood he couldn't tell the one from the other. Perhaps the flesh he had been buried beneath had belonged to one of these men. The only distinguishing feature was an eye hanging from the socket of the second man. The pistol still clutched in his cold hand told Gray it was an officer, and dread dropped into his stomach. It could only be Welsh or Prince.

Swallowing back another bout of sickness, he turned to the third man, who made a low, pained moan. He was still alive, but barely. His hands were trying to cover a gaping wound in his stomach. A large blood covered piece of shrapnel lay at his side.

A thick streak of blood led down the entire wall of the hole where he must have crawled into it with the shrapnel still embedded in his organs.

The hands now resting over the wound shook violently, blood jumping out between his fingers with each slow beat of his heart. Gray leapt towards him, pulling out his field dressing. He tore it open, exactly as he had been instructed, in an attempt to staunch the wound but there was too much blood. Pulling back the man's shaking hands, Gray could see his bare organs as clearly as if he were in a medical lecture. They shone, wet and slimy, in the dim light. The mere idea that he could help was absurd. Gray was instantly aware the man was going to die.

"Please," he whispered. The single utterance looked like the most painful experience of his short life. He touched the rifle at his side. He wanted Gray to shoot him.

Gray stretched out his hand, taking up the rifle without hesitation. He kept his eyes locked on the wounded man's face, which was twisted in agony beyond belief. He pointed the gun and pulled the trigger, but nothing happened. The private cried out, tears racing down his cheeks as the shock wore off and the full scale of his pain seemed to finally hit him.

Looking around frantically, Gray realised he had been separated from his own rifle and fear slithered into him. His eyes fell on the pistol clasped in the dead officer's hand. He clambered over to it, prying it from its owner and bent back over the wounded man.

"Thank you."

The man whispered the words with a smile on his face just before Gray, tears in his own eyes, pulled the trigger for a second time.

A single bullet soared out of the barrel, right through the wounded soldier's head. His hands gave a last violent tremble before they fell back into his ruined stomach. The blood continued to pump out through his dead fingers for a few moments, the speed steadily slowing, soaking the earth beneath them all.

Gray sank to his knees, his hands beginning to shake ever so slightly as they fell at his sides. The pistol dropped to the ground as he struggled not to cry. When his emotions subsided somewhat, he bent over onto all fours, dry heaving on the ground. He reached around into his pack for water, draining it all in just a couple of gulps. The cool liquid soothed his raw throat, and Gray closed his eyes in pleasure, feeling it seep down through his body.

Gaining back his wits, he crawled up the side of the hole, peering over the edge to try once more to gain his bearings. He knew he was supposed to keep going forwards, yet he wasn't sure what way forwards was. He couldn't see anybody else standing — just the odd movement of a wounded man writhing in the dirt.

Gray had been one of the last out of the trench and had been separated from Charlie very early on. Remembering Arthur had been hit, a stab of grief pierced through his heart. He rested his face in the crook of his elbow, willing himself once more not to cry. Taking another shaky, rasping breath, he looked out at no-man's-land.

He wondered what had happened to Prince as he crawled back down into the hole and over to the dead officer. Without looking into his grotesque face, Gray reached into his breast pocket and pulled out his pay book. Ripping it open and staining the pages with the undried blood caking his fingers, he read: Second Lieutenant Fredrick R. Welsh. Relief flooded through him, followed immediately by guilt.

Gray's vision had been knocked out of kilter by the explosion, making everything appear ever so slightly out of focus. His head pounded. Thinking of his own health, he leant against his pack, surrounded by the dead, and patted himself down. He knew he could not go back until nightfall. To attempt a retreat in broad daylight would be suicide. Instead, he tried to piece together what had happened to him.

He felt bruises in several places whilst his muscles burnt with exertion. The only serious injury, though, seemed to be his head. He lifted a hand, touching the spot where the worst of the pain seemed to come from. He felt a sticky wetness beneath his touch, and upon withdrawing the hand, saw fresh blood mixing with the dead man's drying blood, caking his fingers a shocking red. He reached for his field dressings, remembering how he had foolishly wasted them on the other man, and searched the bodies in the hole cautiously. When he found the dressings he removed them slowly almost as if he were afraid of disturbing the dead men.

He wrapped these dressings around his head in a clumsy attempt to stop himself losing more blood. His air starved lungs still ached from the minutes he had spent buried. Gray realised he must have come incredibly close to death. The concussion made his head spin as he tried to stand up again, so he lay down. Unsure of his whereabouts and knowing the German eyes would be fixed on the bit of land he was hiding in, he knew he would be there for hours, regretting finishing his water already.

"What way should I go?" he asked one of the less deformed corpses, laughing slightly at the absurdity of the situation. "Such a good listener, chum." He shook his head, and the pain sweeping through it made him feel violently sick as white spots danced across his vision.

He couldn't sit there, talking to dead people. He pulled out the sketch of his mother and Genevieve, tracing his cleanest fingertip lightly over their features and trying to imagine them sitting beside him. His mother would be stroking his hair tenderly, and Genevieve would be leaning in his lap while making him laugh with her ridiculously embellished stories.

Yet, after a short while of the welcome distraction, he felt wrong. It didn't feel right to bring them there. His memories of them were so perfect, so pure. They didn't belong to the barren land of death.

Needing distraction, he decided to check the rest of the men for identification clues, hoping to find letters he could return to their families. He felt sorry now that he had bloodied Welsh's pay book.

Gray found a photo in the breast pocket of every man, and he pushed them into his own pocket to show Prince when—not if—he reached his own line again. He knew missing was worse for the families than dead, it gave them false hope. He paused by the last corpse, the one he had killed. He touched the man's face, trying to brush off some of the muck. He had been a handsome man, and his skin was still soft and warm beneath Gray's touch. He had been young too, probably younger than Gray.

Snapping out of his daze he checked the pockets, everything he pulled out was completely saturated with blood, so much so it was impossible to read. The paper in his pay book was literally dripping with the warm liquid. Next, his mouth still grainy and dry, he checked each man for water, filling his own bottle with the remnants of theirs to ration it throughout the day.

Leaning back against the wall as far from the dead men as he could get, he tucked his knees into his chest—trying desperately to stop the spinning in his head.

The moaning of the wounded around him grew quieter as the men succumbed to the warm darkness of death—so much nicer than the cold battlefield their consciousness kept dragging them back to. The occasional wail of despair made Gray jump. He felt horrid, sitting there alive when so many were dying. He tried several times to figure out his position but to no avail. Close to one of the lines there was an overturned cart he couldn't remember passing. His empty stomach growled as the day wore on, and he slipped into unconsciousness several times—each time waking further weakened. Fear gripped him every time he realised consciousness had left him. He was terrified he would slip away and not re-awaken.

Once the sun had set, sheathing the field in an impenetrable darkness, Gray crawled out of the hole, feeling off balance and queasy with the movement. His belly was pressed against the mud as he fumbled blindly onwards. He stayed down to avoid being spotted whenever flares were released from the lines, using the light to gauge how far he had come and how far he had yet to travel. After about an hour of slow crawling, his hand slipped, causing his entire body to fall into another shell hole.

He landed with a thud at the bottom, his mouth once more filling with mud. Panic shot through him again, but he managed to crawl out of the hole within seconds. It took him a few minutes for his breathing to slow. His hands were cut to pieces, and his heart hammered against his chest. He was still not sure if friend or foe lay in wait for him and wouldn't until he was faced with them. Although, in the darkness, it would be hard to tell he was a British soldier and he might just get shot down by his own side.

As the fear took over almost completely, those thoughts made his hands shake again like a slower version of the wounded man in the shell hole. He got so close to the line, he could hear the musical sounds of English words—the survivors jovial at their success whilst mourning their fallen friends. Gray thought there had never been a sound so beautiful in his life.

A bullet whizzed past the top of his head when he was within a few feet of the trench. He felt a slight sting in his still open wound and realised the metal shot had flown so close it had touched the bandage around his skull.

"It's me," he croaked, his throat dry and painful, barely able to make a sound. "Private Grayson Brogan. Let me in." He ducked as another bullet soared past him then swallowed, trying to increase the volume of his voice and hoping against hope this was the British line.

"Private Grayson Brogan. Let me in." He was nearly sobbing in desperation.

"Gray?" Charlie's head popped up over the top. The relief washing through him in that moment was almost unbearable. He crawled as fast as he could with Charlie directing him to the gap in the wire. Tumbling down into the trench, he fell straight inside a tight embrace, both him and Charlie clinging to each other in desperate need of a warm, friendly touch.

"Jesus, old chap, I nearly killed you," his friend whispered in his ear, his warm breath reassuring on Gray's neck.

"Thank you for missing," Gray muttered, too exhausted to move.

Charlie pushed him back against the wall of the trench, holding him up by his tunic to look at him. "What happened?"

Gray shook his head.

"I don't know. I was separated from you, and I heard… Arthur, he's—"

The look in Charlie's eyes told him that he had already known.

"I got knocked down by a shell. The shrapnel must have hit my head. When I woke up, I couldn't see anyone, and I didn't know which direction was ours. I just crawled, hoping it would be the right way."

His breathing was coming fast again as the memories flooded into his mind. He was almost delirious with exhaustion, having not slept properly in nearly three days.

"I asked Prince, when he returned, what had happened to you. He said he'd lost you. He thinks you're dead. An M.I.A telegram is probably being written as we speak. Can you stand?"

Gray leant forwards, trying to ease himself up using the wall. No longer powered by adrenaline, his bones felt as if they had turned to jelly. Charlie stayed at his side. Draping Gray's arm over his shoulder, they made their way along the trench. Gray's head felt far too heavy for his neck, and his legs buckled as he tried to take as much of his own weight as possible. Charlie struggled with Gray's bulk, weak from the day's attack.

They each heard the heavy boots falling on the duckboards at the same time. The irregular rhythm of the footfalls told them it was Prince, his limp worse when he was tired or off guard. His hazel eyes fixed on Gray's blue ones, and he stopped dead.

"Gray," he muttered, rushing to his side, taking the other limp arm, and draping it over his broad shoulders. "What happened?"

"Shrapnel. Buried. Wait for dark," he muttered, more than half asleep. His legs were useless, and he slumped forwards, hearing Charlie's laboured breathing in his ear.

"It's all right, Grimsby. I've got him. Go rest."

Gray's body shifted into his leader's safe arms and he was immediately carried off to safety.

Chapter Fourteen

Gray woke to the rich smell of earth in his nostrils and the sounds of shell fire filling his ears. He jumped upright, immediately letting out a loud yell. Clasped within the clutches of a dream, he believed he was still buried beneath the dirt— a soldier with trembling hands at his side and the scent of rotting flesh in his nose. He could see the other man with his eye hanging from its socket, and he heard Arthur's scream as he was hit by the fatal shot. Arthur—so strong, so promising, his entire future laid out in front of him—had lost his life so Gray could live.

What gave him the right to be alive over Arthur? It seemed grossly unfair.

Gray felt a hand on his shoulder and looked to his side, focusing on a pair of green eyes. He sat there, confused for a few seconds, the nightmare still clinging to his vision before Charlie's gentle face came into sight. Gray relaxed, his breathing still heavy. Cold sweat coated his skin and made his clothes damp. Looking down at himself, he saw he was still dressed in his uniform and seemed to be sitting in an officer's dugout. He felt a thick bandage wrapped around his head like a turban.

"You're all right, old chap. Signed off as fit, if you can believe it." He passed over Gray's mess tin, filled with semi-warm soup.

He held it in his hands but didn't eat. "Where am I?"

"Lieutenant Prince brought you into his dugout, as you weren't seriously wounded. Any other time, they'd send you to the dressing station at least, but it's full. As it was only a mild concussion, the medical officer said you may as well stay here. Major Corvin turned up, if you believe it, and gave the order for you to remain in the trenches. Revenge, I reckon. He's only passing through, mind. Conveniently arrived when the attack had finished and left within the hour."

"Coward. Why am I here, though? Prince's being awfully nice to me. It's eerie. Reckon it's just because of my family? You don't think my father's paid him off do you?"

Charlie laughed. "No, seems like a nice chap all round, really. Probably put you here to annoy Corvin. Gave me an extra rum ration today because he thought I'd found you. I didn't correct him."

Gray smiled.

"Probably just scared that you look so alike," Charlie added.

"His eyes are a different colour."

"Nice colour, though. Um, unusual colour, not... I don't look into... They're quite expressive." He laughed, embarrassed and blushing slightly. "Anyway, your father's eyes are a different colour than yours as well."

"My mother has blue eyes."

"Mhmm, eat your soup. There's water here too. We need to go back out soon."

"All right, Charlie, you go. I'll be out in a minute. I think I just need to gather up my wits."

Charlie nodded, retreating up the steps. Gray leant back on the narrow bed, closing his eyes slightly in an attempt to clear his mind of the terrible memories shadowing him. He sat up, swinging his legs off the side of the low bed and easing himself to his feet shakily. He swayed a little at first, feeling dizzy. When his eyes refocused, they fixed on his mother.

He squeezed his eyes shut, and when he reopened them, his mother was still there. Her face peered out of a small photograph tucked inside the lid of a silver pocket watch. The image looked as if it had been cut from a newspaper and portrayed a much younger woman than the woman Gray knew. She was around his age, he would guess. Her hair was piled on her head and she was smiling, though something in her eyes suggested she was far from happy. She was wearing the long, ornate veil she had worn to her wedding.

Gray picked up the watch, running a finger over the cool edge. The quiet ticking seemed loud in the small space. He couldn't remember his mother being that young, but she had been really rather beautiful. Of course, she always had been, but in the picture, she was perfect.

"Ah, you're awake."

He hadn't heard Prince enter. He jumped, snapping shut the pocket watch and whirling around to face his officer. "Yes, sir."

"You haven't eaten your soup. It's gone cold. I know it's terrible stuff, but you really must eat if you're going to get your strength up."

"Oh, erm, yes. I was just about to." He picked up the tin, gulping down the soup ravenously. He hadn't realised just how hungry he had been until he had finished the tin of food, licking the remnants off the sides and wiping his mouth on the back of his hand. He felt his energy flood back into him. His legs became more stable, and the trembling in his hands slowed to a dull tremor. He smiled up at Prince.

"Thank you," he said, looking into his face. "For saving my life."

Prince ran a hand through his short blond hair. "I didn't do anything."

"You did. Your voice kept me moving. It was the only thing that kept me going straight. I just want to say that I will be eternally grateful, and I am forever within your debt."

Prince smiled back at him, his hazel eyes lighting up. Charlie had been right, they were very expressive. Gray paused for a minute with the lieutenant standing in the way of the exit.

"What are you going to do when the war's over, sir?" he asked to fill the awkward silence.

Prince looked confused. "I hadn't thought about it."

"Well, what did you do before the war?"

"Not a great deal of anything," he said in a guarded way, sitting down on the edge of the bed Gray had so recently occupied. "I was already in the army, so I got sent out here the second the war started, and got promoted two weeks in. That's how I came to be back in England with you."

"Yes, but you must have a home of some sort. A family, a wife, or something."

"None of the above, I'm afraid."

"Really?" Gray was shocked. "Parents, siblings, nothing? Where did you grow up?"

"Same place as you, kind of. I have a sister and a brother. I write to them often, but I only see them occasionally. They live somewhere where there are...bad memories, shall I say? People I'm avoiding as well, because it's too painful to run into *that* particular person. Billy can't read, though, so I guess someone reads for him."

Gray's heart lurched, and he felt as if the watch in his pocket was burning.

"I have an uncle named Billy. He's not... He's slow, I guess, but he is the nicest man I've ever met. Genevieve's father. She's the best friend I drew that picture of. A sister really."

He withdrew the drawing of his mother and best friend from his breast pocket again, bringing the photos and pocket books from the fallen soldiers he had met out in the shell hole with it. He looked at them for a minute, seeing only the trembling hands of the man he had shot, the blood pulsing through his fingers. He flinched as the sound of the bullet leaving the barrel reverberated through his mind. His hand shot subconsciously to the pistol now tucked in his belt, caressing the cool metal as if for comfort.

"Did you find these out there?" Prince asked picking up the items.

Gray nodded.

"I'll have them dealt with. The war office will want to know of the dead. Thank you, Gray."

He paused, running his hand back through his hair when he got to Welsh's book. Continuing through them, he unfolded a piece of paper much like the others. He seemed to jump a little as he scanned Gray's most recent letter from his mother.

"Sorry, that one's mine, sir," Gray muttered.

"Oh, sorry." The lieutenant seemed to jump again as if remembering he was in company. His brow creased in confusion. "Why is it addressed to Daniel?"

"Middle name, sir. My mother prefers to address me by it to avoid confusing me with my grandfather, I assume."

"Who...who did your mother get that middle name from?" That odd look crossed through the lieutenant's eyes again.

"An old friend is all she'll say. She told me it was someone who saved her life a long time ago, but she won't elaborate. Jen and I like to say he was an old lover. Jen likes scandalous tales like that. Mother says she needs to behave more ladylike, but I love it."

"And you don't like the name?" Lieutenant Prince looked touched in some way. His hazel eyes had gained warmth, and they shone almost gold. "Before you answer, I should probably inform you of my own first name."

"Oh... I didn't... Yes, it's a fine name."

Prince laughed, muttering his thanks.

"I just prefer Gray. Aunt Patsy flat out refuses to call me Daniel, so when Genevieve was small and couldn't pronounce my full or middle name, they thought of my nickname. It just kind of stuck."

"Tell me about Jen."

Gray smiled widely, sitting back on the bed. He felt the watch slide farther into his pocket as he told him everything about his best friend. Prince laughed as Gray recited one of her funnier tales, smiling reminiscently as he described her slight appearance, and showing Prince the sketch once more so he could explain better. He didn't feel bad bringing her there. It was warm, and she was spoken about in healthy, smiling company—not with three rotting corpses in a shell hole.

As he pointed to the picture, his fingers falling completely free of his sleeves, he noticed the slight tremor again. Prince frowned as he caught sight of it as well. Gray shook the sleeve back over himself, folding his hands in his lap as he tried to continue the conversation as if nothing was wrong. Prince hung on his every word, especially when Gray mentioned his mother. Prince, of course, gave nothing more away about his own life.

"Come on, sir. Surely, there is something to tell," he pried, feeling as if he were pushing his luck. "I've told you my entire life story."

Prince laughed. "Yes, but mine is nowhere near as interesting as yours."

"Have you ever been in love, sir?" he asked a little shy. He watched Prince's face fall ever so slightly.

"Yes," he whispered. "A very long time ago." He gave Gray a tight smile, patting his shoulder. "I think you need to re-join your friends, Gray."

"Friend, sir. Singular. Arthur, see… He…" Gray looked down, running a hand through his hair as if a mirror image of the man beside him.

"The sentry. I'm sorry. I spoke tactlessly. He was…promising."

Gray nodded, feeling his eyes sting in unshed grief. "Thank you, sir." He stood up, saluting his officer somewhat weakly and walked out into the bright sun, his boots squelching in the mud. When he had rounded a slight bend in the trench—engineered to stop shrapnel wiping out the company—he extracted Prince's pocket watch.

Clicking it open, he looked at the photograph closer. The watch itself harboured a lot of scratches. Gray thought this must have been the lucky charm Lieutenant Prince took over the top. What he couldn't understand, though, was why it contained a picture of his mother. Putting it back in his pocket, he found Charlie a little way down the line, a mug of steaming tea held between his hands.

"Ah, Gray, you're back with the living." Charlie winced at his tactless welcome, patting the space beside him for Gray to sit down. "How do you feel, old chap?"

"Good, I think," Gray replied touching the back of his head gingerly and wincing as he found the sore spot. He accepted a cigarette from his friend, taking a long pull on it and exhaling slowly. "What have I missed?"

The retaliating bombardment started up just before nightfall. The light dotting of shell fire had turned aggressive, pummelling the ground ever closer to the trench. Charlie and Gray lay huddled together, desperately clawing to sleep but unable to achieve the simple relief. Screams of full-grown men driven under a sea of terror, echoed up the line as the bombs hit their mark. A shower of flesh and mud rained down on their heads, and tinkled on the mess tins, filled with tea none of them were drinking. Gray held his newly acquired rifle to his chest for reassurance, but his hands trembled on the barrel. Charlie had the collar of his overcoat drawn up over his ears. His tin of cold tea was clenched in his grip as they all attempted normality amidst the barren backdrop of hell.

Another shell exploded only a few feet away. Startled, Gray jumped so violently he nearly toppled over. Both he and Charlie remained silent, each locked in their own thoughts. Gray fixed his gaze on the trench wall in front of him, trying not to think about Arthur. Getting slowly to his feet, he peered through the nearest loophole at the smoking expanse of no-man's-land. The odd body still moved. Whether with gas or life, he couldn't be certain. The stretcher bearers hadn't been able to get to them. Every now and then, a shell would fall amongst the writhing figures, hurling them into an array of different places—their limbs scattered amongst the dirt. Other wounded near the explosions screamed for mothers or sweethearts—full-grown men weeping from the knowledge they would be dead before morning.

Standing on the fire step, he squinted past the horrors in an attempt to see the German line and any movement therein. His head was still sore, the pain pounding behind his skull as he concentrated. The wind stung his eyes until tears leaked out of the corners. He tried to wipe them on his sleeve whilst keeping his gaze on no-man's-land, the pain grew worse until he could focus on nothing more. Images of Arthur falling upon him—a bullet hole in his head— and the breathless feeling of being trapped beneath the heavy earth kept creeping back into his mind.

"You all right, old chap?"

Startled, he turned slightly, nodding at Charlie who stood beside him. "You looked a bit unsteady there. You want to lie down?"

Not wanting to make the other men think badly of him, for their opinions of him as the weak rich boy to be founded, he shook his head and winced as it made the pain worse.

"No. No, I'm all right, Charlie. Thank you."

"You don't look all right. You're awfully pale."

"It's just...the wind, it's in my eyes. It makes them sting a little."

"Oh. It is quite strong. Lucky, though, it makes the shells go off course."

"Mmm, I suppose."

"Have you been thinking about Arthur? Is that why you're lying that you're all right?"

Gray was startled by how well Charlie could read him.

Sensing Gray's unease, Charlie continued speaking. "I know you don't want the men to think you weak, but illness isn't weakness, Gray. You were hit on the head, buried alive, and watched Arthur... Well, that's got to mess with you for a while."

"How do you know me so well? It's just… He died for me, and I don't see why. Why would someone risk their life for a… For… Well, I'm not anything! I'm just a stupid, naïve boy from a rich family. That's not even half worth dying for. He had so much he was good at, that he was going to do, and I took it all away from him. I've still got his blood on me for Christ sake."

He hadn't so much as thought those things until that moment, but he realised they were exactly what he felt.

"Don't feel like that, old—"

"Don't make light of this, Charlie. Please don't try to make this better. You and I both know it should have been me."

Drawing a shaky breath he paused. He was in a fragile state, close to tears. His cushy life had made him sensitive. Quietly, almost inaudible above the howling wind and shell blasts, he continued.

"I feel like I'm barely hanging on by a thread already. My father would be so disappointed in me, so ashamed if he could see me now, but maybe… Maybe I'm just not strong enough, not brave enough—"

Charlie's warm hand touched his shoulder, the thumb brushing over the skin of his neck as he pulled him closer. "Mother says an embrace and a cup of tea makes everything better. I think that only works on women, but worth a try, eh?"

Gray breathed out a laugh, grabbing a fistful of Charlie's tunic around his back. "You're a great friend, Charlie. I think I would have cracked it already without you."

"You're stronger than you look, old chap. You just need to start believing it. I'll get you that tea. If nothing else, it'll warm your hands a little, they're shaking so you must be cold."

The warm touch disappeared, slipping from Gray's searching

fingers. He felt lost without his friend's comforting presence but knew he must continue. He fixed his view forwards upon the barren landscape again, more for his own reassurance. He had been lucky, that was all. No matter what the others said, Arthur should have lived, and he—Grayson Daniel Brogan—should have died.

Chapter Fifteen

The next few weeks passed by mostly uneventful. There were no more planned attacks. The sound of steady shell fire faded into Gray's subconscious, whilst the flinching became nothing more than a nervous twitch he paid no heed to. The smell of rotting flesh and the sound of screaming also held less prominence in his mind now. Death was everywhere, so one more ended life failed to make too much of an impression.

Richards, who it turned out was only fourteen, had been shipped back to England not long after their first attack. His nerves in tatters, he had tried to escape over no-man's-land and was due for court-martial before his true age had been discovered. The government grew scared of repercussions, so they sent him to a mental hospital instead—knowing the degradation of his honour would be punishment in itself.

The men had all begun to make jokes about such people. Feeble-minded and weak is what they said.

One bolder member even, after a little too much cheap beer during one of their rests behind the line, had commented, "I am surprised, pretty boy." His voice was low and he had a beard darkening his heavy set jaw. "I thought you'd be the first to crack it. The rich are usually the first. They're too used to the fine life and not prepared to go without three square meals and a warm bed."

A few days after that incident, they were sitting in the reserve trench, about to travel back up the line. News reached them of a poor lad who, driven so helpless with fear, had put his own rifle in his mouth and taken himself permanently away from the war. None of the men joked about that. The enemy was a fear they could compartmentalise, but the thought of their minds turning against them drove the men half crazed with terror.

Sitting in the trench all day—for there seemed to be a fair amount of waiting around for things to happen, especially when only in the support or reserve trenches—Gray made a lot of sketches. A few of these featured the lieutenant who looked so much like him. Mostly, they were of the other soldiers in various scenarios. His experiences over the top inspired poetry as nothing else ever had. The pencil smudged onto his dirty fingers, making him feel a little more like himself again. Unable to wash, the lead had embedded itself under his nails so thick he didn't see how he'd ever remove it.

He had grown accustomed now to jokes on behalf of this artistic nature. Comments from the men regarding his sexuality seemed rife. He learnt to not be offended but to take the comments in jest and even retort in highly witty, clever ways that always earned him a laugh. Gray would compose jingles for people, often containing offensive or rude rhymes which had them all in stitches. He sent some of the least offensive back to Genevieve, which she appreciated immensely, telling him in her very elaborate writing style just how funny she had found them. The constant reminder of how fragile their lives were seemed to make everyone much more willing to be jovial.

These small moments of pleasure disappeared when he slept. As soon as he closed his eyes, he was faced with a version of Arthur approaching him, his face covered in scarlet blood with his unseeing gaze always fixed upon Gray. Whenever he felt himself losing his grasp on the conscious world, his lungs would falter with the weight of earth crushing down on his chest. His hands trembled violently, blood spurting from between his imaginary fingers as vivid as if he was right back in that shell hole.

He woke up every day with a muffled scream as he huddled against Charlie's shoulder, crammed into a shallow dugout in the side of the trench for warmth. The first smell was that of earth, bringing back that terrifying moment when he had been buried alive, dragging the dream into the first few seconds of consciousness. The tremor in his hands matched his nightmare, no matter how much he tried to hide it. He was jerked awake with every shell explosion. Every bullet whizzing into the air made his eyes wild with fear.

He dared not make any more close friends, aside from Charlie, in fear that like Arthur, they would perish too soon, leaving a void in his life that could never be filled. Every time Prince and the new Second Lieutenant Shepard walked past or crept towards the ladder for their nightly patrol, he was terrified they would be going back over.

Along with this constant fear gnawing the minds of each man, their feet were slowly beginning to rot at the bottom of their living legs. Every few days, officers checked the men's feet and widely distributed whale oil to help keep them as clean and dry as possible, but they could never be kept completely free from the water forever lining the trench.

The poor sanitation meant their uniforms quickly became

itchy with lice, and the warm creases of their joints burnt as if on fire. The insects leapt in joy at the perfect nesting conditions the troops had provided for them. They all scratched without even realising they were doing it. Their grimy skin was raw from the habit, drawing blood on more than one occasion due to the fierceness with which they itched. Some brief amusement came from holding a match close to a seam and hearing the lice pop when they came in contact with the flame. A steady hand was needed for this, so Gray's shirt had become pockmarked with singes from his own efforts.

The conditions meant they were unable to wash for weeks on end. They grew accustomed to the constant smell of body odour, which was a sweet perfume compared to the scent emitted by the less fortunate of their contemporaries, scattered around them. As he had been told on his first day, Gray soon got used to the rats as well. The beasts were everywhere and made for frightfully good target practise.

Gray became quite skilled with his new pistol, taking out heaps of the vermin in a single hour. Nobody questioned where he had gotten the new weapon. All the men had souvenirs from the top, so they just accepted its presence without thought or comment. Everyone knew it should have been sent to the officer's family, but nobody wanted to confront Gray about it when it brought him so much reassurance.

The brief days they got to spend behind the lines were the only things keeping them all somewhat sane. Gray filled himself with potatoes and beer from whatever godforsaken village they found themselves in and bathed in a variety of different makeshift tubs. The favourite seemed to be feeding troughs from barns. Like the first time, he shared the bath with several other men, relishing in the brief relief from the itching lice before the new eggs hidden in the seams hatched spreading the parasites back to their former population within the hour. The previous shyness when it came to this activity faded the longer he spent in France. Yet, he still only undressed when he absolutely must and avoided looking at anyone. He never viewed them in any improper state of undress for too long. The other men didn't seem to have these worries.

The weather slowly became colder, easing them into the harshest winter Gray could ever remember seeing. The ground became solid beneath his feet whilst the water lining the trenches froze, becoming dangerously slippery. One lucky man actually managed to shatter his ankle by falling over and was sent back to England on the next boat. They received reports that he'd ruined the bone so much he would be doing an office job. He was the envy of every man in the company.

Several times, Gray caught soldiers trying to recreate the incident, although, they only ever succeeded in the odd bruise and one court-martial. The men quit the endeavour when the firing squad were called into action. The remaining men sat as close together as they could get, huddled in their great coats, their noses red and stuffy.

On the last day of November, Prince marched down the trench with the news they had all prayed not to hear again.

"We go over the top tomorrow morning, lads. Five hundred hours sharp. We'll hit Fritz while they're still sleeping and take them by surprise. Get some rest, clean your guns, and be ready."

Prince was wearing the deep frown between his brows again. Even this figure of strength was frightened. His eyes locked on Gray's petrified face as he leant into him slightly.

"Remember to keep going. No matter what," he whispered so

only Gray could hear. "And use your gun this time. You're a damn good shot I've seen you. Use that skill, Gray, and… And promise me to stay alive. I'll look out for you as best I can, but you must keep yourself safe above everything else."

Standing up, he addressed the men as a whole. He moved down the line, checking them and making sure they were ready for the morning. He offered them words of encouragement to reduce the terror settling over everyone like a net from which there was no escape. He really was a fantastic officer, going out of his way for the safety of his men.

On the other hand, Shepard—like Welsh before him—only did what his job description stated before retreating to his dugout with a bottle of whisky clasped in his hand. He must have drunk a bottle a day by the look of his bloodshot eyes. He was another product of promotion due to necessity as opposed to skill. Gray was immensely proud of himself for not yielding to the pressure of enlisting under that dishonour.

No matter who Prince was talking to, or what he was doing, he kept glancing back over his shoulder at Gray with concern in his hazel eyes. The company all downed their extra alcohol, desperately trying to drown out their fear. Charlie was making his frequent visits to the latrine once more—swearing loudly every time he got up, running to his destination bent double, and holding his stomach. It would have been comical in a different context.

Gray sat against his pack, smoking an endless chain of cigarettes, and his hands trembling worse than ever. The heavy feeling returned to his chest. Reliving the moments he had spent in a shallow grave made him jump. Leaning forwards, he heaved onto the slippery duckboards, his vomit melting the snow and steaming into the freezing air.

"Gray."

He felt a strong hand on each of his cheeks, pulling his face up. Prince's face was just an inch in front of his, their noses nearly touching.

"You'll be all right, Gray. Listen to me, don't panic. Keep your head straight."

Gray nodded, his face crumpling into tears that he had so long suppressed. He blushed, angry that his emotions had betrayed him to this authoritative figure. The officer didn't seem to mind. He just pulled Gray into his chest, running his hand through his hair. The gesture made him think of both his mother and uncle, and it made him sob even harder.

"You're all right. I won't let you die," Prince muttered, his chin touching the top of Gray's head.

He let himself be held like this for a long while, the debris from a nearby shell raining down on them as he was rocked into a light sleep. He woke up with a start, screaming against the khaki-clad chest of his officer, as Prince's fingers still combed through his cropped hair.

"Shh… You'll be all right. Try to get some more sleep."

But he couldn't rest. His nerves were on edge, his hands shaking and his stomach turning violently. Gray turned around, breaking free of Prince's arms to throw up on the floor again, coughing up everything left in his stomach. Prince rubbed his back, trying to steady him before he got up to fetch him some water. Gray downed it quickly, a cold sweat breaking out over his skin.

"Your hands," Prince stated, prying Gray's fingers from his tin.

He snatched his hand back, covering it with his coat sleeve. "I'm fine, just cold," Gray muttered.

"Please, let me help you."

"I don't need your help! Do you think I'm weak? Because I'm from a rich family I don't belong here? There are men much more worthy of your sympathies, Lieutenant."

Daniel reached out his hand again to touch Gray's shoulder. Gray scrambled back in a sudden fury.

"Why are you so obsessed with me? Are you…you a one of those Oscar Wilde types or something? You know that's illegal, don't you? You'll get put in prison, dishonoured, and shamed."

Prince laughed, a proper laugh from deep within his body as if sharing in a private joke Gray was not privy to. Gray's blood boiled.

"Don't laugh at me. Shove off and help someone else, leave me alone."

Still smiling, Prince stood up to walk down the trench, checking on the other terrified soldiers. Charlie came back not long afterwards, having stayed near the latrines for a while. He handed Gray another cigarette, lighting them both with the same match. They sat in silence while they smoked, a twisted mirror of their first day at training, blowing smoke rings with Arthur. The light from Gray's cigarette moved as he fought to keep his fingers still. At least, in this weather, he could pretend it was just the frost making him shiver.

They got their food an hour before they were meant to go over. Few of them ate much, forcing down a few spoonfuls for energy. Even fewer kept those meagre mouthfuls down.

Lining up at the bottom of the ladders, a couple of men on the fire step, they all kissed their charms and took a last look at the pictures of their loved ones. Prince, at the top of the ladder, kept feeling his breast pocket as if hoping to find something there.

Slipping his hand into his own pocket, Gray brushed his fingers along the cool metal of the pocket watch he had stolen after their first trip over. He hoped Prince would live, he needed to apologise, and he needed to get the watch back to him in private where he could ask for an explanation. He should have done it already, but ironically he hadn't been able to summon the courage.

"Fix bayonets," Shepard shouted, a slight break in his voice.

The sound of metal clanking drowned out his voice. Gray's shaking fingers clicked the bayonet in place much more expertly than the last time. He took a long look at Charlie's handsome face. His curls were just beginning to stick out of his cap where they hadn't been cut for a while.

"Good luck, old chap."

Gray smiled as convincingly as he could, squeezing his friend's hand. "And to you."

Prince placed the whistle between his teeth just like last time.

Gray took a deep shuddering breath and placed his foot on the first rung of the ladder. Time seemed to stand still with only the sound of the air pushing itself through his mouth and down into his lungs, harmonised with the quick drumbeat of his heart.

Prince checked his wrist where a very battered-looking wrist watch sat. He seemed to stare at it for ages.

Gray let out his breath. The world was so quiet. Even the bombardment had ceased in anticipation of their attack. So intent on listening to the strange silence he jumped, his heart in his mouth, as the whistle blew, loud and shrill.

The soldiers all charged, most falling back into the trench before they had even made it to the top. Once over, Gray pointed his rifle towards the German line, shooting blindly as he walked forwards, tripping often on the upturned ground. He splashed his way through rain filled shell holes, skidding on ice as the fierce wind sliced into him. He emptied an entire magazine in seconds, stopping just long enough to rip a new one from his belt and fit it into the rifle. His hands shook so violently he nearly dropped the ammunition into the icy water.

A bullet grazed his face, drawing blood that trickled down his cheek and onto his shoulder. Startled, he stumbled forwards once more, leaping over the fallen members of his company in his rush. The sound of Prince chanting in front of him kept him straight, just like the last time. A strange exhilaration flooded his system. He was alive and walking straight into the face of death. Laughing, a disturbing noise in the chaos and horror surrounding him, he looked down as he stepped over another body.

Realising with horror that it was Charlie, his laughter died on his lips, and he sank to his knees.

"Gray, keep going," Charlie cried, shouting above the noise.

"No, I'm not leaving you behind."

"Just go. You're a sitting duck here. Please."

"No! Where are you hit?"

Charlie groaned. "In the leg. Help me up then. We have to keep going."

Gray slung his arm around his friend's waist, taking most of his weight. Looking around frantically for some vague source of shelter, he spotted a cart wheel. He looked upon this as a sign and stumbled towards it, the sound of pained cries and bullets flying around them. It must have only taken thirty seconds to get Charlie behind the wheel, but it felt like hours.

Setting Charlie down, he reached up, putting his rifle in a gap in the wheel. The movement sent a searing pain through Gray's arm, and he looked down with wide eyes, noticing a bloom of scarlet seeping across his sleeve.

"Where did you get hit?" Charlie asked, noticing the expression on his friend's face.

"Just the arm. I'll be fine." Gray tried to ignore the pain. Adrenaline was pulsing through him at such magnitude he hardly felt it in any case. He pointed his rifle once more. Charlie did the same from his lower position. Gray's aim was perfect. He shot two German snipers directly between the eyes before bringing down a soldier manning one of the enemy machine guns. The soldier was immediately replaced by another, and Gray ducked a bullet aimed for him.

Splinters from the wheel rained down on his bare head. He had lost his cap in the commotion. Crouching next to Charlie, he took out the soldier still pointing his smoking gun at them. They found themselves so close to the German line they could even make out the expressions on the soldier's faces.

Gray fiddled with his belt, pulling out a grenade, made in bulk the night before from an old jam tin. Supplies were short at the front, and they needed to improvise the best they could. The British government sent them all sorts of rubbish with which to try to keep themselves alive. Gray lit the bomb and stood up, throwing it as hard as he could. He screamed when it caused the bullet in his other arm to bury itself deeper and blood soaked his sleeve.

The grenade exploded. German troops flew into the air. Scraps of grey fabric and dirt rained down on Gray's head, along with warmer things that he blocked from his mind.

"Stay here," he shouted to Charlie.

"No, you're hit. Gray!" Charlie screamed back.

Gray ran out from behind his temporary shelter and towards the German line.

"Cover me," he called over his shoulder.

In a blind fury, he shot everything that moved. As if he were floating outside his body, his flesh acted on pure animal instinct. To kill or be killed. It was exhilarating. His heart beat hard in his chest, his breath coming fast. Blood pulsed behind his ears so loud it dulled even the sound of the guns.

Leaping over a lucky gap in the wire and snagging his legs on the razor sharp tendrils, he reached the enemy trench all too soon. He leapt down into it, his boots bashing against the duck boards with a thunk. The trench was at least four feet deeper than their own shelter.

Hearing a shuffle behind him Gray whirled around, thrusting his rifle forwards. The bayonet ripped through the German's chest and his eyes widened. They were a startling shade of blue which made Gray think absurdly of his mother before he twisted the blade, attempting to tear it from the man's flesh. The face was centimetres away from his own, and the bayonet was stuck.

Feeling panicked, Gray wrenched the rifle, forgetting the human form at the end of it. The blue eyes looked at him the entire time, his own panic mirrored inside them. Pain and bravery were there too, but he was trying not to let it show.

Finally, the blade came free. A shoot of red flew with it. The soldier coughed, more blood bubbling on his lips before he collapsed against the trench wall. Gray stared at him for a moment before he heard more running footsteps. He turned to stab, twist, pull. Stab, twist, pull, just like he had been taught in training. He jumped over his victims before he could catch a glimpse of their unseeing eyes. Blood steamed on the snow at the bottom of the trench, splashing up over Gray's boots as he walked. At the sound of another set of heavy footfalls, he thrust his rifle forwards. In the moment before the blade made contact with the soldier, he caught sight of a pair of hazel eyes.

Gray stood frozen, his rifle almost touching his lieutenant's chest.

His breathing was heavy, the rifle shaking in his hands. Blood dripped slowly from his bayonet onto the wood below their feet with a slow, rhythmic plunk. Prince put a hand cautiously on the blade, lowering it whilst looking up at Gray, his eyes falling to the blood blooming outwards across Gray's tunic sleeve.

"I'm fine," whispered Gray, noticing the direction of Prince's gaze. "Where are the others?"

Prince looked back at Gray's face, his eyes flicking for a moment over the deep cut along his cheek.

"I don't know," he murmured. "I think perhaps we're the only ones."

"No, we can't be. Charlie… Charlie's back there. He's alive."

"Did he throw the grenade?"

"No, it was me. Charlie was covering me. He's been hit."

Prince nodded.

"Thank you. You saved my life."

Gray laughed. "Yes, well, you saved mine last time."

Prince smiled at him. "We're quite the team."

"We'll be even better if we stay alive. Let's get out of here before more fritz show up."

"Right. Where were you before? Where's Charlie? We'll stay there until dark then head back. We're outnumbered massively and continuing would be suicide. I don't give a shit what Haig makes of it. I want to die doing something useful, not just for the damned hell of it."

They climbed back out of the trench to the sound of many running feet behind them. They ploughed forwards with their heads bowed, sprinting towards the cart wheel where Charlie was still pointing his rifle, dutifully covering Gray.

"Thank Christ," Charlie breathed sagging slightly against the wheel in his relief. "You scared me half to death. We can't stay here."

Both Gray and Daniel put an arm around Charlie's waist, heaving him to his feet. They stayed bent double for the heavy assault they knew was on the way. With a stroke of luck, they found a deep shell hole just a few feet away, diving in just as the machine guns stuttered into action.

Numb to the inhumanity of their actions, they ripped the magazines of ammunition from the corpses around them, each in varying stages of rot, and piled the bodies at the edge of the hole like sandbags. The blood from their combined wounds ran down the earth to sit in the bottom of the shelter, coating the three living men. Flesh was thrown up and onto them as the enemy guns directed their attentions solely on them. Gray, Charlie, and Prince lay flat on their stomachs, shooting past the onslaught of bullets into the fritz flesh, each distant cry of pain a small victory in their battle for continued life.

The big guns were soon in action, answering the British offensive with their own bombardment. The evening hate had begun with neither side aware the three men in the shell hole were still very much alive.

Gray's hands shook so much that replacing his ammo had become near on impossible. The adrenaline coursing through his blood only made him shake more. He had never been more terrified in his life. In a panic, he whipped out his pistol as another explosion went off far too close to their hideout, sending dirt rain-ing onto their heads as they ducked.

"What do we do, sir?" Charlie asked, his voice shaking as much as Gray's hands.

"I don't know, Private. I don't know." He lifted the hand not holding his pistol and ran it through his filthy hair, knocking off his cap in the process. It rolled down the slope of their hide-out, hitting the bottom with a hollow thump. "Try to stay alive. We'll have to wait until dark to make it back. If the bombardment doesn't let up, we might not even be able to go then."

Charlie groaned, rolling onto his back. Gray crawled to his side, his hands fluttering uselessly over him.

"I have a knife," Prince said. "We can try to cut the bullet out."

"No," replied Gray. "The blade will be dirty. It'll get infected. There will be bits of his trousers in there and all sorts. We can't mess with it. We might push it farther in. The medic can do it *when* we get back. Not if, Charlie. When."

"What about you?" Prince asked, indicating Gray's bloody arm.

"I'll be fine so long as Charlie is," he muttered, flinching as Prince tried to prise his filthy sleeve up over the wound. Another shell ex-ploded, and a particularly menacing piece of shrapnel tore into the ground next to Prince's throat. They sat in shock, looking at it, all wild with fear. How long was it until nightfall? How long had they already been there? It felt like hours, but had only been minutes.

The darkness crept over no-man's-land with deliberate slow-ness, as if mocking their misery. Although, in truth, it was only the early afternoon. When the barren landscape was swathed in an impenetrable night, both the moon and stars having fled the horrible scene of death, the three men in the middle of it huddled together. Their fingers were numb, and the water in their flasks had begun to freeze, making them unable to get so much as a dribble of clean water into their increasingly needy mouths. The water at the bottom of the shell hole was starting to look ever more appealing.

The bombardment around them did not relent. Gray, Prince, and Charlie were forced to remain huddled in the water lining their temporary shelter, their uniforms soaked through and frozen solid. The sun had dutifully taken with it any last remnants of warmth from the air.

They lay like animals in their burrow, their predators hungrily waiting outside for them to emerge. Flares were sent up regularly from both sides, looking for survivors, with entirely different intentions with regards to their fate. The light from the flares made any attempt at a retreat suicidal.

Gray wondered, in his hunger and thirst, whether it would not be wise to just climb out, erect himself to his full height, and let the bullet enter his skull—taking away the pain and fear in one quick pulling of a trigger. His shivering fingertips brushed the metal of his pistol absentmindedly. A new fear gripped him that his mind would allow him such a helpless, vulnerable death. He dropped his fingers from the pistol, stuffing his hands inside his coat where he hoped his body would warm them up a little. Even Charlie's reassuring breath on the back of his neck was cold.

That night brought no sleep for any of them. They shivered both in cold and fear, their energy gone and their nerves held together by a mere thread. The darkness seemed to intensify every noise. They could hear rats scurry across the earth and feel the vibrations in the mud as a shell landed miles from where they hid. The smell of rotting flesh wafted around them, putrid and vile, turning their empty stomachs and bringing the visions back to Gray's conscious eyes.

On several occasions, he yelled, backing away from these hallucinatory figures. The German's blue eyes, and the blood bubbling from his mouth, coming into focus beside the British soldier's trembling, bloodied hands. They both reached for him, smearing his uniform with foul-smelling flesh as the coppery scent of blood rose so far into his nostrils he could taste it. As he backed away, Charlie's solid form closed him in, yet his warmth brought him back to the present. Prince lay on his back to Gray's other side, watching the space where the stars should have been, his breath visible as it escaped his blue lips. He looked over as Gray cried out, his hazel eyes pleading the other man into silence.

Death wasn't what frightened the men, or at least Gray didn't think so. He would have happily taken that end, should it be painless and swift. It was simply waiting for death—the uncertainty of their fragile fate.

The snow began to fall from the black sky at some point in the night. They couldn't be sure exactly when it was, for time seemed to have stopped in the purgatory they were inside. The watch that had been on Prince's wrist before the attack was shattered and useless. Gray remembered the pocket watch he'd stolen as his vision followed the snowflakes. They landed on Prince's familiar face, the features an aged, stronger version of his own. They settled upon his skin, melting into his pores. Feeling them on his own face, Gray stuck out his tongue like a child so the small amount of water could soothe his parched throat. He felt absurd, ridiculous, and vulnerable beyond anything he had ever felt, yet he continued anyway. That night he was acutely aware of only one thing. Any second could have been his last.

Chapter Sixteen

As the night eased into day, their limbs grew heavier, weaker. None of them had eaten much before going over the top. That had been approximately twenty-four hours before, and they all knew there would be at least another ten before night fell again—allowing them the final possibility of salvation.

It was decided they would attempt a retreat come nightfall, no matter the circumstances. If they remained in their hideout beyond that, they would die anyway. Charlie and Gray's wounds were still deep, and the bullets were festering beneath the skin.

The German line eventually relaxed, content in the knowledge the survivors of the devastating attack had likely perished. The big guns and rifles swallowed back their bullets and bombs. Only adrenaline and a determination to live kept the lone survivors fierce.

When the darkness had enveloped the sky once more, the moon still covered by thick snow clouds, they eased themselves out of the hole into the velvety night. To avoid being seen, they pressed down as flat as they could go, coating themselves in ice cold mud within seconds. Bullets rushed past their heads from snipers, no doubt seeing the slightest movement with their keen eye. Gray lay still for as long as he dared, biting his lip until it bled. He was lying with his weight on his wounded arm, and the pain was almost unbearable.

Satisfied it must have been an animal of some sort, the sniper stopped firing, allowing the men to crawl forwards once more. They couldn't go quickly. Charlie had lost the use of a leg, and Gray an arm. Not to mention they were all sleep deprived, dehydrated, and starving.

Helping each other in an awkward, stilted manner, they moved with nightmarish slowness back towards the British line, their hearts hammering in their chests the entire time.

Before the sentry could see them, Prince raised Gray's rifle with a white handkerchief tied to the blood covered bayonet, keeping his head pressed into the mud so enemy guns would have a smaller target.

"Lieutenant Daniel Prince with Privates Brogan and Grimsby. Don't shoot," he bellowed. He didn't sound afraid at all, his voice was strong and sure. Within seconds, stretcher bearers had helped them down into the familiarity of their British trench.

Despite their re-entry to relative safety being incredibly obvious to the other side, no bullets flew towards them. It was likely that, having survived such an ordeal, no-one could bear to kill them now. Charlie screamed as his injured leg slammed into the floor. He fell over immediately racked by violent sobs. Gray crawled over to him, moving with the heaviness of a dream. His over-worked, exhausted body seized up more with every second. He put his uninjured arm around his friend's shoulders to hold him close, letting him cry into the front of his filthy tunic and remembering how the roles had been reversed last time.

The medical officer rushed up, his face bright red with the day's exertion. He wore an apron over his uniform, but Gray didn't see the point, the once white garment was saturated in dirt and blood. Charlie was rolled onto a stretcher, his face growing waxy as he entered into the first phase of a fever that had been initially held off by some fierce determination to make it back to the trench.

Gray, who could still walk, made his own way beside them, clinging to Charlie's slippery hand as he called out for his mother, becoming delirious as the infection sunk its roots deeper.

The hospital tent, set up a fair way behind the line, was packed. There were so many people that some had been moved outdoors. The air was full of the entire company's burnt, rotting flesh. Everyone who had gone over was either dead or wounded, with the sole exception of their lieutenant, who was just in need of food and sleep. Many men lay without limbs, the once white sheets saturated with nasty stains that added to the putrid scent of the enclosure. The nurses looked terrified as they ran around in their starched uniforms, as torn and dirty as the sheets, slipping often on the wet floor. Lines of men, just visible around the back of the tent through a gap in the fabric, lay on the frozen earth outside in wait of a final resting place beneath it. Their unseeing eyes stared upwards at the thousands of twinkling stars. The bright white moon, peaking at last from behind a cloud, illuminated their ghostly pale faces.

Charlie was kept on his stretcher just inside the entrance because there was no room for him any other way. Gray sat at the edge of it, still clasping Charlie's sweaty hand in his own and making his friend's entire arm tremble in his unsteady grip. A cold sweat was breaking out on his own bruised skin. Slowly his head began to droop forwards, his eyes getting heavy as the sweat ran down between his shoulder blades. The shivers moved up from his hands to his entire body. A nurse lowered him down onto the floor, placing his pack beneath his head like a pillow. The two friends lay side by side, the bullets cut hurriedly from their limbs.

Gray's arm throbbed, and the deep cut on his cheek stung from the amount of grime that had found its way inside it. Every pore of his skin felt blocked. His face was black, and his entire body caked in at least an inch of thick mud. The lice inside his clothes felt as if they were running. A sudden energy seemed to seize their tiny forms, making Gray's skin burn like fire. He scratched furiously, growing angrier and angrier when he only made the lice move faster and the itch grow worse.

"Fucking lice," he screamed, trying to rip his uniform from his body, too far gone with fever and discomfort to care who he showed himself to. His hands trembled too much to gain purchase on the dull buttons. He thrashed wildly in his fury.

A nurse, seeing his struggle, placed a soft hand on his unharmed cheek. She brushed a cool, damp cloth over his face, finding and cleaning the wound on his other cheek and lessening a tiny fraction of his discomfort.

As the night progressed, the various screams filling the hospital tent died down as more unmoving bodies were lined up under the stars. Men still called out in despair, always for mothers or sweethearts. They cried for women who would hold them to their breasts as Death prepared to tear them from their tragically short lives.

The fever brought Gray's family into his mind, however, they were always slightly distorted. His mother's face was the one he saw the most, her kind features caressing his vision. He didn't like the visions, for after a while, her eyes would widen and he would feel a warm splatter on his face as blood began to bubble from her mouth.

During one of these vivid dreams, Charlie inched his fingers along the ground, squeezing Gray's. At some point in the nightmare, he had let go. The warmth of his friend beside him spread up his arm just as his mother's bright blue eyes widened like the German soldier's had when Gray had twisted the bayonet inside him. Gray cried out, watching the image of his mother fall to the floor, her vivid eyes staring off into nothing. The warm grip of Charlie's hand brought him slowly back to reality for a brief few seconds before he fell into a restless sleep again.

He finally awoke, feeling more drained than he ever had before—his breathing laboured and his mind foggy. He shifted, startling himself as his legs seemed unable to move. He tried again, still gripped in the last realms of sleep, but they would not obey. Scared, he thrashed all his limbs, realising he was completely paralysed. He screamed, still thrashing before he felt a warm hand enclosing his own trembling one.

"It's all right, old chap," Charlie croaked. "Lie still. You're strapped down. We're on a boat. Earned ourselves a blighty, my friend. A darned lucky one, if you ask me."

Charlie was feigning lightness, although his voice sounded as weak as Gray felt.

Gray slumped back against what felt like a hammock, but he knew that was ridiculous. The bed swayed with his every movement. Having been informed of them, he could feel the straps on both his torso and legs, holding him in place. Despite his cold, wet uniform and the pain searing through his every muscle, Gray felt an odd warmth flood him as soon as Charlie spoke. His limbs slackened with relief that they had both reached the other side of their fevers unscathed. A near on impossible fate.

Lying on his back, the only thing he could do was run his

eyes over his surroundings. Even that one simple movement was exhausting. He noticed the sheer number of people that seemed to be around him first, registering their many groans of both pain and weakness. They appeared to be strapped on stretchers, piled up in the belly of what looked and felt like a ship.

The stretcher above Gray could only have been a few inches away from his face. If his arms were not bound, he could have touched it without much effort at all. A steady drip could be heard from somewhere above as a wounded soldier emptied fluid onto the man beneath him. Strapped into their beds they were both powerless to stop it. Their stretchers rocked sideways with the movements of the boat.

Gray smiled suddenly, glancing sideways at Charlie, who appeared to have drifted back to sleep. Despite the foul smell, itching uniform, and oppressive heat, they were going home.

Gray was half-conscious of the boat docking some hours later. He was packed into the back of an ambulance in a hurry. Like the nurses in France, the look on their faces was impassive. They were used to this scene. Although, unlike the nurses at the front, they were dressed in clean, white uniforms whilst their hands and nails held the softness of regular washes.

Some of the men had not survived the boat journey, and they were heaped silently into other vehicles to be cleaned and shipped to family members. Or, at least, that was what Gray assumed. To lie in a clean, peaceful graveyard, buried at the hand of their own kin, was a rare luxury for the dead those days.

The hospital was extremely clean. The usual smell of disinfectant hit his nose immediately. The wards were filled with soldiers in khaki uniform and women with creased, worried faces, fiddling restlessly with their skirts or gloves as they tried to remain strong for a loved one. The ward he was placed in was long and jammed with too many beds and too few nurses. Gray refused to be put anywhere other than at Charlie's side, and his friend made the same demands. They became almost hysterical when the doctors attempted to separate them.

To avoid a scene and having witnessed many close bonds between soldiers by then, they were placed in the same ward. Their narrow beds were pressed together to form one larger one due to the lack of space. To rid them of the coating of clay and mud, Gray and Charlie were quickly stripped and washed—causing a lot of exasperated sighs from the nurses when they had to refill their bowls of soapy water numerous times —before they were redressed in thin, button down pyjamas with an almost cold efficiency. Both men were tucked into crisp sheets, clean and warm for the first time in weeks.

Gray rolled onto his good side to face his friend as he fell asleep, the familiar sound of Charlie's gentle snoring once more lulling him into a slumber, safe in the knowledge they were both back in England and so close to the people they loved most in the world.

He awoke convinced he was in Hoddington Manor. A soft feather pillow was beneath his head, and a warm hand brushed back his hair. The hand on his head felt so real he started—eyes flying open wide and focusing on his mother's beautiful face. He flinched away from her touch, still thinking she was a vision. He squeezed his eyes shut again, unwilling to see blood bubble from her lips or her eyes turn glassy.

"Shh, Daniel. It's all right. I'm here." Her lips tenderly press against his forehead. "Mother's here, sweetheart."

"Mama," he moaned. "Are you… Are you real?" He opened

his eyes tentatively, watching her. She smiled, her eyes scanning his face and a worried expression lining her features.

"Of course I am," she whispered.

Gray's eyes started to fill with tears, his arms moving upwards to snake around her back.

"Oh, Daniel," she breathed in his ear, folding him to her breast.

Immersed in her comforting scent, and feeling the familiar feel of her arms around him, tears seeped from his eyes into the expensive material on her shoulder as he let himself be rocked like an infant.

"You're all right," she whispered, over and over again, in a reassuring tone.

After a while, when Gray's eyes had once more gone dry, Annabel unwrapped her arms from her son and cupped his cheeks in her palms. She smiled down at him.

"I've arranged for a car to take you home, Daniel," she said, wiping away the last remnants of his tears with a silken handkerchief. "We'll be leaving in a couple of hours, so we should be home by dinner time."

Gray nodded. Remembering Charlie, he turned away from his mother towards the sleeping man at his side. His mouth was open, one arm hanging limply from the bed, whilst his short dark curls framed his pale face on the pillow. A feather was stuck to his lip, and it moved slightly every time he exhaled.

"Mother, Charlie has to come too," he said.

"Yes, the nurse said you were both quite insistent on staying together. He can come back if he wants to, but surely he has his own family to go see."

Gray nodded again, feeling silly that he hadn't thought of that.

He leant his head back onto his mother, and she placed her arm around his shoulder—her cheek resting on the top of his head.

Charlie's family arrived just before Gray left, rushing to his side as the two men sat propped up on their pillows, wolfing down a meagre helping of bland stew. Charlie's face split into a huge grin, food leaking out of his mouth and down the front of his pyjamas. Gray laughed, taking his almost empty bowl out of his hands before he could get any more on himself.

Charlie threw his arms around his mother, holding her far too tightly. Neither person seemed to mind, they were just over-joyed at the sight of each other. Quickly his sisters caught up and surrounded his bed in an endless exclamation of joy and concern. Both of the soldier's needed further attention, but the hospital was too packed and so they were discharged without a second glance.

Still in his pyjamas, a freshly purchased frock coat thrown over his shoulders, Gray silently left his friend's side and made his way outside to a waiting motor car. One of his arms was in a sling, and his mother gripped the other as she helped him inside. His legs were still unsteady, and his thoughts were slow as he tried to tell his limbs to move.

Hoddington Manor was only a couple of hours by motorcar. Gray spent the entire journey with his forehead pressed to the cool glass window, taking in the unchanged English countryside. They arrived home just as the light was beginning to fade. He sat in the car for a little while, staring at the house in all its grandeur. A warm feeling reached down to his toes, but his heart felt a little cold at the thought of so many men out on the front line of numerous horrific battlefields whilst he was there among opulence.

"Daniel, are you all right?" Annabel asked, taking his unin-jured arm.

Gray nodded, following her numbly. His hands, tucked inside supple leather gloves, continued to tremble.

"Gray!"

He whirled around, hearing Genevieve's beautiful voice call out to him. All the sadness he had felt evaporated in an instant. She was running towards him at full speed, her skirt hitched up to her knees in her rush. She slammed into him. He groaned in pain, but threw his arm around her, to hold her with equal force. He had forgotten how small she was. He had imagined her somewhat larger than life, but in reality, she only just reached five feet. Her waist was barely there at all.

Genevieve sobbed into his neck. "What'd you get shot for, you fool? You promised me you would be fine. I can't lose you."

A single tear slid down his cheek, landing in Genevieve's hair. "I'm so sorry, Jen." He couldn't think of anything else to say to quell her concern, so he remained silent.

She leant back, kissing his cheek. "I still love you, you bastard."

They laughed in unison, walking up the steps into the grand entrance hand in hand. "There's a huge dinner laid out for you, you look starving."

"Daniel, my boy. My brave, brave boy." Theodore strode forwards, folding his son in a tender embrace but being careful not to jostle any of his injuries. He patted Gray's untainted cheek. "I'm so proud of you, son."

Gray smiled to mask his disappointment in himself. He wasn't proud of anything he had done in France. The image of that first man, his hands trembling as they clutched his open stomach, flashed into his mind—followed by the gurgling German. Gray stumbled backwards. Letting go of his father and running his hand through his hair, he started to walk up the stairs towards his bedroom. Annabel immediately made to follow him, but her husband put a hand on her shoulder.

"Let him go," he whispered. "He'll come back down when he's ready."

The gentle clipping of his mother's heels retreated down the foyer and into the family parlour. Genevieve stayed at the bottom of the stairs as well. Gray could feel her gaze boring into his back before he disappeared around the corner.

Once in his room, he shrugged off his coat and kicked the boots from his feet before crawling under his black silky sheets and pulling the fur throw up to his chin. He breathed in the familiar scent of his private sanctuary, his hands trembling as violently as ever. A few minutes later, he felt the mattress beside him dip with the comforting weight of his best friend.

"Was it really bad?" she whispered when she had slithered under the sheets beside him.

Lying to Jen was impossible so Gray chose to remain silent instead.

Genevieve continued. "Everyone says it's so honourable. They just blindly believe the Jessie Pope version of events." She tried to laugh but stopped, knowing nothing about this was funny. "I don't see how it can be a good thing if people are dying like they are. Some of them are suffering a fate even worse than death. The blacksmith's son came back blinded with no legs. How's he supposed to carry on with his life now? May as well have just died."

Gray rolled over to look at her. The expression on his face seemed to tell her everything she needed to know, and she reached up, tracing the cut on his cheek.

"How did you get this?"

"Does it look terrible?" Gray's voice was quiet, as if he was afraid of being too loud in the otherwise quiet room.

"Yes. It's really deep. Give you a nice manly scar, though, I shan't doubt."

"I think it was a bullet, but it could have been shrapnel. I was… There was a lot going on at the time, so I don't really know what happened."

"Jesus Christ."

The way Genevieve completely understood him, as she always did, without having to say a single word was a rather beautiful thing. She wasn't fooled by the government's shameless propaganda like he had been. Just one look at Gray's wild eyes had told her the truth. She put his quivering hands in hers, kissing his fingers softly. He didn't try to hide them from her because she'd have seen through him in seconds.

"I don't want to go back, Jen." His utterance was almost inaudible. Gray felt his cheeks colour with shame from voicing his cowardice.

"Uncle Teddy tried to get you a safe posting, something away from the front, but there was some general or major or someone who was adamant that you went to the front. They need people out there so badly that even your father couldn't sway their decision. Seeing his desperation to keep you safe was quite pitiful really. We definitely got lucky with the family we were given. I reckon I'm just about the luckiest girl alive, to be honest. I don't know how I'm going to live with you gone again, though. The worry was driving me insane."

The two friends were silent for a few moments. Each listening to the sound of the other's gentle breathing.

"We can hear the guns sometimes, if the wind blows the right way. I always think of you under them, and I hate it. I shake all over when they're going."

Slowly the darkness settled over the room. A maid came in silently to stoke the fire just as before. Everything was still exactly as if he had never left. The two best friends, altered by war and loss, discussed every little thing that had taken place back at home, and Gray told Genevieve some of the things that had happened in France—leaving out the gruesome details. He had to live with the memories, but he could protect Jen from them at least. Annabel crept into the room about an hour later, seating herself next to her son.

"Are you coming downstairs, or would you like dinner on a tray?"

"No, I'll come down, Mother." He sat up, still weak from his recent illness but knowing sustenance and the social element of eating with his family would most likely revive him somewhat.

Annabel plumped his pillows behind him before going through to the bathroom. Gray could hear her turn on the taps, the hot water gushing out of the pipes and hitting the wide bathtub. When he walked in several minutes later, it was to see her knelt on the floor, her sleeves rolled up past her elbows to check the temperature of the water and swill around the soap—encouraging it to form bubbles. She could have easily called a maid to do this entire process for her, but it was a comforting site to see his mother undertake the task.

Gray wondered, as he had done numerous times, what had happened in her youth. Surely, no proper society lady would even think about drawing a bath herself. When she had turned off the taps, the bath full of fluffy bubbles, she opened his wardrobe.

The hangers squeaked across the rail as she searched through his many clothes.

Annabel turned around, letting Gray settle himself slowly amongst the bubbles so that none of his body was on show. Once he was covered she crouched down next to the tub to help him clean his various wounds, rubbing the sponge over his back where he couldn't reach. Once more, he felt like an infant, resigning himself to the tender care of his mother. He was far too exhausted to protest, so he just sat there, resting his chin on his knees until Annabel stood up.

"I'll let you sort yourself out now, sweetheart. I'll see you downstairs when you're ready."

Once alone, he dried himself off and dressed slowly. His aching limbs protested every movement. The shaking of his hands made the doing up of his buttons difficult as the nightmarish images flashed before him every time he so much as blinked. As he attempted to push the button through its adjacent hole, he looked around for his valet but seemed unable to locate him.

Seeing himself in front of the mirror, dressed in his normal expensive attire, he felt strange. His battered body was stuffed into a suit to pretend everything was fine. After he'd rang the bell a few times his valet eventually came to help him with his suit jacket. Using a square of black satin, he fashioned Gray a sling to blend into the tailored outfit.

Dinner was brilliant. The food was not rich—something his mother had insisted upon, knowing how it would affect his malnourished body—but it tasted divine. Gray ate until he thought he might burst, laughing as Genevieve told many exaggerated stories about her time without him.

She was evidently trying to make his parents happy by

diverting their attention from their wounded son and helping him to disguise his frightened eyes and shaking hands. For that, he was extremely grateful. Jen told him how she had been courting a young man from one of the mansions down the hill but how she didn't really like him all that much, which earned a few laughs and exclamations of surprise. However, she talked mostly about how she felt useless. She wanted to be a part of the country's war effort. A nurse perhaps.

Gray just smiled at this, knowing she only spoke so highly of the war because of Gray's mother. Jen wanted her not to look at him like he would break just as much as Gray did.

"Some of the men and I are going hunting tomorrow," his father cut in whilst Genevieve was taking a much-needed breath. "I think you should come, son. You were always a good shot, but you must be first rate now. Why you never became an officer, I'll never understand."

"Because I didn't want to. I've told you that already. And I don't know if shooting people well is something to be proud of, Father," Gray muttered taking a large gulp of wine, lifting the glass to be refilled by the footman behind him for the fourth time that night. Theodore looked a little taken aback.

"Of course it is, my boy. You're helping your country by stopping the fritz. I'm incredibly proud of you."

"I'm not proud of killing people."

"Killing Hun, not people."

Gray stood up so suddenly his chair toppled backwards. "They are still people!" he shouted as he ran an agitated hand through his hair. "You think they don't have families too? Mothers, fathers, and friends just like I do? Most of them have children as well. You didn't see his face, Father."

"Who…whose face?" Theodore stuttered, confused by the sudden outburst.

"The man I drove a bayonet through. I watched the life leave his eyes. His blood all over me. I can still smell it. I can still hear it dripping off my rifle. Still see his face every time I close my eyes. There's nothing honourable or brave about that."

"Daniel." His father stood and approached him slowly. "You've had too much wine. I didn't mean—"

"Yes, you did. This war isn't nice, Father. It's not fun. It's some grotesque means to no end." With this statement still hanging like an unwanted presence in the room, he stumbled away, stopping in the smoking room to snatch up a crystal bottle of whisky from his father's small collection. Not bothering with a glass, he made his way upstairs.

His feet carried him subconsciously to his writing room. Standing at the door, he surveyed the space that had always been a sort of sanctuary to him. His pen was still resting, the lid off, on top of an unfinished poem. Approaching it, he read the verses depicting some joyous day in the park. He thought them shallow and ridiculous.

Screwing it up he threw the paper into the raging fire without another thought, watching as the corners curled into the flames, and it disintegrated to ash. He took another large gulp of whisky, feeling it burn its way down his throat, and spun around to look at the other sketches and poems pinned to the walls.

As he read the words, scribbled in his own flourished hand, he grew angrier and angrier. They were unimportant. Just silly letters that meant nothing anymore. Reaching up with his uninjured hand, he started to tear them up in a blind rage. His face felt hot, and his hair fell into his eyes. The words he had written, back when his life had been simple, rained down to the floor.

He took up a sketch of a man sitting in a tree, a carefree nature to his leg swinging from the branch. He threw it, but just before it landed in the flames, he started. He looked into the eyes of the pencil drawing as it fell downwards onto the embers. The curly hair was suddenly illuminated to a fiery colour as the flames licked eagerly at Charlie's face. He tried to claw the picture from the fire, but it was of no use. The sketch he had unknowingly drawn of his friend had turned to ash, staining Gray's fingers black with soot.

Even angrier than before, he ripped off the sling, relishing in the pain now shooting up his injured arm. Once the walls were mostly bare, he grabbed the pen—now laying on the floor, a dark ink blot spreading slowly across the rug. With harsh lines, completely void of his usual tender care, he sketched the face that haunted his every dream, and the blood bubbling at his mouth. He embellished it with hands resting on an open stomach.

The pen pierced the paper in his anger as he put the image into rushed, raw verse on the back. His hands trembled so violently that the words were hardly legible. Tears leapt off his nose, blotting the page further. He stumbled back to look at the paper, taking another deep gulp of whisky. Without realising it, Gray had balled his hands into fists to stop the shaking. The pen he was still holding snapped, causing the sticky black ink to run over his fingers, joining the soot already staining the area.

He turned back around to the fire, his gaze going to the spot where Charlie's happy face had been just minutes before. Seeing his words staring up at him from the flames, the rage boiled over again, hot and fast. He screamed, throwing the half-empty bottle at the wall, where it smashed. The liquid ran down the wooden panels and onto the floor, soaking his dismembered verse.

Gray jumped at the loud noise the crystal made as it smashed.

Looking at the destruction he had caused, he fell to his knees. His trousers tore as he landed on the broken shards, small spots of blood speckling the paper around him. Still shaking, he pressed his hands into his stomach, angrier still that he couldn't control their movement.

Gray, lost in other memories left over from his time in France, didn't notice his mother's entrance until she crouched beside him and pulled her son to her. One hand cradled the back of his head, and the other rubbed his back. He seized the front of her dress, crying into her chest with such force he could hardly breathe. He collapsed into his mother's reassuring warmth as his anger subsided completely, turning into a vulnerable sadness.

"I'm so sorry, baby," she whispered into his hair. "I'm so sorry."

Chapter Seventeen

Annabel and Gray sat on the floor until Theodore entered, his dress shoes clicking on the wood and crunching on the broken bottle. Gray felt his father's arms around him, and he let himself be pulled up into the air. He burrowed his head into his father's shoulder, Theodore's strength more reassuring than anything else at that moment. He was carried into his bedroom where Theodore helped him into his pyjamas and tucked him in bed as he had every night as a child. He felt his palm against his cheek and leant into the familiar touch.

"I love you, son. More than anything. You're the very best of my life and always will be."

Those words, also repeated every night to him when he was a child, filled Gray with more warmth than any embrace ever could. Teddy kissed his son's forehead before retreating. Gray heard him kiss Annabel on the way out as well.

Once they were alone, Gray felt the mattress dip as his mother crawled up beside him. Putting his head back on her chest, he let her rock him to sleep.

He woke up some hours later, screaming at the top of his lungs and thrashing wildly against the imaginary dirt smothering him and pressing him into the ground. He felt hands on his face, the sensation making him think of warm flesh and rats on his skin. Images of the men he had killed clouded his conscious eyes, making him thrash even more vigorously to get away from the clawing, undead hands.

"What are you doing? Gray? It's all right. Come on, Gray. Wake up, Gray, please."

He came around slowly, taking in Genevieve's face directly in front of his own. The sheets were wrinkled around her lap, suggesting she had taken over his mother's post at some point in the night.

Gray was covered in sweat, which quickly cooled on his skin, making him shiver. The sheets were damp beneath him. His face crumpled into tears once more, heating up beneath Jen's palms in embarrassment. Peeling his friend's hands from him, he lowered his face into his arms, his shoulders shaking. The room was filled with the scent of sweat and urine. Gray wanted more than anything to disappear, to simply cease to exist.

His eyes caught sight of the pistol resting on top of his pack by the door. It seemed to beg him to hold it, its shape made for his hand alone. Questions would surely arise when the news spread that a grown man—a soldier and son of the most powerful man in the country, who was supposed to be the very image of masculinity, courage, and honour—had wet himself like an infant.

Without saying a single word, Genevieve climbed off the bed. Her long nightgown swished in the silent air as she walked from the room. Next came the sound of running water from the adjoining washroom. Approaching his bed again, she put an arm around Gray's waist, helping him to his feet and steering him towards the perfume scented bath. Tears still clouding his vision, Gray fumbled with his pyjama buttons, the trembling in his hands rendering him useless. Seeing his struggle, Jen did the job for him. Once his top hung open, she slipped away, allowing Gray the little dignity he had left. Sinking beneath the warm soapy water Gray let out an involuntary sigh as the last clinging remnants of the dream crept out of his mind, the warmth loosening his tense muscles.

He sat in the tub until the water had turned almost completely cold before drying himself with a soft, warm towel and slipping on an undershirt and fresh pyjama bottoms. When he walked back to his bed, he noticed the sheets had been changed and the window cracked open to eliminate the smell. He perched somewhat awkwardly on the edge of his mattress, feeling the cold air from the open window glide over his face, cooling the embarrassed flush still evident in his cheeks.

Gray had quite given up hope that Genevieve would return. He was sat on his pillow, his chin resting on his knees, when she crept back in nearly two hours later. Her hands were creased as if they had been submerged in water for a prolonged time. He realised from the soapy smell of her, the same smell that clung to all the linen in the house, she had just washed his sheets herself so no-one else would know about his accident.

He felt a huge surge of love for this sister figure as she leant in and kissed him lightly on the cheek, letting him know she didn't think badly of him at all. She lifted the clean sheets and crawled under them, waiting for him to do the same. Snuggling back down into bed, he folded his arms around her and kissed her dark hair.

"Thank you," he whispered.

"Don't be ridiculous. You can return the favour when I'm old and withering somewhere."

"I love you," he murmured into her hair, letting out a breathy laugh that moved the strands.

"How could you not? I'm brilliant."

They laughed quietly.

"I love you too, little brother."

"I'm not that little."

Jen laughed again, making him feel warm. In that moment, he completely forgot his nightmare. He thought, just as he was drifting back to sleep, if Genevieve went to the front, she would likely stop the entire war in seconds. No-one could get mad with her next to them.

Chapter Eighteen

Gray woke to a cold breeze caressing his face. A bright line of sun shone through the open window. Despite the large quantities of alcohol he had consumed the day before he felt considerably better than he had in weeks. Stretching, his eyes still closed, he noticed a pain in the bullet wound and a slight headache behind his temple. He was also incredibly thirsty. His bone-dry tongue stuck to the roof of his mouth.

He smiled as he opened his eyes, wincing at the sunlight that hit his pupils. His mother was standing over him, a cool glass of orange juice in her outstretched hand. He took it eagerly, downing it in just a couple of large gulps. She settled a tray onto his lap, and he immediately took a bite from a piece of toast liberally spread with strawberry jam. The scene was so familiar he could have cried.

"How are you feeling?" Annabel asked, plumping the pillows beneath Gray's head.

"Good," he replied, his mouth full. "I'm sorry...about yesterday." He swallowed the food, placing the toast back on his plate where he picked at it with his fingers, remembering his appalling behaviour from the day before. It hadn't exactly been the homecoming he had planned.

"Don't worry about it, sweetheart. Just don't throw your father's best whisky next time." She smiled, her voice falsely bright and cheerful. Her eyes were fixed on him as though he were a wild animal, likely to pounce at any moment.

He lowered his eyes to the breakfast tray so he couldn't see the hurt he had caused—that he kept causing.

"Father's going hunting today, will you join him?" his mother asked, still watching him cautiously.

He nodded, desperate to prove he wasn't going to break. He needed them to see the strength in him before he had to return to the front. Thinking about the trenches, the toast he had just raised back to his mouth fell from his hand, clinking against the china plate. He thought he saw his mother's eyes glance towards the offending fingers, but she seemed to put the sight down to her imagination and stood up, smoothing down her yellow skirt, before going to inform his valet that he would join his father's hunting party.

"They leave in an hour," she called back.

Gray groaned whilst Genevieve laughed beside him.

"Have fun," she joked. "If it's anything like yesterday it's freezing out there."

He shoved her sideways and she fell against the heavily stuffed pillows. This made him roar with laughter until the valet arrived.

Downstairs, he was handed a riding crop which he hit rhythmically against his boots. Gray decided these boots would replace the slightly ratty pair he had worn to the front. He greeted his father's friends with his usual polite charm, shaking each of their hands in turn. Theodore's associates were all convinced the British line ate roast beef every night, killed Germans like flies, and would be home just after Christmas. Being only three weeks until that specific holiday, it was deluded to think they'd make the festival itself. The second Gray was given a rifle, his facade started to crack. His hands shook as he reached for it, holding its heft limply at his side and trying to touch it as little as possible.

"Come on, boy," one of the men boomed, his rotund belly bouncing as he laughed. "What you looking so scared for? You've been shooting down Hun for weeks. A little bird should be child's play."

"I-I don't even know how we're going to find anything to shoot, it's the middle of the bloody winter," Gray stuttered.

"Let him be," his father answered the fat gentleman, clapping his son on the back. "I don't think the war's quite as simple as all that, Horace."

"Of course it is. Isn't that right, boy? You're all having the best time out there. The war office tells us it's a doddle. I can't see why you're still employing that coward valet of yours, though. He's an absolute disgrace to our country and should be court-martialled if you ask me. A perfect specimen."

"Yet, I don't see you enlisting," Gray muttered. He'd always been sensitive about people bullying objectors. If his valet didn't want to go, it was his choice. Who was this fat man to tell him he wasn't entitled to his freedom?

Horace looked taken aback, a hand now resting on his obscenely large stomach. He laughed, his cheeks going red. "I'm too old for that. Besides, we want fit young things like you to—"

"To die for you. I get it. And my valet is the perfect *specimen*, did you say? Yes, well, you're far too important, surely. Your excuses are nothing more than just that. Empty excuses. Yes, let the peasants and the young people die, but surely not the great fat

Horace because he needs his three meals a day and can't possibly get brains in his hair."

"Excuse me, boy. I do my bit." The man looked seriously offended. "I help the war office directly and help organise attacks. Much more important than some private."

"That's going too far—" Theodore tried, but Gray cut him off, stepping towards the humungous man whose face was now purple.

"Have you ever even gone within five miles of the front? You order men to war like cattle for slaughter without a single clue what it's really like!" Gray spat on the man's shoes. "That's what I think about your war effort, *sir*." He saluted, exactly as he had been taught. A grim expression played on his face as he strolled out the door in a rage, his hands shaking more than ever.

Walking straight past the horses, wanting to feel his own muscles working out his anger, he briefly looked back to see Horace waddling out the door towards a waiting motor car. His cheeks were puffing from the rare exertion. Gray's father came out looking angry as well, catching his son's gaze before he went back in to rejoin his guests.

Knowing that his father and the others would catch up, Gray began to jog out of the manicured grounds and into the acres of unruly meadow beyond. He felt the wind on his face clearing his head, allowing him to forget about the rifle still gripped in his fingers. He slowed to a halt to let the others catch up, leaning against a tree. The odd image from the front crept back into Gray's mind, although he tried to suppress them. He kept his eyes screwed shut, willing his thoughts back to his present setting. As he leant heavier against the bark, his arm still sore, a gun shot rang out over the meadow.

He jumped, tripping on a root just behind his foot. As he land-ed, the wind was knocked out of him. A second shot rang out to follow the first. He lay there, winded and fighting for breath, and the wound on his arm ached from the impact since he hadn't bothered with the sling that day.

The struggle for breath brought back the feeling of being bur-ied alive. He could feel the earth on top of him as if he were right in that moment. The flashing images of the dead flooded back with renewed force. Another gunshot rang out, and he crawled along the grass, seeing the mud of no-man's-land instead. He hid behind a large oak tree, burying his head in his knees and pressing his hands against his ears as he rocked backwards and forwards, desperate to block out the guns. Surely, he couldn't survive this third trip over the top, he had been too lucky already. He felt a hand on his shoulder.

Reflexively he raised his rifle, plunging it forwards to spear the German with his bayonet. He heard a sharp exhale of breath and saw his father, his face crumpled in pain, clutch his stomach. Gray looked down at the rifle in his trembling hands, dropping it as if it had burnt him. His eyes were wide and wild, relieved that there was no bayonet, but mortified he had caused pain to his father. He stood up, his legs shaking.

"I'm sorry," he muttered, stumbling backwards.

"Daniel, wait," his father called, wincing as he got to his feet.

Gray turned around and ran in the opposite direction. The tears blurring his vision made him stumble on fallen branches as he moved farther into the small collection of trees, desperate to block out the sounds of the hunt behind him. As soon as he reached the manor, he ran up to the servant's door, climbing the narrow stairwell and easing himself into Genevieve's bedroom at the back of the house. She wasn't there, so he sat on her pink covers, staring out the window, still in his riding hat and boots.

His father found him about an hour later. Out of breath and walking stiffly from the bruise on his gut he was trying to pretend didn't hurt.

"I'm sorry, son," he whispered, taking a seat next to him. "That was really stupid of me. I should have known better than that." He placed a hand on Gray's arm.

"Why can't I do it?" Gray muttered.

"Do what?" His father looked on confused.

"Be strong like everybody else." His voice caught, the tears flowing freely once more. He brushed them away furiously, embarrassed at the show of weakness. "Father I'm... I'm scared. I don't want to disappoint you, but that's all I seem capable of doing."

Theodore draped his arm around Gray's shoulder. "You can't disappoint me, Daniel. It's impossible. I don't care how you act in those trenches, so long as you do everything you can to come back to me and your mother."

"But you would be disappointed if you knew—" he cleared his throat shifting tactics. "That man back in the house—"

"Is a fucking imbecile."

Gray looked up, shocked. He had never heard his father swear before. He laughed softly as Theodore continued.

"Well, he is. I told him to leave my house and never return. Nobody gets to speak to my boy like that."

"Is he powerful? I haven't ruined an important relationship or something, have I?"

"Stop worrying, Daniel. None of them are as powerful as I am, and they know it."

Gray laughed softly again, and his father smiled back.

"There we go, a smile finally. You're going to make a girl very happy when you return with looks like that, my boy." He smiled even bigger.

Gray, for some reason, thought of Charlie and how he was getting on back in normal society. He wondered if he was faring better than himself.

"Right," Theodore said, getting to his feet. He winced as he straightened. "Let's have a whisky, shall we?"

Gray stood up as well. "Sorry I broke your last bottle."

"It's fine. I can always buy more whisky, I can't, however, buy another you. Not with all the will or money in the world. Look after yourself, and stop worrying about your mother and me."

"I'm sorry about back there as well." Gray looked at his feet, shuffling in embarrassment.

Theodore approached him again, taking his son's face in his hands so he was forced to look at him. "I said it's fine, Daniel. Lord knows what you were seeing when you did it. If I could take that pain from you, I would in a heartbeat. Sorry that you've had to see such things."

"I was seeing a German." His father's question had been rhetorical, but Gray felt he had to tell someone. "He was right behind me, and I stabbed him. I watched the blood bubble up on his lips and the life actually leave his eyes. I stabbed a lot of Germans that day. It felt... It felt like it wasn't me doing it. I can't explain it, the feeling of just stabbing and jumping over them like they were sandbags back in training. The German had the same colour eyes as Mother." Gray looked up, and Theodore grabbed his shoulder.

"It will get better, son. I promise you." He squeezed and let go. "How about that whisky then?"

Gray left the house just five days later, summoned to stand in front of a medical board. He hid his shaking fingers beneath his cuffs and was thus passed fit to return to the front. When the time of his departure came, his mother held him so tight he couldn't breathe. He squeezed her back just as hard, feeling her tears soak into his neck.

"Come home, sweetheart. I don't care what you must do. Just come home to me."

He nodded, kissing her cheek. His father held him next.

"Remember what I told you, son. All right? I love you. Please stay safe."

Genevieve waited until his parents had gone outside to make sure the car was correctly loaded before pulling him to her.

"Don't get shot again, understand?" she said.

Gray laughed. "I'll do my best, Jen."

"Make sure you do. I love your stupid face. Don't make me miss it for too long."

He kissed the top of her head, closing his eyes to take in her scent and trying to hold it to him so he could remember it in his worst moments.

She stepped back, taking his hands in hers. "Your hands are shaking again," she whispered.

"I'm fine," he muttered, trying to take them back.

She just squeezed harder. "You can't pull the wool over my eyes, brother. I know you're very far from all right, but you won't listen to me." She smiled tightly, taking in his new, pristine uniform and brushing away an imaginary piece of dust from his shoulder. "Keep writing that brilliant poetry, all right? Let me read it when you get back."

Gray nodded. "You hate poetry. I'll send you a letter when I get back. I promise."

She held him to her once more and then turned sharply, running up the stairs so she didn't have to watch him walk out. Putting on his hat and taking a deep, shaky breath, he turned to walk outside and slid into the leather back seat of the car that would take him to the harbour, where he'd get the boat onto France. He would arrive back at the front just two weeks before Christmas.

Chapter Nineteen

W elcome back, old chap."
    Gray heard the familiar voice just as he took his first step onto the boat. His face split into a genuine smile as he hugged Charlie. "How are you?"

"Yeah, the leg still hurts. Still can't put all my weight on it. The board wouldn't permit me any more recuperation time, though. I did try to milk it as much as I could. They told me it was a very lucky wound, if there is such a thing. How about your good self?"

"I'm all right," Gray replied.

Giddy at their reunion, they discussed the events of their leave.

"As I said, it was great," Gray concluded. "But it wasn't the same."

"I know what you mean," Charlie said. "Everyone thinks I'm the bravest man ever born. They're completely oblivious to what's really happening over there."

Gray nodded. "I spat on a man from the war office."

Charlie laughed, clapping Gray on the back. "Jolly good, old chap. Jolly good."

The sea was calm that day making the journey across the channel a lot smoother than the last two times they had made it. This time they weren't strapped onto stretchers or heaving over the side. Instead they were seated on the deck beneath the bright sunlight, wrapped in their thick, clean coats to block out the icy winter chill.

"Nice boots," Charlie commented as Gray lifted his feet up onto the railings.

"Riding boots, leather. I couldn't wear those old ones any longer. The shoe was starting to peel away from the sole. Tell you what, I'll write to mother and get her to buy you some for Christmas."

Charlie's eyes lit up. "Would she? I mean no. I couldn't possibly. They look really expensive."

Gray shrugged. "I don't actually know how much they cost, but if I ask, she'll get them. You forget my mother and father own the largest fortune in England. Apparently, more money than the King. The price of one pair of boots won't make a difference. They could buy the whole army new boots, and it wouldn't make a difference. Anyway, my blood got you into this mess. It's the least I can do."

"Well, when you put it like that, old chap. Thank you."

Charlie smiled the rest of the way over, his eyes flicking between his tatty, ill-fitting boots and Gray's custom made ones. The lines on their faces only began to tilt back downwards as the first explosion came into view. A distant glow lit up the horizon like lightning—although they both knew the true source of it.

Upon arrival, the men were marched back up to the small village they had spent that first few nights. Stuffing themselves with potatoes and beer, they relished in their last night of sleep before being sent back into the trenches. The company had moved farther down the line, so it was a mission just to find them again. On their first night back, they were told they would spend Christmas day in the front line. News that reduced their mood significantly.

To acclimatise to trench living again, and give their wounds a final chance to heal, they were stationed in the reserve trench for the week before they marched up to the front with a new platoon full of inexperienced men to restock their company. The work was tedious and boring, sitting for endless hours in the icy cold, their collars turned up against the bitter wind.

They fixed trenches, their numb hands frozen around the handles of their shovels. They cleaned their guns an endless amount of times, although they always found a way to get dirty again in a matter of seconds. And they waited for something to happen. The waiting was probably worse than the event itself. A constant fear, of what could possibly be around the corner, filled everyone.

Gray wrote to his mother, requesting new socks, gloves, and a hat—along with the promised new boots for Charlie.

Fresh snow began to fall the second they set foot on the front line.

The men, already half frozen, tried to dig small dugouts in the solid side of the trench, putting their coats over the opening to keep out the bitter wind. Small fires were made in the holes that didn't have a man inside, causing a lot of friction with a new second lieutenant called White, who said it would make them more visible to the Germans. A ridiculous theory because the Germans already knew exactly where they were.

Prince, who was still alive and well, much to Gray's relief, sat next to his men as much as he could, huddled around the fires despite the warmer alternative of the deep dugout he slept in. The new men liked him instantly for this. He had made himself known as a member of the team, rather than distinguishing himself as a leader.

On Christmas Eve, parcels began to arrive.

"Brogan."

Gray heard the voice echo down the trench and leapt to his feet. "Yes!"

"At ease. I'm only delivering parcels for Christ's sake. That one weighs a fucking tonne."

The foul-tempered, yet slight, man shoved a large package into Gray's hands. The parcel was wrapped neatly with brown paper and had a piece of bright red ribbon tied around the outside. It would have been perfect if not for the muddy fingerprints. Gray paused for only a second to admire the package before carefully unwinding the ribbon and tearing the paper open. Inside, there was a new pair of boots for Charlie, as promised, as well as thick gloves, scarves, and socks for them both.

Accompanying these was a bottle of expensive champagne, and a bottle of whisky. A solid gold, bejewelled cigarette case was wrapped in tissue at the bottom of the package beside a Christmas letter full of good wishes. Leaning against the trench wall with a rare smile crossing his features, Gray caressed the red ribbon, letting it slide between his fingers. Hit by a sudden idea, Gray jumped up, grabbing a dead branch that lay just on the edge of the trench and stabbing it into the hard ground between the duck-boards before wrapping the ribbon around it.

"There you are, lads," he said, getting laughter from them all.

They had all seen his whisky and were desperate to get some.

"Not until tomorrow," he continued, noticing the direction of the men's gaze. He slid the bottles underneath his makeshift tree, trying to put it as near to the fire as he dared to stop the liquid getting too cold.

That night was full of laughter. The glowing fire fooled the men into thinking they were somewhere more jovial than their actual position. As Prince's watch, still tucked in Gray's breast pocket, ticked towards midnight, the air grew suddenly silent. The guns, which the men had ceased listening to a long time ago, had stopped firing on both sides. At first, the silence was eerie. All the men immediately stopped talking, sitting bolt upright to survey their surroundings. A clatter could be heard along the trench as they all grabbed their rifles. A few men even poked their heads slightly above the top to look out onto the stillness of no-man's-land.

Before long, the laughter resumed. Everyone becoming giddy in the peaceful air, although, they knew they were supposed to remain vigilant. They could even hear deep laughter from the opposing line. Adding to their Christmas spirits, Prince started to sing softly. The men looked at him, enraptured by his beautiful voice. He sang a festive song that was taken up by the other men after just a few lines. A domino effect took hold, and the men up the line started to sing as well until it echoed all over France. In a slight state of shock, Gray heard the German line start to sing with them. He laughed, a great booming sound that echoed across the barren landscape.

"Can you hear that?" he cried.

The others nodded, raising their voices. The German's did the same, Prince's voice carrying both sides through the notes with ease. He was by far the loudest of them all. His hazel eyes positively sparkled. When the song ended, another was struck up immediately. A few soldiers started singing their own songs, but they all soon converged into the same one.

Some of the men snuck off during the night to get some sleep, resting properly for the first time on the front line, but there was always someone to keep the tune going. The singing only ended when the sun began to rise above the white horizon and coco was brought up the line for the men to warm their hands. Gray poured a small drop of whisky into all the steaming mugs in his company to loud cheering from everyone.

Christmas day remained silent, even the wind had stopped to honour the festivities. Gathering in the trench around lunch time and expecting their usual watery stew or gruel, they were surprised yet again by a full Christmas dinner. Albeit not nearly as elaborate as his usual Christmas meal, or in fact, any meal at Hoddington Manor. The dinner was accompanied by a steaming plum pudding. They couldn't believe their luck. The meat was dry and rubbery, the pudding over steamed, and everything still had the acrid taste of chloride, but to Gray, it was the best meal he would ever eat.

Beer flowed like water down their throats, only improving the mood further. Just after lunch, the singing from the German line resumed, quickly picked up by the British with much more vigour than they had possessed with their sober tongues. One more daring soldier raised a stick with a white flag attached to it, heaving himself out of the trench, still singing. He carried with him an unopened bottle of beer. His tentative stride grew more confident as the air remained void of the sound of gunfire. Everyone was silent, their mouths agape, waiting for him to get taken down, but it never happened. Instead, they could see a grey uniformed soldier appear on the other side. He didn't look like he was even carrying a gun.

Gray heaved himself up over the top. Charlie grabbed his leg, but he just shook it off, jogging to catch up with the first private who had gone over. One by one, the rest of the company seemed to swallow their fears and emerged beside him. The same happened on the German side. The two groups, the grey and the khaki, met slap bang in the middle of no-man's-land.

Seeing everyone happy and weaponless was surreal. They all shook hands in a slightly awkward manner—in disbelief, Gray assumed, as they all realised each person was nothing more than human.

Many men carried with them small gifts of alcohol, which they all began to drink without hesitation, passing the bottles around like old friends as opposed to sworn enemies at war with one another. Gray sprinted back to the trench, tripping on the uneven ground in his drink-clouded mind, to seize his bottle of champagne. Before drinking it, they each agreed to use this truce to bury their dead, sobering their moods for the fallen. Digging shallow graves that warmed their muscles, they recited all the prayers they could remember.

Meeting the Germans once more, members of both sides wiped tears from their faces with their grubby sleeves, and Gray popped the cork off the champagne. The pop of it emerging from the bottle as if it was desperate to be free, lifted everyone's hearts immediately.

To fill the silence, Prince started to sing again, choosing a more solemn number that Gray had never heard before. It appeared no-one else knew the song either, but it fit the scene perfectly. He took a seat on a stray mound of dirt.

There was champagne and music, so Gray took it upon himself to provide dancing. He stepped in front of Charlie, coaxing him into a slow waltz. They both laughed, stumbling on the churned-up ground.

"You're good at this, old chap." Charlie laughed, looking at his feet, now clad in his new leather boots, and frowning as he tried to follow Gray's step. Soon the entire party was dancing. The drunker members just swaying by themselves, holding a bottle in their gloved hands. Khaki danced with grey until the two opposing sides were no longer distinguishable. At last, they were equals.

"Come on, Lieutenant," Gray called, holding out his hand whilst Charlie took a much-needed rest. "Have a little dance."

Prince snorted. "I don't dance."

Gray took another step towards him. "No, you just don't know how. I'll teach you." He grabbed Prince's hand, forcing him to his feet with a laugh.

"I'll be the girl. You lead," Gray said to a laugh from Prince.

He placed Prince's hands in the appropriate hold positions, counting as he remembered his own dance teacher doing. Prince fell often yet they laughed so much tears ran down both their cheeks.

"Well it's a good thing these boots have steel toes, officer." Gray chuckled when the lieutenant stood on his feet for about the hundredth time.

"You're a damned professional. How am I supposed to keep up?"

Gray laughed again stepping back to do a little tap dance on the snow, joining in with a song being sung behind him. Prince joined him in this endeavour, much more comfortable singing than dancing.

"You're a damned professional, sir," Gray imitated, earning himself a wide smile.

Just as darkness fell, Gray linked his arm into Charlie's in a drunken imitation of his high social position and stumbled around the open expanse of no-man's-land with ease. They had both taken up speaking in elaborately high-class accents, their chins pointed towards the sky.

When their legs became fatigued from walking and dancing, they were both content to simply observe their surroundings. Gray pulled a fresh piece of paper out of his folder and, seated on the ground, began to sketch. His pencil seemed to be an extension of his arm as if it was meant to rest between his thumb and forefinger for the rest of eternity. He found himself smiling as he conveyed the joyous event to paper.

A new day was beginning to stir when Gray and Charlie re-entered the trench. The morning light had just begun to poke its head optimistically over the horizon, as if unsure what it would see. Both men fell asleep almost instantly, curled up together to feed off each other's body heat. Gray actually felt happy as he drifted into a dreamless slumber. His breathing was even, his mind clear, and his hands were still as he tucked them inside his tunic for warmth. Charlie's gentle snoring was close to his ear, a sound he thought he may never be able to sleep without.

Everyone stayed asleep until nearly lunch time, having had far too much to drink the night before. The first thing Gray noticed as his mind slipped slowly back into consciousness was the silence. The guns were still quiet. The melodic song of a bird drifted over the battlefield. Nobody wanted to be the first to fire. They had now known their enemy as equals. They had humanised them.

The guns remained silent for days. The war office, clearly annoyed by the lack of death, eventually ordered the company back behind the lines under the pretence that they were being relieved. None of the men bought the lie. In reality, they were being swapped for men who had not experienced the truce—men who no longer felt.

Prince led them away, forlorn looks on all their faces. Their collars remained turned up against the fierce, icy wind whilst their noses were all red and stuffy.

As the company reached the reserve trench, the first shells were heard. The firing was light at first, unwilling, but it was still there. Every man jumped at the shrill whistle as the bombs flew through the air. They winced, their ears sharp once more as the bombs found their targets, fracturing into a million pieces as they hit the earth. The shaking of Gray's hands took back up with the first shot.

Chapter Twenty

The bombardment grew heavier as they reached their destination. Gray flinched with every explosion, the muscles in his neck taut with the frequent movement. He tried to cover his ears to block out the sound, but it was to no avail. The noise was burnt into his memory. His flight instinct seared. The only thing keeping him on the road was the tightly packed company around him, pushing him forwards.

Gray and Charlie's platoon was placed in a shabby room in the first ruined village they came to. It was a large enough room for fifteen men but contained just one double bed with thin, tatty sheets. The justification for this was that the men were all supposed to have their own bedding. The fact it was caked in mud was beside the point.

One redeeming factor was its adjoining bathroom, containing a chipped, stained bathtub. The toilet was outside, down a narrow, bare wooden staircase that creaked ominously with every footfall. However, compared to their former living conditions, the men couldn't believe their luck. Perhaps the best thing was there wasn't a scrap of corrugated iron or a sandbag insight. To them, that meant it was a luxury billet if ever they saw one.

They grinned at the peeling dark green paint on the damp

walls and jumped on the bed like children. A large dust cloud puffed up around them as they stirred the sheets. To them, the grotty room almost felt like home. They threw their heavy packs under the bed for safe keeping before heading downstairs to order the largest portion of greasy potatoes they could from the estaminet and drink pint after pint of watery beer. They quickly forgot about the death being inflicted at that exact moment on the front line.

Gray, however, couldn't forget.

He went through the movements, smiling in all the right places as he stuffed potatoes into his mouth without tasting them. He drank his beer numb to the fear he felt inside.

"All right, chaps," Charlie boomed when they first arrived. "How is it going?"

They all roared their response, having had much more beer than Charlie and Gray by that point. They appeared to have interrupted a rather vulgar conversation about the local brothel. Gray buried his face into his drink. The conversation went on for almost an hour.

"Anyone going?" one of the younger men asked.

Gray and Charlie both just laughed.

"What?" scoffed an older soldier, his left eye swollen shut by a recent injury. "I don't even know where it is. My wife is at home waitin' for me. I'm not going to get my end away whilst she sits at home worrying whether I'm still alive."

Gray laughed whilst his hands still shook violently.

"Well, there's split sections, would you believe it. Separate whores for the officers!"

The men all roared.

"You're jokin'?" one of the younger ones said.

"Nope, the war office thinks it keeps up the moral."

The older man choked on his beer as he laughed around a huge gulp of the sour liquid.

"I feel dirty just talking about it. I'm going for a wash." Charlie eventually declared, standing up, a little wobbly from the large quantity of beer he had consumed in such a short space of time. He was blushing profusely.

"I'll see you in a bit then," Gray replied still with half a bowl of potatoes left. Despite the odd turn in conversation, he wanted to soak up the joviality to dull the nightmarish images still flashing through his mind every time he closed his eyes.

Once he had finished, noticing that the other men were likely to stay in the estaminet all night, Gray stood to offer his farewells. Perhaps, if he managed to get into his pyjamas quickly, he'd get to sleep in the bed. What a luxury it would be to be able to wear bedclothes.

Charlie was still in the small washroom when he returned. He could hear the water being moved around. Alone in the room, he removed his tunic and sat on the bed in his shirt and trousers. Lice crawled against Gray's skin, and he couldn't help longing for a wash himself. He placed his toes against the heels of his boots, hearing each of them thud against the wooden floor when they finally broke free of his feet. As his toes rejoiced outside of their confinement, he realised that he hadn't removed his shoes for at least three days. Gray crinkled his nose as the smell of them filled the room.

"That you, old chap?" Charlie called.

"Who are you calling old?" Gray replied, laughing. He heard Charlie laugh as well, and a feeling of warmth spread through him from making a friend smile. The door opened after a few minutes, and Charlie made his way into the bedroom—stark naked and his hair still wet from the bath.

During the war, the men couldn't afford to be self-conscious, and thus not much shocked them anymore. However, seeing his friend emerge from the bathroom—his muscles toned beneath his skin and the water dripping off the ends of his curls—induced an odd feeling in Gray.

The room seemed to get very warm all of a sudden. He flushed a deep shade of red and tried to look away, but it was too late. As if deciding what to do, Charlie seemed to stand in the middle of the room for ages. Slowly, he approached the bed. Sitting on the edge, he reached out a hand, cautiously touching Gray's cheek. Gray gasped, inching back against the wall.

"Get the fuck off me," he said, but there was no conviction in his voice.

The two men looked at each other for a while, confused as to what was happening and by how right it felt. Both their breathing had turned heavy.

Their desire seemed to win out at the exact same moment. Lunging for each other, their teeth clashed in a violent kiss—each man fighting with the other in a refusal to accept the intense emotions they both felt.

Gray pushed Charlie off the bed with as much force as he could muster, jumping to his feet and rearranging his clothes. He ran his hands through his thick blond hair, his eyes wild with desire and fear.

"No, no we can't do this." He gestured to Charlie. "This is wrong. It's illegal. Christ!" Gray ran from the room with one last look at his companion. He barrelled down the stairs in a daze, desperate to feel the cold air on his skin and to get as far away from Charlie as soon as possible so he wouldn't be tempted to go back.

When he thought about it, he knew he had always known this about himself. He'd shunned it from his conscious mind, knowing it was wrong. His family would never even begin to accept it. He tried to put it down to the war. Shock perhaps, or the fact they had been surrounded by men for months without a feminine touch. Either way, it was unnatural. He could be put in jail or even killed. His parents would never even look at him. They would be so disgusted. They might even disown him. He wouldn't survive that.

He ran until he reached the house at the edge of the village where he knew the other normal soldiers went to see women for a small fee. He pushed his way inside, fighting off the memories of the evening. His sock-clad feet, now sodden from the wet ground, slapped against the stone floor. He thought he must look desperate. He was ushered into a room as soon as he showed them his fistful of mucky coins.

The room was dim with a small bed against the wall, surrounded by tacky drapes in shades of pink, and a screen erected in the corner. It wasn't anything special. Just a back room in someone's house. The woman, only a few years older than himself, was waiting for him, clad in only her undergarments.

"Get undressed behind there and tell me what you want."

He understood her French perfectly, but he just stood there with fear on his face.

"Do you understand French?"

Gray nodded his head. A crease crossed the girl's brow.

"This your first time?"

He shook his head this time, blushing as she approached and slowly unbuttoned his shirt for him.

"What you afraid of?"

"I-I don't know." His fingers trembled, but the rest of his body was stock still.

"You were right. You do speak French. What do you like?"

He thought of Charlie again, and he blushed deeper.

"Don't be embarrassed, tell me. I've heard it all." She ran her coarse fingers down his bare arms, pimpled from the cold.

"It's not men, is it? I've had a few of those."

She coaxed him over to the bed. His hands trembled as much as they would have if he were going over the top. At the mention of his deepest secret, he blushed even deeper. He looked down at himself, standing there in a filthy brothel, and wrenched his hand out of hers.

"It is, isn't it? You're one of those men that gets turned on by other men. Is that why you're here? For me to cure you? I don't think I can, honey, but I can arrange something else if you like."

She touched him, trying to arouse a response, but he flinched involuntarily. Tears formed in his eyes at his shame.

"I'm sorry," he muttered as he walked out, his whole body trembling. He ached with the need to find Charlie, but his mind refused to let him go back there. He wanted his brain to simply stop working.

The blue-eyed German with blood on his lips flashed through his mind. The image was so sudden, so violent, Gray stumbled with the force of it. As he walked, the man's last gurgled breath filled his ears as loud as if he were right beside him, as if the breath were his own. Feeling pain in his chest, the ripping apart of his flesh as the imagined blade dug itself into his organs, he cried out.

Gray wanted more than anything to stop feeling and for the horrid images to stop haunting his every thought. His next trip to the front would be his last. He knew that with certainty. His luck had run out. The thought of spending more time in the trenches, waiting for his inevitable end, drove him mad with panic.

Tears rolled down his cheeks, his breath struggling to push past the lump clogging his throat and the pain searing in his chest. He couldn't stop thinking about home, knowing he couldn't return there. No-one would love him there after they realised who he really was. He was a disgrace in every way, but he couldn't hide it for the rest of his life. Genevieve could read him like a book. He would be a liar and a cheat.

The light from the shells exploding on the horizon shone off his wet cheeks. Tears and mucus dripped off his chin and onto his thin white undershirt. He had no idea where he was going, he just knew he had to get out of there. Wherever there was. If he went back to the front, he'd be killed. Yet, if he ran away, he'd be shot for desertion. There was no way out. Stopping dead in the middle of the road, Gray reached down to his belt where the pistol—his first souvenir—sat in its holster. The handle was cold to the touch. He couldn't keep purchase on the weapon for long. He dropped it several times whilst cocking the gun. Reaffirming his grip with long, elegant fingers, Gray looked down the dark barrel. He gave one final, shaky salute and pulled the trigger.

Part Two

Chapter One

30th December 1914

Annabel jerked awake. She had heard a gunshot. She was sure of it.

"Wha's the marrer?" Teddy sat up beside his wife, his eyes bleary as he hovered on the border of sleep.

"Did you hear that?" Annabel sat up beside her husband.

"'Ere wha'?" He rubbed a hand over his eyes and shifted beneath the blankets.

"The gun."

"What?" He was suddenly wide awake, staring at Annabel in shock. "What gun?"

"I heard it. I just—"

Teddy threw the thick covers off his legs and rushed over to the window. His form was silhouetted in the moonlight, the outline of his body visible through his nightshirt as he drew back the curtains. He let out a small sigh, surveying the grounds below.

"There's no-one out there, Annabel. No-one at all. These windows are really thick anyway, you must have dreamt it."

"No, I…I felt it. I definitely—"

Teddy turned towards his wife after redrawing the curtains. He approached her slowly, placing a tender hand against her cheek. Stroking the thumb in small circles, he kissed her. Looking into her eyes he rested his forehead against her's. Annabel knew he could read the worry there.

"Daniel's fine, my love. You read that letter he sent. He's doing well. There isn't any fighting at the moment. He's safe."

He paused, and Annabel felt him draw in a breath as if he were trying to convince himself as well.

"Please, go back to sleep."

"I...I can't," Annabel stuttered. "Knowing he's there, under those guns. How bad must it be if we can hear them from—"

Teddy's lips came down on Annabel's again, this time a little firmer than before. He was trying to distract her, to take her mind off the worry eating her alive. His hands cupping her face, and his breath against her, was so warm and familiar. So safe. She closed her eyes as her husband continued to kiss her, slowly easing her back against the pillows as his lips found her neck.

She put her hands in his thick, dark hair, hoping he would find encouragement in the gesture. This was just as much about distracting him. Teddy never spoke about his worry, never let his wife be burdened with it, but she could see it in the creases around his eyes and in the deftness of his touch. He was just as crippled as she was.

Teddy hovered above her for several minutes, his hands moving down from her face to shift her nightgown upwards. In turn, she did the same to him, trying to help him with her touch. Teddy buried his face in Annabel's neck before letting out a frustrated groan that tickled her skin. His breath was fast as he rolled off her.

"I can't... I'm sorry," he whispered into the darkness. He rubbed his hand over his eyes, letting out another sigh.

Annabel moved towards him, resting her head above

Theodore's heart and listening to it beat against her ear. Teddy's arm wrapped around her, holding her against him.

"I'm sorry," he muttered again, his breath slowing as he drifted back towards sleep.

Annabel envied how easy sleep appeared to come to him. "It's all right," she whispered in response, pressing herself closer to him. "It's all right."

Yet, as hard as she tried, Annabel couldn't believe her own words. As her husband's breath regulated, and his hand against her back slackened, she couldn't stop thinking about her son, so many miles away, in unimaginable danger. No matter what she told herself, she just couldn't shake the feeling something was wrong.

Chapter Two

The next week passed in a groggy daze. Annabel had hardly slept or eaten, her stomach constantly churning with worry. She just knew something wasn't right. The world itself felt off balance. She wanted desperately to hear from her son. It was the only thing she could think of. So long as her child was unharmed, the rest of the world could continue spinning.

On the day when everything fell apart, Annabel was sat in the family parlour, a cup of lukewarm tea between her cold hands.

Genevieve came in not long after Annabel and sat beside her, trying in vain to instil a smile upon her face. It seemed she had felt something the other night as well, some shift in the atmosphere of their own private world.

Just as Annabel was about to get up, she heard a metallic tinkle outside. Glancing out the window onto the sunlit drive, she saw a flash of red from the post boy's bicycle. Genevieve stiffened beside her, her spine perfectly straight. A hard knock came from the main door. Neither woman moved. Perhaps if they stayed perfectly still, time would stop, the news that bell insinuated would never be read, and all would be as it should. A few seconds later, a butler entered the parlour, carrying the silver mail tray. Annabel's heart hammered against her chest.

"A telegram for you, m'lady." The butler sounded a little shaky.

Genevieve glanced at Annabel before moving forwards with a tentative step to take the bright white telegram.

"Would…would you like anything else?" The butler was trying desperately to act normally whilst they all knew the contents of that envelope. He took his leave without being dismissed, closing the door as silently as he could.

With a shaky breath and tears already sliding down her porcelain cheeks, Genevieve took the telegram out of its envelope and began to read. A pained moan escaped her small mouth and her face crumpled. The telegram floated to the floor, where it landed face down at Annabel's feet.

Annabel stayed in the chair, her eyes still fixated on the spot where the tray had been. Her face had gone deathly white. The only sign of life was the ever so slight trembling of her bottom lip.

Genevieve fell to her knees with a thud, her shoulders shaking in sorrow. The door opened, and Annabel half registered her husband's presence. He took just one glance at the distraught girl before falling to his knees beside her. Without missing a beat, he took her in his arms in a fatherly embrace, resting his chin atop her hair. He ran a hand lightly up and down her back as he had done when she was a child. Looking around the room for the source of the upset, his gaze fell on the telegram and his composure crumpled.

"No," he moaned. His eyes turned glassy, swimming with emotion. He didn't need to read the impersonal words to understand. "No."

"Gray… Gray's… He's d—"

"Don't you dare say it, Genevieve. Don't you dare." Annabel

had re-awoken and there was venom in her voice. "He's fine. It's just some stupid game he's playing. He's my boy. He can't... He isn't."

Theodore looked as ashen as if all the life had been pulled from him in a matter of seconds. Words could never describe the pain a man feels when they lose their son. His appearance was unbearable to watch. He reached out a hand to rest on his wife's knee, but she slapped away his consoling touch. It never crossed her mind that he wanted to receive comfort just as much as he wanted to give it.

To Annabel, comfort equalled acceptance, and thus she refused it. She stood up sharply, walking from the room without looking back. The echo of Genevieve's agonising cries grew more distant as Annabel made her way up the stairs, leaning heavily on the bannister as a sudden fatigue seeped into her every muscle.

She had no particular aim in mind, yet within a few moments, she found herself outside her son's bedroom. Slowly, she reached out her hand, brushing her fingertips along the shiny door handle. Turning it, she let it swing open. Taking in the sight of his neatly made bed covers, she remembered how she had held him and rocked him into a peaceful sleep just a few weeks before.

She took one step inside, trailing her hand over those silky sheets and thinking about how excited he had been when he had purchased them. Next, she ran her fingers over the fur throw slung over the foot board. She thought of him as a toddler, wrapped up inside the blanket whilst pretending to be a wolf. She laughed softly, a flood of similar memories entering her thoughts until she was laughing almost manically.

Alongside the happy memories came images of him standing in the entrance hall in his battered uniform, his eyes so much older than his years after seeing suffering she had sworn her life she would protect him from. Finally, she pictured the telegram, lying unread on the floor, and the laughter quickly turned to tears. She leant over the footboard of Gray's bed as the sobs ripped through her. Just as her knees threatened to give out, she stopped crying. Willing herself to stand up straight, she wiped her eyes and walked back out of the room, heading to her office to compose a letter to her son. Her heart knew he was dead, yet she was certain she wouldn't survive the news. So her mind blocked it out, continuing to deny the obvious.

My beautiful son, Daniel.

I do hope this letter finds you well. You will never believe the things they are saying about you here. I am actually rather angry with whoever writes these telegrams, as there must be a family somewhere completely unaware their son has been killed. The stupid people sent it to our house instead! Poor Genevieve is quite beside herself. So do write to us soon, my love.

Look after yourself and come home quickly. I love you so very much. Mother.

Having sealed and addressed the envelope, Annabel walked over to her arm chair. She stared into the fire, watching as it died down to nothing more than a pile of smoking embers.

It was past midnight when she made her way to bed, undressing and climbing beneath the golden covers in something of a daze. Theodore was not in the room. As she had passed his office, she had heard him crying gently. That room was full of pictures of his beloved son and wife throughout the last eighteen years. Pictures of Gray smiling, laughing with his arm slung over the shoulder of his father, or sitting up close to his mother. There were drawings from Gray's own hand, from his childhood year's right up to the present. Annabel's particularly favourite photo was one of their son tenderly kissing the cheek of his best friend on a picnic a few years earlier.

Annabel didn't sleep. She simply went through the motions of pretending.

The next day, Annabel rose at the same time as usual, dressing herself in a beaded beige skirt suit and pinning a wide-brimmed hat adorned with flowers in her hair. Without further ado, she walked out of her room, pausing only briefly to look into Gray's room—perhaps hoping to find him in there and that it had all been an elaborate dream.

Her heart soared when she saw a figure beneath the silk covers, and she ran towards it, reaching out to touch her son's shoulder. She realised just as she laid her hand against the warm form that it was Genevieve. The young girl rolled over at Annabel's touch, tears etched onto her cheeks. She reached out her arms like a small child begging to be folded into the embrace of a mother's love. The need in Genevieve's eyes made Annabel give into her, and she held the girl close, remembering her as an infant and how she had helped to bring her to this safe place she called home when she was a tiny baby. She had promised to shelter her from pain as well. This was another person she had failed. Her throat burning, she kissed the young girl's dark hair, rubbing her back as she had done in that stable so many years ago.

"It's all right, sweetheart."

"No, it's not." Genevieve's voice was thick, catching with every word. "N-nothing is w-without him. H-he was everything."

Annabel closed her eyes against the pain piercing through her heart, regaining her composure in seconds as she had been trained to do her whole life.

"He's fine. You'll see." She pulled back, cupping Genevieve's face between her palms and kissing her forehead. "You'll see."

She got up slowly. Genevieve whimpered behind her. Her arms were still outstretched, pleading to be back inside Annabel's arms where she could pretend, however briefly, that everything really would be all right.

Annabel turned away and made her way down the stairs, the letter to her son clasped in her hand. As she started to walk down the drive, she felt the cold air on her face sobering her thoughts. The sun, to Annabel, was yet another omen her boy couldn't be gone. Surely, if the world had lost such perfection, even nature would be mourning him.

Chapter Three

Annabel's state of denial lasted for the next few days. She continued to wear her usual pastel colours in defiance of the telegram still lying face down on the floor of the parlour. The staff looked at her cautiously as if she might break at any moment. Her husband had tried and failed to comfort her on multiple occasions. His eyes were constantly puffy, from crying when he thought she couldn't hear.

Sitting in her window seat, her lap covered in a pale pink and gold skirt, she looked out at the forest as she had done so many times over the years. Surrounded by her finery she remembered the horror of that place and the incomparable happiness she had felt in the older Daniel's arms. She hadn't seen him in nearly twenty years but wondered daily what had become of him. Her son had talked of a Lieutenant Prince, which she wouldn't let herself believe was the same one. Had he really met his father?

She knew Patsy kept in contact with Daniel, but she never asked after him. Patsy never talked of him either. It would hurt too much to be told of his new life without her. Annabel knew that was selfish. Patsy had her own family to worry about without having to look after Annabel as well.

Still lost in thoughts of the past, she glanced down, seeing a figure walking up the drive. It was a man in a khaki uniform, blond hair poking out the sides of his hat. She jumped to her feet, her heart soaring. She knew she had been right. Taking the stairs two at a time and stumbling over her feet in her haste, she threw open the door just as he was walking up the steps. The butler frowned in confusion. Annabel came to an abrupt halt as the man removed his hat, revealing a pair of hazel eyes.

"Daniel," she stuttered, putting out a hand to lean against the door frame, her sweaty fingers leaving marks on the polished surface. She had forgotten just how much her son had looked like him. The familiar features, even after all this time, made her heart ache with longing.

"Lady Brogan." He bowed his head.

The formality with which he addressed her hurt. He had changed over the last almost twenty years. He spoke more eloquently—almost as if he were a gentleman—and there were deep lines between his eyes. However, Annabel still wanted to touch him, to throw her arms around his shoulders and press her lips against his like she was eighteen again. She knew she couldn't. The ring on her left hand seemed suddenly white hot, burning into her delicate skin.

"P-please, call me Annabel."

They stood there, looking at each other in awkward silence. Regardless of the fleeting joy of seeing him again, it was accompanied by the most crushing disappointment of her life. She wanted him to be a different Daniel, the little boy she had raised in this house. As she surveyed him, she realised his uniform was different from her son's. He wore a stiff leather belt and had the stripes of an officer embroidered on his sleeve. Just like his son, although much more potent, there was a haunted sadness in his eyes. The same sadness that had been in Daniel his whole life. Something else was there as well. She realised with a jolt that it was pity.

Taking a deep, shuddering breath, she invited him inside, leading him into the family parlour. He looked around at the finery of her house in astonishment. He looked strange beneath the enormously high ceilings and crystal chandeliers—small and vulnerable. How many times had she imagined him there? Now the daydream had become a reality, it felt wrong. This wasn't how they were supposed to be reunited.

Once in the parlour, Daniel removed his pack, propping it carefully against the wall, a worried frown on his face as the dirty item touched the clean, expensive carpet.

"I'm so sorry, Lady…Annabel."

"For what?"

"Weren't you sent a…a telegram…? I know you were. I wrote it."

"Oh, that. Well, don't be sorry. Daniel's—" She looked up. "Gray is fine."

"No Anna—" The line between his eyes deepened. "Anna, listen to me."

"No, you listen, I'm his mother, and I am telling you he is alive." The determination in her voice was heartbreaking. "I would know instantly if he was… If he… He isn't. I just know it." She blocked the moment she had awoken to the imaginary gunshot from her mind, as well as the cold feeling she had held in her bones ever since. It was as if half her soul had been removed as she slept.

"I-I saw him, Anna." He looked as if the phrase physically hurt him, but as if he couldn't keep the information in any longer.

Annabel continued to stare at him, but she could feel her composure slipping, slowly collapsing piece by carefully sculpted piece.

The denial that had been keeping her alive the past few weeks tumbled through her feet and evaporated. She shook her head, her eyes pressed tightly closed as if by not looking at the world around her she could pretend it didn't exist.

"We found these in his belongings. I thought you might like them. I just wanted to give them to you. I thought it might be easier coming from someone you know. Or used to know. I won't stay long."

He handed over a small parcel. With shaking fingers, Annabel pulled apart the brown paper, the crinkling sound reverberating around the silent room. Inside was a thick folder. The smell of leather crept up to her nose, followed by the familiar scent of her son. Cautiously opening it, she noticed his leather folder. With a small smile, she saw it was full of poetry, written in Gray's elaborate hand. Along with the verse, there was a series of sketches, each depicting a different scene or person he had met. She flicked through them in a daze, a single tear falling from her eye and landing on a soiled picture of herself with Genevieve. Mud stained the faded outlines where it looked as if his unwashed finger had traced their features.

She hadn't believed the words, but this was the proof she had hoped not to find.

"How did it happen?" she asked, her voice wobbling dangerously.

Daniel said nothing, he just ran his hand through his hair—a gesture that reminded her so much of her son she nearly broke down.

"I said, how did it happen, Daniel?"

He looked up, his hazel eyes fixing on hers. Seeing that familiar gaze, her emotions boiled over into anger. She shoved her former lover in the chest. The papers fell from her hand. When she glanced down, Gray's signature was scattered around the floor.

"He was…was killed in action."

Annabel closed her eyes again and took a deep breath. "Yes, but how exactly did it happen. You must know. You said you saw it!"

"No, I just heard it. I saw him afterwards. I'm certain he died instantly and didn't suffer."

"How can you tell me he didn't suffer? Did you see him before? When he came back here, he was a wreck. Barely able to stand up because he had seen such horror, and his eyes…" She stopped speaking, drawing another deep breath to steady herself. She put a hand on the back of a chair to keep herself upright. "I don't believe you. There's something in your eyes. You're not telling the truth."

"Don't contradict me, Anna, please. You haven't been over there to the front. You have no idea the kind of horror… You don't need to know. I'm the lieutenant of Gray's company. I saw him every day. Christ, I held him for the entire damn night before he went over the top that second time. He was so scared. I was terrified that something might happen to him or to his friend. I saw what happened to the other men. How can you stand there and tell me I'm lying about something like this? After everything we had together, do you not know me at all?"

"Of course I know you. You and him are identical in every way, and I know my son better than anybody."

"*Our* son, Annabel. Everything I've told you has been the truth. Can you say the same? You didn't even tell me we had a son. He was the best…the best man I ever met." Daniel's voice broke with the expression of love for the boy he had unknowingly created. He moved closer to Annabel, his voice lowering. "Why didn't you tell me, Anna? I could have been a good father, but you never gave me the chance."

"How could I tell you? You were in prison for the first ten years of his life. He would have grown up a convict's bastard if I'd waited for you. Theodore is the best father I could have given him. He was there for him through everything."

Daniel nodded slowly. "That's why you said what you did in the prison, isn't it? Damn it, Anna, you should have told me, if I'd known—"

"It would have torn you apart. You believed I didn't love you. You got over it and moved on."

"No, Anna. No, I didn't." A heavy silence hung in the air.

Annabel stumbled slightly, her grip on the chair tightening.

"I'm really sorry for your loss, Lady Brogan," Daniel chanted, putting his hat back on his head as a mournful look crossed his face. He bent down to pick up his pack.

Letting go of the chair, Annabel stepped backwards blocking his path. "Daniel, please just tell me how it happened."

"I've already—"

"No, you haven't. Don't I have the right to know what happened to my own son? Please, tell me the truth." Her eyes were clouding over in tears, desperate to find out her son's fate. A part of her still clung to the idea he was fine. If Daniel hadn't seen Gray's death properly, maybe her son had escaped. Maybe he was in a French hospital somewhere waiting for her. "He's our baby boy. Please, Daniel."

"Annabel, I can't. I've told you what you need to know. Please get out of my way." His jaw tensed in anger and sorrow, desperate to keep his emotions at bay until he was alone.

"I won't move until you tell me what happened to our son."

"Move, Anna."

"Tell me what happened!"

"No! I can't, Anna. Let me go. Please."

"Tell me."

Daniel let out an aggravated groan. The truth on his tongue, and he looked terrified it might slip out.

"No," he repeated with steel in his voice.

Annabel rushed forwards, grabbing his arm. The touch they had longed to share for so many years made them both jump.

"I can't, Anna."

In an equally sudden gesture, Annabel let go, her hand striking Daniel's cheek with a loud slapping noise. The skin turned red immediately.

"Please, just let me go. I can't do this."

"Do what? What happened to our boy? What did you do?"

Daniel stumbled backwards. "You think… No." He threw his hat to the floor in anger. "Read the telegram, Annabel. Killed in action. That was the cause of death. He was my son too. How dare you say I had a hand in his death? How dare you?" He whispered the last utterance, and somehow, it made it seem even more menacing.

"What happened? What did he— Did a British soldier do it? Did he do it himself? Every image in my head gets worse and worse, Daniel. I can't take it."

Daniel turned around, looking at her with sadness and shock. One of her guesses had been correct. Annabel's eyes narrowed.

"That's it, isn't it? A British bullet killed my son."

"No, Anna it wasn't—"

Annabel leapt back out of Daniel's reach. "Don't touch me.

Who killed my son?" But the look in Daniel's eyes told her that her latter suggestion had been the correct one. She covered her mouth with her hand. "It wasn't— No, he couldn't have done it. Tell me that's not how—"

Daniel squeezed his eyes shut, running his hands through his hair. "I shouldn't have come here."

Annabel's eyes glazed over in shock and misery as if every drop of life was seeping out of her. "He wouldn't. He couldn't." She swayed on her feet. "Why would… Did you come here to torture me? Some sick way of getting me back for hurting you twenty years ago?"

"Shit, Anna! I'm sorry. I shouldn't have come. It would have been best if you hadn't known. Why did you make me tell you? Gray had war neurosis. Shell shock, they've started calling it. He wasn't in his right mind. He was as much killed in action as any man I ever saw. I've seen men with shock do impossible things. I'm sorry. I should… I should have seen the signs. His hands… They— I'm so sorry."

He reached for her arm, but she shook it off, reflexively taking another step back until she was leaning against the wall. Her breathing grew faster as the knowledge of her son's death finally seeped into her brain. She tried desperately to convince herself Daniel was lying.

He was her little boy. The boy who had run around in this very parlour stark naked at the age of three. It was there she had helped teach him to waltz so beautifully. The same boy she had nursed through every illness and every sadness since the day he was born. The world could not be without such a boy. It simply couldn't continue to spin. A pure, undiluted despair played out on her flawlessly beautiful face as she began to shut down, cell by excruciating cell.

Daniel's voice caught as he tried to speak reassurance to her whilst his own sorrow still seemed so raw. He hadn't let himself grieve yet.

"Annabel, he was such a wonderful boy. So brave and polite. Such a brilliant soldier. He was so beautiful. I loved him so much. I'm so, so proud of him. No matter how short a time he spent here, he was the proof of our love, and he was perfect. In every way. He was our perfect boy."

Annabel's breathing grew faster still, tears sprung from her eyes at this stunning declaration of love. How many times had she imagined Daniel saying those things about their son?

All of a sudden, the last threads of Annabel's hope snapped. Hearing the raw emotion in Daniel's voice brought the truth to her like nothing else ever would, and she collapsed with a piercing cry. The scream was so full of agony it tore through the soul of everybody within earshot. Even birds took flight at the noise, escaping the evidence of such pain. Daniel rushed forwards, grabbing her limp body just before she hit the ground, his own tears falling freely as grief finally set in. Sobs ripped at both of their throats.

Annabel continued to scream her mournful song, distraught beyond measure at the loss of her entire reason for existence. She grabbed at the rough material of Daniel's tunic desperately, pressing her face into his shoulder. The soapy smell of him filled her consciousness, causing twenty years of suppressed emotion to burst forth. Nothing had ever felt like this. Even leaving Daniel, hearing him calling out her name from behind the bars, was a mere scratch upon this hurt. This was a wound so deep, so severe, she knew it would never even begin to heal. The pain would continue as raw as it was at that second—crippling her every movement for the rest of her life.

The love she and Daniel had shared was shattered, blown apart and rotting in a hole in France. Daniel had shown her the first blossom of true love, but Gray had lit up her world with such brilliance that she was blinded in this sudden darkness.

When her body could no longer suck in enough air to scream, she fell against Daniel's lap. She hoped then, with every fibre of her being, that her mutilated heart would cease to beat, allowing her to once more be with her son. With every breath, the pain ripped through her again, with renewed vigour.

Daniel held her to him as tightly as he could. Annabel could feel his tears soaking into her clothes as he rocked her slowly.

When the room had fallen into complete darkness, Annabel felt herself lifted into Daniel's strong arms. Opening her eyes, she saw Theodore standing in the doorway. The two men exchanged a glance. She hadn't noticed her husband entering, nor did she know how long he had been there. He looked distraught and un-focused—his aristocratic features drawn down and his eyes void of their signature sparkle—from the loss of the heir he had taught, chastised, and loved with all his heart.

Annabel knew this image would have broken her heart once, but her heart was beyond that now. No piece big enough to break remained . That day, she couldn't even muster the energy to care.

The two men looked at each other in silent understanding. Theodore was slightly taller, although, Daniel's shoulders were broader and his muscles larger. He bore all the physical and emo-tional scars of a life lived far beyond his years and full of suffer-ing. He was the complete opposite to Teddy in almost every way, their only similarity being that they were both completely in love with the woman now curled in Daniel's arms and the boy whose death had caused her undoing.

"Can…can you show me to her room? I want to make sure she is safe before I leave." The vibrations of Daniel's voice went through Annabel's body. Once she would have craved that feeling, been revitalised by it, but not then.

"How long have you got?"

"Only a week. I-I won't stay that long. I just came to check to see that she was… Not all right…but something like it. I'm sorry I just couldn't stay there after… After it happened."

Daniel sniffed back more tears as Teddy nodded stiffly, turning to lead him up into the east wing. Teddy didn't seem surprised by Daniel at all. It was almost as if he had expected his arrival for years. Annabel watched his elegant back as he walked. When they reached her room, Teddy glancing momentarily at Gray's closed door on the way, Daniel placed Annabel's limp form onto her bed, slipped off her shoes, and pulled the covers up to her shoulders. He brushed a rough finger along her cheek before turning to leave.

"No," Annabel croaked. Even her voice sounded lifeless, catching as it left her mouth. "Don't leave me."

The tears were falling once more. She could feel them soaking into the pillow case beneath her raw cheek. Daniel rushed to her side at once. Crouching down beside the bed, he took hold of her hand. His fingers felt exactly as they had all those years before. The sensation made a new lump rise in her throat for her lost past and she sank back into violent sobs. Annabel felt Daniel's other hand once more on her cheek.

"I'm not going anywhere, my love. Not this time."

Chapter Four

Annabel slipped in and out of unconsciousness. In sleep, she gained blissful moments where she could forget everything and pretend in a dream she was with her son. Billy came in at some point during the night with a loud expression of joy for his long-lost brother. Genevieve came in just as Billy left.

Annabel felt the mattress dip as the young girl curled up beside her. Clinging to Annabel's waist, she buried her head in her breast, seeking comfort from the only maternal figure she had ever known. They both cried with renewed vigour, needing each other in equal measure as they once more remembered the perfect boy that would never return home.

Annabel imagined the gossip Jen and Gray would have had if they'd been able to see Daniel at Annabel's side. They would have both relished the story. She clung to the young girl tighter.

When Annabel and Daniel were once again alone, she opened her eyes. Even that one simple movement took almost all her energy. Daniel was looking out at the forest he had called home for over half his life, watching the gentle sway of the trees through the tall window. A wistful expression clung to his face as his chin rested against his knees—perhaps a childhood habit to make himself appear as small as possible.

"Daniel," she croaked.

His head snapped around. He winced at the sudden movement but returned to her side immediately.

"Tell me how it happened."

The crease between his eyes returned, but she wanted to know so badly. Every time her unwilling mind pictured the scenario, trying to imagine the pain he must have been in, her heart rate increased dangerously—making her chest heave. Each image that flashed behind her eyes was worse than the one before.

"You need to rest, Anna. I've told you what happened."

His voice was low and smooth, exactly as she remembered it.

"Please, I need to know what happened to our little boy." Her voice broke, another tear falling onto her sodden pillow. The moisture seemed to burn as it trickled down her saturated face. The moonlight flooding through the window was making her feel sick.

"I've told you enough."

"No, please. I keep picturing it. I need to know. However bad."

Daniel seemed torn. Eventually, he exhaled a breath that dislodged several strands of Annabel's messy hair. He reached up to brush them off her face.

"I...I don't know exactly what happened. Before I mean. I don't know the reason. I... We were behind the lines. There were bars and things, hot food, you know? It was meant to build our morale or something." He let out a laugh, a dark humourless sound full of untold anger. His eyes were fixed on a point somewhere off in his memory. "He was staying in a room, not far from my own, with his platoon and a private named Charlie Grimsby. His best friend I think. They did everything together." Annabel remembered Charlie from the hospital, his youthful curls looked ridiculous in the khaki uniform, as if he were just playing soldiers.

"I'm a lieutenant," Daniel continued. "So I get different billets than the privates. Different bars as well, I don't know why exactly, some authority thing. I saw him briefly. He was eating as he sat next to Charlie, as always. I didn't stop. I should have stopped, but I didn't. He looked happy, a little distant perhaps, but he was smiling."

Annabel sobbed quietly as Daniel kissed her fingers absent-mindedly, his voice thick.

"I was sitting in the officer's bar, right at the edge of the town, with my back to the window. The other men started to look at something outside, but I didn't turn around. I was so tired. I just wanted to eat and go back to my room. One of them, Shepard, nudged me. They had this joke that Gray was my secret child because we looked so much alike. Ironic really.

"They were all laughing because he wasn't walking straight. They thought he was drunk. As soon as they said his name, I turned. When I saw him, I knew he wasn't right. He wasn't wearing any shoes, so he must have been freezing. He was crying, and he… He stopped in the middle of the road. He was fiddling with his belt, trying to get his pistol loose.

"He shouldn't have even had a pistol, but he came back from his first show with it. I should have taken it back off him, but it seemed to offer him comfort, to reassure him in some way. He dropped it twice because he was shaking so much. I should have noticed the shaking in his hands before. I did notice, but I just… It had been so cold at the front, everyone was shivering. Especially with him having come from this place, he wouldn't have been used to the cold. So, I thought that's all it was. Why would I think anything else?

"When I saw him, I got up straight away and tried to get out as fast as I could, but it was so busy. Once I got outside, I called to him, but he didn't hear. I was running towards him when I saw him salute, and then… Then I heard the shot."

Daniel's eyes were bright red and streaming, his entire body trembling. "I was so scared... I've never been so scared, so—" He sniffed, squeezing his eyes shut in an elongated blink. "I was too late."

Daniel cried uncontrollably, clasping Annabel's hands with a white-knuckled force. She didn't mind, she barely felt the physical pain. Her emotional hurt was too great.

"I kept thinking of you... How I… I failed you, and I failed him. I loved him so much, but I let him down. The first and only time he needed me to be his papa, and I failed. I wasn't there for my *son* in his one goddamned hour of need." He broke down again, rendering all speech impossible. His head fell forwards resting against the mattress.

Annabel felt empty, she curled up against Daniel. His arms came around her back, and they held each other so tightly neither of them could breathe. Joined in the knowledge they had failed in the most important task they were set on this earth. To keep their child safe.

The day progressed slowly. Each tick of the second hand pounded through Annabel's skull. Food was brought in at various points in the day, but neither person looked up. What was the point in eating when their reason for life had ceased to be?

Annabel heard Theodore enter the room a little before nightfall. However, seeing Daniel and Annabel lying together in their despair, he turned swiftly around. She assumed he would spend another night in the armchair in his office. There were, of course, plenty of spare bedrooms in the manor, but he seemed to seek the discomfort of a chair instead of a comfortable bed.

The next morning dawned sunny, mocking the mood of every occupant living inside Hoddington Manor.

Daniel rose early, just as the sun was cresting the trees, making long shadows on the cream carpet. His soft, warm lips pressed against Annabel's forehead, lingering for a second too long. He kept his hand against her cheek as she opened her eyes, rubbing the pad of his thumb in small circles. She smiled, still in the clutches of a dream. She reached up her hand, grasping his rough one as the dream fell away from her conscious mind. Her heart sank, her eyes filling once more as she caught sight of her son's immortalised picture in a golden frame beside her bed. His wavy hair had been cut short, and a small close-lipped smile played on his handsome features. Every breath that entered her lungs felt as if a knife was piercing through her flesh, the blade twisting inside her.

"My baby boy," she whispered dropping Daniel's fingers to stretch out a hand instead towards the picture. The movement felt strange as if she were no longer in full control of her body. "My darling baby boy."

Daniel pulled her closer for a few minutes before loosening his grip to look into her face. His eyes looked sad and haunted.

"I think he knew about me. When I… When I found him, he had my watch." Daniel reached into his breast pocket, extracting a long silver chain with a watch dangling on the end of it. Annabel rested it in her palm as Daniel clicked it open. As it opened, she stared at her own face. It was the image that had made it to all the newspapers in England following her wedding.

"He's so much like you," she whispered, still staring at the picture of herself. The image behind the glass held a small smile—a smile for the unborn child she had been carrying. "I'm sorry you got so little time with him."

"He was perfect. I just wish I'd known him under better circumstances." He paused, drawing a breath as if steeling himself to say something. "Annabel, I've got to go back."

She fixed her gaze on him, an element of her former strength coming back into her.

"No, you said you wouldn't leave me." Her strength crumbled as quickly as it had arisen. "Please don't go," she pleaded, her voice defeated.

"I have to, my love. I will be court-martialled if I stay. Your husband needs you here, and my company needs me at the front. It wouldn't be right if I stayed."

Annabel nodded slowly, rolling onto her back so the tears fell into her hair. She felt Daniel move away from her side and heard her water jug clink against a glass as he poured some, downing it in one gulp. He poured another glass, holding it to Annabel's parched lips as he placed a hand behind her head to stop her from choking.

When she had drained the liquid, she turned her back on Daniel, not wanting to watch him walk away from her. She felt his lips press against the bare skin of her neck. His hot breath was fast as if he was holding off tears again. The door clicked as it closed behind him. Annabel heard a second, lighter pair of footfalls approaching the closed door.

"What's your name?" Theodore asked.

The sound was muffled through the polished wood, but Annabel could still make it out. She knew the scene would have terrified her just a few weeks before. It was the moment all her carefully constructed lies fell apart.

"Lieutenant Daniel Prince, sir."

"Daniel. Of course." Teddy sighed. "I… I know what you and Annabel must have shared. I knew it, I think, before I even married her. She always had such a sadness in her eyes. Something I couldn't place."

"You knew Gray wasn't—"

"Of course I knew. She wanted nothing less than to marry me and then suddenly wants the wedding to take place immediately. When she told me she was pregnant, it all made sense. He was born so early. I can put two and two together. I'm no fool. Yet, by that point, I was too in love to fight it. Once Da— Gray was born, I loved him even more than Annabel, if that's at all possible. I still do. How could I walk out on such a beautiful family? He is *my* son, Lieutenant."

"I understand. I didn't even know about him until he ended up in my platoon. I promise. Your wife was a faithful wife, sir. I just wanted to see Anna. To… To apologise for not keeping him safe. You were much more his father than I. Thank you for that. I am truly grateful. He was a perfect gentleman in every way. Please know that, if I could take his place, I would in a heartbeat. I'm so sorry I failed him."

Silence followed Daniel's words as the two men seemed to drink them in.

"I trust you won't be returning soon?"

Teddy didn't say the words in a malicious tone. Annabel believed they were said with understanding. Theodore, it seemed, knew he would always come below Daniel in Annabel's heart, but he was still her husband. He wished to cling to that last positive element his life still possessed.

"No, sir. I won't."

The words cut through Annabel.

"Look after her."

"Always. I'll get my driver to take you to the station. Good luck, Lieutenant, honestly. And thank you for the most beautiful son I could have ever wished for."

Annabel listened to Daniel Prince's heavy footfalls as he walked out of her life for the second time. She shook with renewed grief, holding her chest as if afraid she would physically fall apart. Reaching under her pillow, she pressed her fingers against the small carving Daniel had made for her nearly twenty years before.

The beauty of Theodore's words cut her so deeply that her pain intensified tenfold. He had known the whole time, yet he had continued to be the best father she had ever laid eyes on. He was more remarkable than he had ever been. A few days earlier, the confession would have made her weep with relief, now she felt only sorrow.

She didn't even look up when she felt the mattress dip beside her a couple of hours later. She hadn't the strength. A familiar pair of arms pulled her into an embrace, and a hand stroked her hair rhythmically in comfort.

"I came as soon as I could," Patsy said close to her ear. "I'm so sorry, Anna, so, so sorry."

Annabel let herself be held, her will too weak to resist. She laid her head on Patsy's shoulder as the woman rocked her like a child, her own cheek on the top of Annabel's head.

"Daniel," Annabel whispered. "He's—"

"Shh, I know. I saw him just now. He looks like hell."

"Our baby boy's gone," she sniffled, the words searing her throat as she uttered them. "It hurts so much, Patsy. Please make it stop."

Patsy continued to rock her, ignoring everything else around her. She concentrated only on comforting this distraught shell of a woman, as only a best friend would do. Annabel's tears didn't flow this time. Instead, she felt as if her insides had frozen, leaving her completely numb but for the searing pain festering in her heart. She didn't see how she would ever feel happiness again. She couldn't even remember what the warm fingers of joy felt like.

"Genevieve," Annabel whispered.

"She's in his room. I think she's slept there since she found out. Teddy and Billy are taking turns checking on her. She'll be all right, eventually. Let's just focus on you."

"I can't be all right."

"Shh," Patsy cooed, her voice thick.

Gray had touched everyone he had ever met. The entire town mourned once the news had spread that they would be forever without him. Women who had hoped to be his wife were swathed in black and shop windows were darkened. Even the horses seemed to walk around with their heads bowed against the weight of such news.

*

Over the next few weeks, Annabel ate no more than what was necessary to stay alive, and even then, only because Patsy made her. Her body quickly deteriorated until it was nothing more than skin and bone, the sharp angles digging into the mattress painfully. She hardly ever changed her clothes, and she never washed.

Patsy returned to her family in the evenings but spent the days practically running the manor, leaving the two mourning parents to manage only their grief.

Theodore and Annabel no longer slept in the same room. In the early days, Theodore had entered the room often, trying desperately to comfort his wife and seek some comfort for himself in return, but she wouldn't let him. She shrugged off his kind touch or pretended to be asleep when he spoke. The very smell of him sparked an excruciating hoard of memories, the pain so intense she silently begged for death.

She refused even to look at the man who had been her husband for the best part of twenty years because he wasn't the son she so desperately needed to see. She would have done absolutely anything just for one more minute with him. Just to touch his cheek one last time and tell him everything would be all right. To tell him she loved him with all her heart.

*

The twenty-eighth of March dawned with a heavy sense of despair and anticipation in Hoddington Manor, for it was the day of Grayson Daniel Brogan's nineteenth birthday. Desperate to feel close to her little boy, Annabel slipped out from her protective shell of bedding. Waiting until she could no longer hear Theodore's anxious footfalls in the corridors, she crept out of her bedchamber. She stumbled slightly on her weak legs, unused to holding her meagre weight. Her shoulder rested against the wall, the thin material of her nightgown drowning her frame and caressing the floor with a quiet whisper. Her feet were bare, so her toes turned cold as they moved along the soft carpet.

She sang in the cracked, low voice of a person driven to the brink of madness.

Upon reaching Gray's room, Annabel stretched out a hand, resting it on the cold door knob for several seconds as she had done when the telegram had first been received, back in those blissful days of denial. Twisting the handle, her son's scent hit her hard in the face, making her almost collapse with longing. Her breathing turned heavy once more, her chest heaving beneath the thin fabric. The room looked exactly as it had the day he had last left it. His clothes were still thrown carelessly over the back of his dressing table chair. His shoes lay on their sides in the middle of the room. Annabel tripped over them as she had so many times and smiled at this piece of familiarity. The staff should have tidied up once he'd gone, but she was glad they hadn't.

Cautiously, she ran her bony fingers over the tweed jacket on the back of his chair. It was the one he'd worn hunting. Without thinking, she placed it over her shoulders, the sleeves fell past her hands. The silk lining was cold against her arms, raising pimples on her skin. She folded herself on the seat, hearing it creak as she lowered her body into it.

Annabel gasped as she caught sight of herself in the mirror. Her eyes were sunken and shadowed, her hair hung over her shoulders and down to her waist in a tangled mess. The formerly envied waves were now limp and peppered with grey on her waxy scalp. Her fingers fumbled along the dressing table, taking up a small comb. Her eyes stung once more with tears as they fell on the silver object, for there were still several short strands of blond hair clinging to the dull teeth. Bringing her knees up to rest under her chin she let the tears go for the first time that day. Falling into a numb state, not far from sleep, she found she could finally be with the one person that had made her shallow life worth living. Even if it was only for a short time.

Genevieve found her a few hours later, curled up so tightly in Gray's chair her legs had cramped. A shooting pain stabbed her muscles with every slow beat of her heart. She had clutched her son's comb so tightly as she cried that the teeth had dug into her palm. Blood dripped down onto the shiny surface of his dressing table. Genevieve rushed over to her, helping her to unfurl her fingers from the comb. It clattered as it hit the polished floor.

The young girl wrapped the elder's hand in the same piece of black material Gray had used as a sling on his last visit home before helping her to her feet, and, eventually, to her room. The entire time, tears had raced down the young girl's porcelain cheeks. She stopped every few seconds to wipe them away in an almost angry frenzy.

When Annabel was back amongst her gold embroidered bed clothes, Genevieve slipped from the room like a breath of wind, with no sign she had ever been there at all.

She reappeared several days later with a fierce expression on her face.

"You remember the hospital Gray and his friend were taken to once they got back to England?" she announced, charging into Annabel's room and making the woman jump half out of her skin. "I've written to them, and they're looking for nurses. Of course, I know nothing about nursing, but I thought perhaps I could be of some use there at least. More use than sitting around here, dreaming of a boy who I will never lay eyes on again."

"You don't need to work, Jen. That's why you were brought up here. I wanted to protect you from ever seeing hardship. Both of you."

"I know, Anna, I do. Aunt Patsy told me everything right after Gray died. But I can't sit here in purgatory, forever waiting for something that will never happen, a past life I will never play out."

Seeing the determination in her young eyes, a spark that had been absent for far too long, Annabel nodded slowly.

"You must go, Genevieve."

"Really? You honestly believe that?" She almost smiled.

"Yes, you mustn't waste your youth here. There is nothing left for you in this miserable house. You'll be perfectly safe in England. I've known for a long time I couldn't keep you here forever." Annabel tried to look happy as she remembered the former Genevieve's fiery personality—the young girl who had always been beside her son. They'd always been two peas in a pod. Seeing her without him was painful, but Annabel knew Jen would move on, eventually. She was young, and time would heal her.

Genevieve came over to her quietly, leaning forward so that the bedspread sighed beneath her, and kissed Annabel's frail cheek.

"I love you, Anna. I am so grateful for everything you've done for me and everything you continue to do. You've been a true mother to me. I want you to know that."

"And you're a true daughter. You're more than I ever hoped you'd be, my love." She smiled wistfully. The first smile she'd offered in months. "Now, go. Enjoy your youth as much as you can. Be happy, dear girl, please."

"I don't know if I can." It was just a whisper. "He was everything to me. My brother, my best friend, and the other half of my soul. I believe soul mates can take all kinds of forms, not just romantic ones, and he was mine. How can someone continue to live with only half their soul?"

"You'll find a way. Trust me. You have so much to offer the world. Don't waste it."

Jen left the following day with nothing but a small suitcase in her hand. She was clearly seeking her own way of being close to him whilst hoping to find work hard enough to forget about her pain.

Annabel was glad she left. Seeing her in the manor without Gray was wrong. She no longer belonged there without him.

Chapter Five

28th March 1916

The months slipped past Annabel without her realising their different meanings. Seasons became empty. Summer held no delight, and the first frost of winter was no longer magical. These small things only made the yearning to see her son grow stronger.

The first year without him had been long, dragging on in an endless stream of days and nights, leading up to that one joyful moment when she would be allowed to slip into unconsciousness forever and the pain would finally be over. The hurt hadn't even dulled, and her wounded heart hardly had the strength left to beat.

Annabel filled her days drifting slowly in and out of consciousness, huddled against the world. Her mind never let her forget, not even for a minute.

Patsy had employed a group of maids to care for Annabel, their sole duty to make sure she ate and drank enough to keep living. They had given up trying to get her out of bed long ago. Patsy and Genevieve were the only people who could get her up, the only people Annabel now wanted to impress. Genevieve had moved out long ago.

Annabel's parents had tried to get her out of the house. They had tried sympathy, kindness, even anger, frustration, and violence, but none of it had worked. A parade of mourners, young women who had hoped to be Gray's wife or even mistress, had paraded around the house over the months. All manner of high society members had hoped to take advantage of the family's vulnerability to climb the ranks. Their cards had remained unread, now gathering dust on Annabel's bedside table. The women had grown bored with waiting and left, muttering insults about the Brogan's ungrateful attitude or spreading rumours about the crazy people holed up in the white palace.

They put on a good show of their grief. Annabel had seen them from her window, trying to state the largest claim on her deceased son for a slice of the most thrilling drama that was an upper-class death on the front. The news was splashed across every paper as if Gray's life had been nothing more than a piece of fiction from a tragic Dickens novel.

The entire thing made Annabel feel violently sick with disgust. None of them had ever met grief. None of them knew sadness at all.

The day of Gray's twentieth birthday dawned with Genevieve back at Annabel's side. Outside the long window the sky was overcast. Even the birds, always so joyfully singing, seemed to sense the need for silence. The staff continued about their work, quieter than mice.

Genevieve's tears fell on Annabel's shoulder. Her hair was pinned up in a sensible bun, and her body clad in a simple black dress. It hurt to see her presented like that. She and Gray had always taken such pleasure in shopping and fashion, dressing as elaborately as they could get away with. Her only adornment that day was a well-worn diamond necklace—a present that Gray had carefully picked out—clasped around her neck. She looked up after a while, her eyes red.

"I just… I know it's hard for you, but…today, I just wanted to be with someone who loved him as much as I did… Do."

Annabel gave a weak smile, the unused muscles in her face protested in their stiffness. She patted the girl's cheek, relishing the feel of her warm skin.

"I know, sweetheart."

"I miss him so much. It still hurts like it was yesterday. I thought it would get easier. Everyone said it would." She looked down at her hands. "Please get better, Anna. I can't bear it. I think if you got better, I would be able to as well."

"A mother never gets better when she has lost a child, my dear, I'm sorry."

Another tear slipped from Genevieve's eye, and she kissed Annabel's cheek, standing back up.

"You still have me. You've been a mother to me my whole life, you told me yourself I was like a daughter to you as well. Help me by helping yourself. Please just try." The young girl took up her leather bag, walking slowly over to the door. "Lots of people still love you, Anna. Very much."

Before she turned to walk out of the door, Genevieve smiled, but the smile didn't shine as it had done when Gray had been alive. She seemed to walk with a slight hunch, as if her torn soul physically pained her.

Annabel contemplated those words for a long time after her niece's footsteps had receded and her car had pulled away from the drive. Her thoughts were only disrupted when Theodore crept into the room.

He looked thin, a good ten years older than he had just a year and a bit ago. Grey was now scattered in his dark hair, and his eyes were wrinkled and downcast. He was holding a piece of white paper. For a brief flash, Annabel thought of that dreaded telegram and a shot of pain seared through her, causing her to clasp her throat. Theodore slid the form across the covers. She knew, seeing his gaze on hers, she also looked older than her years. Her skin was stretched over her bones obscenely whilst her eyes held a depth of pain that was all too rife within this era. Looking down at the paper, Annabel frowned.

"What's this?" she whispered, the first words she had spoken to her husband in months. She knew exactly what the form was but needed to know her eyes were deceiving her.

"My form to enlist in the army," Teddy replied simply.

"But... But..."

"They're drafting people out soon, forcing them to go. We're running out of men. I can't just sit here and do nothing."

"But I thought it was just... Surely, you're too old. Besides, you have businesses to manage, and... And you're part of the war effort. You're just working from here. You can't go."

Theodore laughed bitterly, his feet shuffling. "How will that look? Sending all the young *boys* to war whilst I just order their deaths from my manor? I can't do that, Annabel. I'm going."

"G-going where?" She was using her favourite tactic, denial.

"To the front."

"No." Annabel sat up straight, her head spinning with the sudden movement. "I've already lost a son, but you would stand there and have me lose my husband as well?"

"This isn't a marriage anymore. I ceased to be anybody to you the day our son died. Annabel, I see him in every room of this house. I can't take it anymore, I need to do something."

"P-please, you're needed here." She swung her feet down to the floor and tried to stand.

Theodore grabbed her arm as she tottered, a slight shiver passing through his body at the long denied touch.

"No, I'm not. I keep thinking of something Daniel said the day I took him hunting. To that man I told you about, the one who told him a private wasn't as important as a politician in the war effort." He laughed again, a single bark without humour. "Daniel retorted brilliantly and spat on him of all things. He told him that he did nothing more than order men into battle like cattle for slaughter, and that he was too used to finery to live in a trench himself. I don't want to be like that, Annabel. I want to make my son proud. I want to show him—"

"You can't show him anything, Teddy. He's... He's dead."

Annabel looked down, clinging to her husband's arm with white-knuckled force. He leant into her and planted a tender kiss on the top of her head. She gave into him, letting herself be held this once. In her mourning, she had forgotten how good a man's embrace felt, in particular this man, the one whose body had become as familiar to her as her own. She had spent her life wishing for something that had happened twenty years ago whilst forgetting to enjoy the brilliance she had possessed the entire time in Theodore. They had loved each other. Despite what she had thought all those years ago when she had walked away from Daniel, their marriage had been happy.

"Am I too rich to die, is that it?" he whispered into her hair. "My son can die for his king and country, but I can't?"

Annabel closed her eyes tightly. She could feel Teddy's jaw brushing the top of her head as he spoke.

"I'm going to finish what he started, Annabel, and drive the Hun straight back behind that line in honour of our beautiful boy." He pulled her even closer, his arms clinging to her as tight as he could before tilting her chin upwards to look into her eyes and absorb her face.

She stepped out of his arms, reached under her pillow, and presented the silver pocket watch with her face on their wedding day secured inside. The watch fell into Teddy's hand, and he squeezed it in his fingers.

"Goodbye, my love." He kissed her fiercely, desperately, without the tender touch of their usual kisses. Holding his lips to hers as long as he could, he finally spun out of her grasp, walking away without looking back.

"I love you," Annabel whispered as he retreated. Those were the three words she had hardly ever said to him, although he deserved to have heard them every day. She realised, as the phrase passed her lips, she meant them with all her body and soul. Although she had never loved Teddy as passionately as Daniel, she had loved him just as much. They had raised a son together and had shared a bed for almost twenty years. Her life was, and always would be, fused with his. Annabel thought she saw Teddy's step falter at her words, as if he was about to come back.

"I love you too," he whispered, his voice thick as he carried on, out the door.

Annabel sunk slowly down into the window seat behind her, the glass steamed up with her breath as she watched her husband climb into a waiting car, a suitcase in his hand. Everyone was leaving her, one by one. She hung her head, too numb to cry, too weak to move.

As night shrouded her, Annabel regained a little strength and crept out of her room. It was now another place tainted by bad memories.

Without fully deciding on a destination, she found her feet moving towards Gray's writing room, a place no-one had entered since he had broken down in tears on his last leave. It was the night Annabel had held him as he cried, reliving horrors she could never even begin to imagine.

As she entered, her heart skipped a beat. The room seemed to still contain her son as if his spirit lived amongst the words of his poems or the lines of his carefully composed sketches. It was the one room in the house without that constructed façade of perfection.

The whisky and glass had been cleared away, and the torn poems and sketches had been piled neatly on the edge of the ink-stained desk. Some poems remained pinned to the wall, the one's that had been too high for Gray's injured arm to tear down in a hurry. Her breathing ragged, Annabel stepped over the threshold.

Reaching the desk, she gasped at the sight of each letter written in her son's hand, like a friendly smile from beyond the grave. Reading to the end of one of the pages, Annabel looked around for the adjoining pieces. She realised whilst she was searching, she had only ever read a handful of her son's poems and wished she had told him more often how beautiful his written word was. She had been too blinded by his presence to see his talent in its full glory.

Annabel spent hours spreading the poems out on the rug, piecing together his last words like a giant jigsaw. Laying them in their completeness over the floorboards, the room became carpeted by her son's hand. Walking between them, a crinkling noise coming from beneath her feet when she accidentally stepped on a page, she felt immersed in him.

The passion in his pen was clear. This was his entire life's work. Gasping once more, she sprinted from the room to fetch the folder containing the very last of Gray's work—the things he had written and drawn during the war—from where it still lay atop the cabinet in the parlour. No member of staff had possessed the heart to pick it up. They had simply just cleaned around it.

Annabel took a deep breath before opening the folder. She'd read the words briefly when she had first been handed them, however, none of them had gone past her eyes. She knew these verses would not be full of sunshine, countryside, and romantic fantasy but of inhuman horrors and nothing more. Picking up the first page once she had re-entered Gray's sanctuary, she read quickly, absorbing the stanzas with a numb distance so she wouldn't feel the fresh hurt burying into her heart from the things her son had suffered. The things she had sworn to protect him from but had failed to do so.

There were several sketches mixed in with the poems, the most striking depicting a trench full of men, lined up as if waiting for something. The trench looked a good deal worse than even her darkest nightmares had imagined. It was little more than a hole in the ground. Breathing raggedly once more, she peered at the sketched figures. There were many depictions of Charlie, in various poses and activities, as well as a few of the infamous Lieutenant Prince. The pictures were so lifelike they told the tale of a thousand words, with an honesty she found stunning. A fresh wave of pride coursed through her veins, so strong it almost doubled her over. Her perfect son had told the truth until his dying breath, living only for the exact thing he most believed in. He felt everything with the sharpness that only an artist could possess.

The curtains, still closed the way Gray had liked them, meant the room sank into darkness much faster than usual. The only daylight entered through the open door. Annabel turned on the lamp sitting on the desk, watching as the long since settled dust whirled in front of the light. The musty smell she had experienced when she had entered the room was fading, along with the faint smell of the fire that had been lit on Gray's last day within these four walls.

Catching sight of the desktop as the light spilt over it, she saw a new page. It was smudged by Gray's furious, trembling hand. She lifted the paper to her face, blowing the dust away. She coughed as it tickled the inside of her nose, her dry eyes prickling with tears she had not shed for a year. A drawing, done in ink, came into focus before her. The lines were harsh, rushed as if drawn in anger or another extreme emotion.

The sketch depicted a face she did not know, but the eyes were haunting. They were lifeless, dead, and blood bubbled on the thin lips. This was the man that had haunted his dreams. This was the German he had killed just an inch from his own face, skewered through with a bayonet blade. The image was crudely drawn, but the pure, undiluted distress was evident in every stroke.

Amongst the images was the most evocative poem Annabel had ever read. The verse depicted his nightmares—the feelings of anger, sadness, and betrayal that had led to his death. More dramatic detail was housed in the four stanzas than others had managed in entire novels.

Annabel sank into Gray's chair, the leather creaked as dust puffed up around her. She put a hand to her mouth to mask the sob clinging dangerously to her lips. Annabel surveyed the room, taking it in from the angle her son would have seen it as he'd sat there, covered in ink and brushing his hair out of his eyes with that frustrated expression on his face.

Her eyes stung at this vivid image. She had almost forgotten what his true face looked like. She saw the porcelain depiction of him in photographs but had forgotten his expressions, the emotion he held within him always. She had forgotten the grace with which he'd made every movement, the feel of his light head on her breast, how soft and silky his wavy hair had been beneath her fingers. His laughter in her ear and velvety soft voice, had all but erased itself from her mind. Sitting there brought it all back. She was overcome by the beauty of the moment, first beginning to smile and then to laugh softly in the gloom, surrounded by the memories of her son.

She laughed until she cried, and cried until she could no longer form a thought. Sitting in that chair all night, she was filled with the closest thing to joy she had felt for far too long. Only in the morning did she bend down to the floor and pick up the poems, stacking them—in their completed forms—back into Gray's leather folder. Annabel determined then and there she would publish them. Her son's work would be seen. The entire world would hear the truth in his words and would see the war for what it really was, if it was the last thing she ever did.

Chapter Six

Just as the first rays of dawn sunshine filtered their way through the doorway Annabel opened one of Gray's draws, placing a piece of pristine, blank paper in front of her. She intended to compose several letters. It was the first contact she would have with the world outside the manor since Gray's death.

Pausing with the pen that had last been clasped in her son's elegant hand resting in her own aged one, she realised she had no idea about this industry. Standing up, she walked out of the room, still in nothing more than her thin, white nightgown. Glancing around one more time, she eased the door shut behind her. Annabel made her way into her own writing room, instructing her maid to contact someone immediately who could help her as she clutched the folder of her son's life work to her breast.

The maid returned about an hour later with a laden tray, making it clear that Annabel had to eat. Despite her lack of interest in the food, her stomach growled on instinct. Whilst she ate, feeling a sense of energy absent from her system for over a year flood back into her limbs, the maid lit the fire and draped an embroidered robe over her mistress' shivering shoulders. Annabel ate quickly and pulled her arms through the sleeves, grateful for the warmth the garment provided.

"We've telephoned a Mister Smith," the maid said just before leaving. "He'll be here by this evening. I will notify you when he arrives."

Annabel smiled her thanks. With the fresh energy the project had given her, she went to her bedroom, washing and dressing quickly and simply. Her black frock hung off her slight frame in a most unflattering way. A maid approached her just before she left her dressing room, pinning her damp hair atop her head and placing a few tucks in the fabric with fast, practised hands that somewhat synched the gown into Annabel's shrunken waist. Heading back to her writing room, she copied out all Gray's poems in her own hand so she could at least keep the torn, battered originals.

The house was alive with Annabel's apparent recovery. Her mother, whom it appeared had been staying back in Hoddington Manor for months, entered Annabel's office. It was the first time Annabel had seen the old woman in at least a year. She wore a light grey dress, having come out of mourning some months earlier.

"Annabel you have to get over this soon," she announced after standing in front of her daughter's desk for a few silent minutes.

Annabel refused to look up. "Get over it? Would you have *gotten over it* if I had not returned from those woods?"

Her mother's eyes briefly fell at the painful memory. "No, but I would have done so on the outside. I would have put on a show to the public to prove this family's strength."

"I don't have any strength, Mother. It was Daniel who had that. Now that he is no longer here, this family will die with us, so what's the point?" She said this with her head bent over the current poem she was copying out. She could almost hear Gray whispering in her ear, muttering insulting words about the prudish grandmother he had despised. His voice, so loud and clear in her memory, made her smile.

"You're still just about young enough to mother more children if you're quick about it, Annabel."

"Theodore's enlisted. If you'd been interested enough in my affairs, you would already know that. Besides, I'm not replacing my son with another. How crude of you to suggest it."

"I never said… You're impossible. You should have had more children when you had the chance. You were too besotted with that one sensitive child to bother making another should something happen to the first."

Annabel winced, but her mother continued regardless.

"He clearly didn't feel the same love as you. He went and got himself shot."

Annabel put her pen down, cursing when it blotted the page.

"Don't you dare say a word against my son! He was the best of my life. Anything you have against him is my fault, not his. If I hadn't had him, you wouldn't have a grandson at all. Do you not think I tried to have another? A companion for Daniel, who was always so surrounded by women? Theodore and I slept in the same bed for nearly twenty years, Mother, and our marriage was a happy one.

"It didn't happen, but I will be forever grateful for the opportunity to mother such a perfect child for however short a time I was allowed the privilege. He was a man, not an antique vase to be exchanged for monetary value. Your indifference sickens me. Get out of this room now. I can't look at you. Get out." She looked sternly at her mother, who looked back at her daughter with equal fire. The smell of too much perfume rising from her mother's dress intensified Annabel's disgust.

"I will not be ordered in my own house, Annabel."

"It is not your house, and it never was. Get out," Annabel screamed, her face red with fury.

"Don't shout. It's not becoming."

"What use have I for being becoming? I have lost the best of my life, the two sole reasons for my existence. My husband raised our son with all his heart, knowing full well he wasn't of his own blood, and has gone off to the same ghastly fate. All the while, you stand here gloating about how I should have listened to you. I should not have gotten kidnapped and attacked. I should have stayed here and mothered as many children as my body could hold, to marry them off to whoever would yield us the largest profit. As if any of this mess was at all in my own control. I know I can make children, Mother, I have proved that. It's my husband who cannot. Why are you still here? Get out!"

Her mother, shocked by her daughter's outburst, stood stock still. Annabel had never admitted to being assaulted, and she had never even hinted Gray was not Theodore's child. She felt she had nothing to lose by admitting it now.

"So… So Grayson wasn't…? He was a bastard? You gave this great family a bastard grandson? A bastard grandson made from a violent thief."

"Don't you dare insult him! Your anger is at me, not him. He was everything you could have ever wanted in an heir. You put me on a pedestal from the day I was born. I was never going to meet your standards."

Looking as if she might throw up, Annabel's mother turned away, leaving the room with tears in her eyes at how messed up her daughter's life had really been. Her hands were clenched into angry fists.

Annabel sat reeling for a few moments, before she buried herself back into her son's work, choosing to block out the present world for the warm comfort of the past.

At precisely five in the evening, Annabel received a small, scrawny man of about thirty years old into her writing room. He introduced himself, politely and with a strong stutter, as Mister Lewis Smith. Ink was caked under his nails, and he had that aged look to his eyes that told Annabel he had served in the war. He'd clearly seen things no person ever should, and he leant heavily on a wooden stick. The last two fingers on the hand holding it were missing, leaving behind only a long, vivid looking scar where the wound had been crudely sewn together. A wedding ring hung around his neck where it would otherwise have sat on his missing finger.

There were a few minutes of useless small talk whilst tea was poured and sipped from fancy china cups. The sound of Mister Smith's teaspoon clinking against the side of his cup, and the smell rising from the freshly sliced lemons and bowl of thick honey, filled the room. Shifting in her seat, uncomfortable in the unfamiliar formality, Annabel slid the stack of poems, written in her own flowery hand, across the desk. Evidently relieved to reach the point of their meeting, Lewis took up the pages. He read the poetry with his face lined up into a frown, the paper shaking in his hands as the emotion in the words brought back his long suppressed memories.

Annabel had sorted them as she thought proper, placing the happy, pre-war poems at the front whilst saving the most emotive pieces, that had been written in the last few weeks of Gray's life, for last. She clasped and unclasped her hands in her lap, playing with the large diamond on her left hand.

"They...they are g-good, ma'am," he stuttered, once he had finished.

Annabel smiled knowingly.

"But not pub-publishable, I'm afraid."

"What do you mean?"

"P-people want the Jessie Pope version. This... This won't sell."

"That's absurd, it's a man's dying wish. He died fighting for this goddamned country!" She was flustered all of a sudden.

"There are a lot of dy-ying wishes now-nowadays." The former soldier squeezed his eyes shut as he spoke, desperate to get his words out and seemingly frustrated by the effort the simple task took. "The first few p-poems I could publish but...but they aren't good enough."

"What? Yes they—"

"I'm sorry. Th-they aren't. He was your...your son and I...I understand, but no-one would pay for them. The last five or six, they are really good, but...but I can't. Not yet. May-may I keep them 'til...af-after the war?"

Annabel nodded weakly. "Why can't you publish them now? To hell with anything else."

Smith laughed. The noise sounded alien as it erupted from his haunted, pinched mouth. "That's ea-easy for you to say in this man-mansion but the real... The real world don't work that way. I'd get court...court-martialled."

Annabel lowered her eyes. "I'm sorry. I didn't realise."

"It's fine. I do really li-like your son's work. I'll hold...hold onto them 'til af-after the war. If there...if there ever is an end. When I'm thin-thinking of pub-pub-publishing I'll contact you and see if you want to put an in-intro-introduction."

Lewis sighed, taking a deep breath. He tried to get to his feet, leaning heavily on his stick, but it slipped from his deformed hand. Annabel rushed to his side, helping him out of the door.

"Thank you for your help, Mister Smith."

"Cor-corporal, Corporal Smith," he muttered. "But the title don't... Don't matter now. I'd rather not have it and still have my nerves."

"You seem in full health to me, Corporal."

He laughed heartily, a small glimmer of humour in his eyes this time. Annabel looked into his face, seeing who he must have been before the war for the first time.

"Thank- thank you, but you're lying. I offer my full con-con-dol-condolences for your son. Too many deaths. I fear the worst isn't...isn't over."

The humour left him as quickly as it had surfaced, and they walked the rest of the way in silence. Annabel thought of her husband and fingered her wedding ring again. Corporal Smith tilted his head towards her at the door and hobbled to a waiting car. He seemed in more pain both emotionally and physically than when he had entered. He must have come from some institution, or snuck out from under the watchful eye of his wife.

Annabel felt suddenly exhausted. She leant on the bannister, digesting the news that her son's verse was unpublishable, contrasting with the hope the end of the war would see him in print. Of course, the corporal had been wrong, people would buy his work if only to own something with the name Gray Brogan printed on the front, but Annabel didn't want him to be known for something imperfect. Feeling ever so slightly closer to her son's beautiful dreams, she crept back upstairs to bed.

Chapter Seven

The next month saw Annabel in a slightly more improved state. She ate more and even found the strength to walk about the house. Each morning, she wrote a letter to her husband, who in turn wrote to her. They poured their love into these letters in a way they had never been able to do in person. Receiving Teddy's correspondence, waiting on a silver tray in the parlour, had begun to dull the constant pain in her heart. It appeared Theodore had found some shred of peace being surrounded by people similar to his son whilst Annabel found her own peace in his love.

In her new mindset, Annabel even took over some of her former duties with regards to running the house. There were some days where survival was possible. It even felt as if she were finding herself again—healing, perhaps. However, other days hit her hard. It was on these days she remained beneath her sheets, unwashed and undressed for hours on end. It was often at the strangest, most inconsequential moments when the moods struck—whilst she was stirring her tea or simply walking down the stairs. The pain was unpredictable and ruthless in its ferocity.

Genevieve, when she was off from her new job at the military hospital, seemed cheered by her aunt's slight recovery. The commute was long and the work hard, so she visited rarely, telling

Annabel ridiculous stories about the small apartment she rented with some other nurses and the soldiers she had come to know in her care. She came by one particular day, one that had yielded no letter from Annabel's husband, full of a strange optimism and shining with almost her former joviality.

"Anna!" she greeted cheerily.

Annabel sat on her window seat, wrapped in a nightgown and robe. She looked towards her niece smiling. "Hello. You look well."

Genevieve smiled a little, putting her warm hand onto Annabel's forehead. "What has become of you?" she whispered, almost to herself.

"Too much," Annabel whispered back, smiling in a motherly way.

"Although, alas, you look better than last time I saw you at least." The young girl paused as if for dramatic effect and then, unable to keep the news inside anymore, flopped down on the edge of the bed facing her aunt. "I've met someone. An officer."

Annabel beamed. "Is he good to you?"

Genevieve nodded, her curled hair bouncing with the movement. It seemed an age since Annabel had seen Genevieve with curled hair. Her entire face was split into a grin that Annabel had not seen since Gray had last been home.

"I'm glad you're having fun, sweetheart."

"I hardly think fun is the word for it, but yes, the hurt has dulled. It doesn't feel right to admit it. It feels like an insult to his memory." She sniffed, a single tear falling down her youthful cheek.

Annabel sat up properly, instinct kicking in at the sight of this girl's tears. "It's not an insult, Jen. He would love you to have found someone. He would have held you so tightly and asked for more details than you could remember."

Genevieve laughed a little.

"You're young, sweetheart," Annabel continued. "Don't live your life in the past. Remember him, but don't be hindered by the shadow of his death."

The two women sat there, looking into each other's faces, reassured by their shared feelings.

"What about you?" Genevieve whispered.

"What about me? You will understand when you have your own children. There is no living when you've lost a child. I don't want there to be."

"But you must try."

"No, *you* must. Be happy. You have so much to give."

Genevieve stood sharply, her skirt rustling as she made her way to the window seat. Annabel was cheered by the fashionable cut and lighter colour of the garment. Genevieve sat beside Annabel, taking up her hand. The young girl's small touch was warm— the kind of warmth that heated her right down to her soul.

"Tell me about him," Annabel said after a while, trying to make her expression as joyful as she could manage.

"Second Lieutenant Andrew Morris." Genevieve grinned again, shifting her feet in giddy excitement. "He just won the Victoria Cross. Seized a machine gun post, taking out dozens of enemy soldiers, and then crawled out of the trench under heavy fire to rescue five of his wounded men. Got shot in the shoulder and the head for the effort. Poor man's nerves are in tatters. The helmet protected his head slightly, and the bullet just dented his skull, but his shoulder's shattered and the arm's near on useless."

A line appeared between her eyes as she frowned in concern.

She looked down at their hands. "He's getting better, though, he's been at the hospital for two months already. We went on our first proper outing last week, to the picture palace in the town. We had to get a bus, it was dreadfully exciting. The other girls teased me for never having been on one before.

"When he was first brought to the hospital, he lit a candle and put a white handkerchief on his bedside table to look like a restaurant table hoping to win me over. I joked it was because he had been shot in the head and was not in his right mind. I suppose I wasn't at the time either. Well, when he *first* got there, he was pretty messed up, but once he opened his eyes and got used to the whole idea of being wounded—" She laughed, looking off into a memory. "He is so handsome, though, Anna. You'll love him."

"Yes, I would. You must bring him to lunch."

"May I? He is able to walk about now, and he says he wouldn't have made it if it wasn't for me, but I think he is just being sweet. He is awfully funny. Reminds me of Gray a little. Not much, but a little. He has blond hair like him. It's a little darker, really curly, and looks awfully amusing in the morning with it sticking up in all directions. He's only two years older than me, but he's seen so much that I daren't ask him about.

"Sometimes he tells me, but he doesn't like to. I hear him muttering in his sleep, though, and he's always restless. He wakes screaming most nights. The nights are dreadfully loud in the hospital... So much screaming. So many nightmares. I used to request a night shift so I could sit with them all, especially him. I think it helped a little, and I don't mind doing it. As I said, he's getting a lot better. He improves almost daily now."

Annabel let a genuine smile cross her face. "He sounds lovely."

"No, I didn't do him justice. I made him sound like an invalid. They all hate it when I dwell on their wounds, and so would I. Let me begin again. His name's Andy, and he's really funny and kind. A proper gentleman. He loves birds. I don't know why, but he has this book of them. He tries to teach me about them, but I haven't a clue. A little sparrow landed on the windowsill yesterday, and he was quite transfixed. He really enjoys the pictures as well and has his own camera. He films absolutely everything. I tell him the countryside is nicer when one views it from one's own eyes.

"He's so considerate, though, Anna. He doesn't care a shred for his own well-being so long as I am all right. He makes me feel ever so special. We've talked for hours, but it only felt like minutes. Like some romantic novel. When I'm away from him, I feel… empty. Like I've been looking for him my entire life but only just this minute realised it. I always knew I loved Gray, he was my brother for all intents and purposes, and my soul mate. Andy's who I intend to marry." She looked Annabel in the eye with a fierce determination on her face.

"When he is discharged, bring him back here, and I shall greet him properly," Annabel stated. "If you deem him good enough, then I trust your judgement. Daniel would be thrilled." She smiled again. The future shone for one of them at least. That made her, if not happy, something like it.

"He would. I've written Gray letters, loads of them, but I put them on the fire as soon as they're written. I know it's mad, but this whole world is mad now, so why can't I join in? Anyway, enough about this silliness. You must get washed and dressed. We are going out for lunch, even if I have to drag you, no questions. I've been to see Papa already so we needn't hesitate."

Genevieve crossed the room to fill the bath tub and lay out

a deep black dress. It was a new dress that Patsy had ordered for Annabel, having seen her ever so slight revival. Her hair was arranged in an elaborate bun when she had finished bathing and a hat secured in place. She went along with Genevieve to amuse her. To make the younger girl happy meant more than anything in the entire world. Jen had been the most important person to her son, which in turn, made her the most important person to Annabel. Thinking about the sick baby in the stable all those years before, made Annabel fiercely proud of the woman Genevieve had become.

Despite the happiness of seeing Jen's excitement, a slight anxiety fluttered in Annabel's breast as she made her way down the stairs. She had not left the manor's walls in almost two years. A bright red motorcar sat expectantly on the driveway waiting for them.

"It's the car Uncle Teddy got me," Genevieve exclaimed in answer to Annabel's dumbfound expression, as the young girl stepped up into the car and slid behind the wheel. "What? He didn't tell you? Well, I was whining about the time it took on the train to get here and how sparse they are. Next thing I know, Uncle Teddy is driving up the road in this beauty. Of course, I told him I couldn't possibly accept it, but he practically forced it on me. I drive it ever so well, Anna. Uncle Teddy taught me you see."

Without missing another beat, Genevieve shoved the motorcar into gear and pressed her foot down on the accelerator. Their first movements were jerky, and Annabel's hand went reflexively to her hat whilst her other hand gripped the supple leather seat as they sped off down the hill. Annabel loosened her grip on the brim of her hat as the warm wind whipped into her face, the smell of freshly cut grass pervading the air.

Genevieve had tied a large ribbon under her chin so she could keep both hands on the wheel whilst remaining in possession of her own, more fashionable, hat.

They parked outside an airy looking tea room of Genevieve's choosing—the window filled with elaborately iced cakes. It was apparently quite a fashionable place to dine now. Climbing out of the motorcar, Annabel looked around the wide cobbled street. It was a fair few miles away from the town centre, so she didn't recognise it.

"Gray and I used to come here often. It was always just far enough out of the way that we could get ourselves pickled without it making the front page." Genevieve laughed at the memory.

Annabel, having ordered an array of cakes and sandwiches, soon received the full account of Genevieve's various meetings with her officer and found she did indeed like the sound of the man. Other women, all dressed in the highest fashion and behaving with impeccable manners, turned at the sight of Annabel. They openly stared at her altered appearance. She was obviously still deep in mourning for her son. In contrast, Genevieve, in a light blue dress with black ribbon lining the hem and collar, sat across from her. The younger girl chattered like an excited school girl not even bothering to keep her expressions of joy to herself. She was in love, and she wanted everyone to know it.

Annabel was past the point of caring about societal opinions. She hadn't so much as touched a paper for the past year. Instead, during lunch, she focused on nothing but getting utterly lost in this young girl's happiness. It was hard not to feel positive when looking upon Genevieve's beaming face, surrounded by the tastes and smells of sweet sponge and the tinkling sounds of idle chatter.

Annabel even found herself laughing as Genevieve recounted

a particularly funny joke of Andy's, with all the enthusiasm she had used with Gray. The expression of humour felt strange on her face, but she couldn't help it. The image of Genevieve's beaming face clung to Annabel's memory as she watched her car recede into the distance in a cloud of dust. She was due back at the hospital the following morning.

It could have been a bias opinion, but she could see why Andrew Morris would have clung to Genevieve during his darkest hour, and in doing so, had fallen deeply in love with her. She epitomised warmth in a way most ironic to the circumstances within which she had been brought into the world. Humming subconsciously, a tune she had learnt in the forest all those years ago, Annabel picked up her stack of letters from the silver tray beside the door. Flicking through them as a maid unpinned her hat, she noticed without surprise, her husband's elegant hand. The letter was dated a week before. Annabel tore open the envelope, almost desperate to hear Theodore's gently familiar voice in her head.

My dearest wife, Annabel.

I hope I find you as well as possible. News of your health will cheer me greatly. I'm sorry I have not had the chance to write for a few days, but we have been on the move. We have finally been brought to the front and have been under heavy bombardment for a solid twenty-four hours.

I am in my dug out, and the very roof is crumbling. It falls onto my hair and the page you are reading now. I have to keep stopping to brush it away.

A fresh, fierce pride for our son has been born inside me after seeing what it is truly like here. I only feel saddened that I did not take more heed of his warnings, and sickened to have had a hand in sending young men to this fate. I'm filled with admiration for our boy, for remaining so strong. My nerves are slipping already. I can feel it.

We are about to launch a big push, which I'm told should end the war. It is nothing short of chaos here. Of course, I am not permitted to tell you the details, but please know, whatever should happen tomorrow, I do everything thinking of you. Should I perish, my final thought will be of your face. In the event of such a conclusion, you should not fret for I shall be reunited with the pride of my life. Our beautiful Daniel. I am filled with enthusiasm at continuing his noble quest for peace.

Please write back of home as soon as you get the chance. A bottle of brandy would be much appreciated if you get the time to send some.

I love you with all my heart and more.

Teddy.

Clutching the letter to her chest, Annabel crept up to her bedroom, her earlier positive mood diminishing as it did every time it raised its timid head higher than despair. Another person she loved was at the front.

Would this war never cease to haunt her?

Chapter Eight

The next day saw Annabel sitting in her writing room, reading over her son's poetry for the millionth time. She had just finished composing the letter she'd been ordered to write to Patsy, informing her of her continued recovery. Which, of course, was all vastly exaggerated. The lunch with her niece had restored some small amount of life within her, yet it was still only just enough to continue getting out of bed every day.

Patsy checked up on her often, although, she could not continue her daily visits as she had when Gray had first died. She turned up at random intervals without prior notice, which Patsy claimed would keep Annabel on her toes.

Annabel missed her friend when she was gone. She understood her like a sister and seeing her happiness spurred Annabel into feeling a slight warmth in herself. Patsy, having gone from utter ruin, with the most miserable, destructive upbringing a person could have, was happily married to a man who loved her deeply and held a comfortable lump of money to his name. They had three beautiful children who doted on her in the way all mothers dream of.

Just as Annabel reached her favourite poem, depicting a pleasant walk on which she had been present, there was a timid knock at the door.

"Enter," Annabel called in confusion. She had not eaten that day, so she figured lunch would be the reason for the call. However, when the butler entered, he was not carrying a tray. He held only a small white envelope and a look of fear in his eyes.

Annabel took the envelope with a cold fear of her own.

The butler bowed but did not leave, clearly anxious for the outcome. Annabel remained still, unwilling to open the envelope. She thought she could pretend its contents were good so long as the telegram remained closed. The longer she sat, the more her body shook. The memories of the last telegram she had received were flooding her mind.

She had never read that telegram, but she knew her husband would have kept it somewhere. What if this telegram brought foul news of him? Surely, he couldn't have been killed in his first week at the front. Teddy was the most powerful man in the country. No, it would just be a standard issue telegram informing her that he was well.

She ushered the butler out of the room with more impatience than he deserved. His presence was setting her teeth on edge. Convincing herself the telegram was nothing more than correspondence of good health, she tore open the envelope and slid it out, reading as quickly as she could and holding her breath the whole time. She took in only a few lines of the hurriedly composed, mass produced note.

Lady A. Brogan,

It is my painful duty to inform you that a report has this day been received from the war office notifying the death of your {husband/brother/son}.

Rank: {Captain} Name: {T E Brogan} which occurred on the {1st of July 1916}. The cause of death was {killed in action}.

His majesty commands that I offer my deepest condolences for your loss. Any correspondence—

Annabel stopped reading. Rage at her late husband bubbled up. How could he have left her when she was already so fragile? Surely, her frail soul could not claw its way any further beyond this point. Her heart must surely cease to beat. She closed her eyes, wishing with all her might that it would. To die now would be the sweetest path her life could take.

Without a second thought, she got up, throwing the telegram into the fire. She watched as the flames destroyed all evidence of Teddy's death. Perhaps she could sink into the comfort of denial as she had the time before. Although, even as she thought it, she knew it wasn't possible. Her husband had been one of the most financially powerful men in Britain, there would be people arriving at the house the second the newspapers published the news. All these thoughts filled her with even more anger. He had left her to deal with these worries on her own.

The one constant thing in her life had been Teddy's presence, and she realised, too late, how she had never properly thanked him for everything he had done over the past twenty years. She had loved him, despite all evidence to the contrary. He had raised her son, knowing he had not been formed of his own blood, with all the love and strength any son could ever receive. Yet, she had been cold and distant from him the one time he had needed her. For the third time, she had failed someone she loved, only to become aware of it when there were no remedies to be sought.

She sat on the floor by the fire, huddled on the fluffy carpet and shaking like a leaf in a storm. Her breathing was dangerously fast. Her skin began to prickle. She was far too close to the flames, yet she paid them no heed. She just kept her eyes glued to the spot in the fire where the telegram had disintegrated into ash as her wounded soul did the very same thing inside her.

Some time later, the fire no more than a few glowing embers, her mother entered carrying a small brown package, crudely wrapped and dirty. She placed the parcel on the nearest chair with a look of disgust on her aged face. She bent towards her daughter and attempted to stroke her hair. Annabel flinched away from this woman's touch, remembering the scorn with which she had last addressed her.

"Annabel, please let me comfort you." When she got no response, she continued. "I want to help you, my child. You have shamed this family, but you are still my daughter. It pains me to see you like this." The flatness in her voice contradicted her words.

"Teddy's dead," Annabel whispered, her body limp. She was slouched over her knees, a corpse in every way bar the frantic movement of her maddened eyes.

Her mother shifted beside her. "I know. He was a wonderful man, a perfect husband and father."

Annabel continued to stare into the embers. Her mother, frustrated with her grieving child's lack of response, seized her chin and forced her face upwards.

"Annabel, you must snap out of this. You cannot sink the way you did when Grayson died. People need someone they can look to for reassurance, someone strong to help them through this ordeal. Plenty of men are dying, not just ours."

A single tear trickled down Annabel's cheek, landing on her mother's palm. Both women looked at the glistening droplet for a while before Annabel snatched her chin from her mother's grip and once more glared into the fire.

"I didn't expect you to be in peak health the day you found out about your husband's death, my dear, but you must at least pretend." She clambered back to her feet, her heavily beaded black gown creaking as she straightened her ageing body. Annabel let her mother leave without a single word.

When the room grew dark once more, Annabel turned her head towards the brown package her mother had brought in. With stiff fingers, weak from nearly two days without food, she tugged at the string, watching as the paper fell away to reveal a splintering wooden box. Easing open the lid, she saw a pocketbook lying on the top so similar to Gray's it sent fresh waves of hurt through her lifeless heart. Picking it up with shaking fingers, she saw "Captain T.E. Brogan" written on the first page. As she brought it closer a photograph fell out of the front cover and into her lap.

Looking down at the picture, she saw her smiling face, a few years earlier. Gray sat beside her, laughing, with his arm over her shoulder. Teddy sat at her other side on a checked picnic blanket, holding a crystal glass of lemonade. Annabel smiled at the memory. She could hear the soft voices of these two men in her ears once more. Remembering the rhyming poem Gray had made up about a fat woman walking in front of them, Annabel recalled how they'd all roared with laughter, earning a stern look from the woman adorned in far too many frills to suit her large shape.

She had been hurt in the forest all those years ago, and had believed herself too heartbroken to continue, but she had ended up with such a perfect family. Not only did she ache for her son, she wanted Teddy back as well. His comforting familiarity, his kindness, his love. They had been friends, as well as partners, sharing their every thought as they lay side by side at night. What would she do now?

The smile she was wearing slid off her face as her fingers moved aside a piece of muddy material, ripped hurriedly from something or other, to reveal what must have been Theodore's revolver. She touched the cool metal, lifting it slowly from its box to balance in her palms. It was heavier than she thought it would be and was still loaded, fresh from her husband's dead hand.

With tears once more falling silently down her cheeks, landing on the gun to wash away some of the mud, she grasped the gun tightly. She slid her index finger over the trigger and lifted it up, as she imagined Gray had done, resting it against her temple. Caressing the photo on her lap with her other hand, she tried to lose herself in the happy memory as her final thought.

Too lost in her own pity to be aware of her surroundings, she hadn't heard the door open. A warm hand folded around her own, drawing the gun from her head. Annabel looked up, her cheeks glistening, to find Patsy, who prised the gun from Annabel's tight fist and folded her into her arms. Annabel cried with such vigour the floor seemed to shake beneath her. Sobs ripped from her throat with a scratchy, gulping sound as her lungs fought for breath.

"Oh, Annabel," Patsy sighed. "What more can life possibly throw at you?"

Chapter Nine

Patsy only left Annabel's side when the morning sun had begun to shine through the window, seeking a butler that could carry her friend into her bedchamber. The gun had been removed and disposed of accordingly.

Lying limp on the carpet, Annabel caught sight of the discarded picture of her family. Crawling over to it, her limbs hardly working in their exhausted state, she traced her late husband and son's features mournfully. With a sudden determination, she heaved herself up to her feet, swaying as dizziness flooded her head. Her feet tripped over each other as she dragged herself into her room as fast as her wasted body could muster.

In an urgent frenzy, she knocked a trunk off the top shelf of her dressing room, throwing clothes and undergarments into it at random. On top of these items, she tossed in the small wooden carving Daniel had made for her all those years before, along with the folder of Gray's poetry and sketches. She put the picture in last, the smiling faces of her lost loves staring up at her just before she clicked the lid closed.

There were hurried footsteps before Patsy raced into the room, her face bright red. The door banged against the wall in her rush. Seeing Annabel hunched on the floor over her trunk, surrounded by clothes dislodged from their shelves, she let out an audible sigh of relief.

"I heard the bang, and I thought— Oh, God." She knelt next to her friend. "Wh-what are you doing?" She tried to gather back her breath but was still panicked. Annabel could see her heart beating beneath the deep purple material of her dress. Patsy had rushed from the house so fast when she had heard the news, she had not had time to change into the appropriate mourning gear.

"I'm leaving. I can't do it anymore, Patsy." Annabel's voice sounded choked. "I can't do it."

"You'll find a way," Patsy soothed. "You always do." She stroked her hand rhythmically through Annabel's hair.

"Not this time."

Noticing the packed trunk again, Patsy eased it open as quietly as she could and paused, catching a glimpse of the carving resting atop the muddled clothes. "You kept it." Her eyes drank in the delicate wood, and her lips parted in a dumbfounded expression.

"Of course I did."

"You still love him, don't you?"

Annabel's eyes misted over in a sense of betrayal to her husband, not even cold in his grave as she nodded. She didn't long for Daniel body and soul like she had in those first few months of marriage, but he had taught her what love was and had given her what she needed to love her husband. He had given her his child, the most perfect part of her life. For that, she would always love him in some sense.

Patsy got to her feet, glancing uncertainly down at the trunk. Her fingers twitched at her sides. "Where will you go?" Her eyes moved rapidly inside their sockets as though she were reading some imaginary book in front of her.

"I don't know yet. But I can't stay here, Patsy. There are too many ghosts. I catch their scent when I least expect it, and see them move in every shadow. I can't stay here." She gestured towards the bed she had slept in for most of her life. "Teddy slept there for nearly twenty years.

"I heard that most married couples don't share a room, but we always did. After the stable, I just couldn't sleep alone anymore. Teddy was a really quiet sleeper, and it worried me sometimes. He was always so pristine, but when he first woke up, his hair would be all messy and there were lines on his cheek from the pillow case."

Annabel's voice broke. "Sometimes... Sometimes, when he was little, Daniel would come in if he'd had a bad dream. Teddy would hold up the blanket for him, didn't even open his eyes. He'd just kiss the top of his head and hold him. It was beautiful. He could have called a maid, but he never did. Not once. I would stay awake just to watch them sleep. Daniel's little fingers would trace Teddy's ear. It was a habit, like Jen sucking her thumb. Daniel worried I'd be left out, so he would make sure Teddy had his arm around both of us. He'd find my hand and make sure I was stroking his hair too like Billy does. He always liked that."

Remembering was so painful that Annabel's words were almost illegible. Patsy started to cry, hearing the undiluted love in Annabel's tone.

"I love them so much. Your brother... I'll always love him, but Teddy brought so much to my life, so much to our son. I had mere weeks with Daniel, with Teddy I had a lifetime. Why can't I just die with them? I keep... I keep hoping I'll open my eyes and this will all just be an elaborate nightmare."

"You can come back to mine," Patsy exclaimed, coming to a

decision. "Margret and Eloise already share a room. You obviously couldn't share with Rupert. Oh, I'll just put him in with the girls for a little while. He's only eight, it won't bother him. Then you can stay in his room." She put a hand to her head, pacing. "I'll summon my driver. I'll tell him he isn't to tell a soul that you've left. He's a very trustworthy man." Her voice was spilling out this information thick and fast, her mind reeling.

She ran from the room, returning with a tall glass of water and a mug of soup which she poured into Annabel's mouth. She was too weak to refuse.

Once Annabel had eaten, Patsy repacked the trunk, folding all the items properly and making sure everything Annabel may need was inside. The nicest, warmest coat was then selected and draped over Annabel's shoulders, before her arms were coaxed into the sleeves and her hair re-pinned.

They arrived at Patsy's house in the middle of the afternoon. Annabel composed her face as best she could as she climbed the front steps towards the red brick townhouse. It was a homely place with tall, white-framed windows looking out across the park. The children crowded around her as she walked through the door.

Patsy whispered to her husband Victor, a chubby but kind-natured man with slightly receding, mousy hair. He ushered the children outside with him.

"Aunt Anna is feeling a little poorly, so we're to be extra good for the next few days, all right?" he whispered to them as they went. "We have to let her get better. Don't go asking Mummy too many questions either. You know it has been hard on Anna since she lost Gray, and remember, I told you this morning that Uncle Teddy has gone to heaven as well?"

The words were not meant to be heard by Annabel. Closing her eyes over the pain, she tried to smile at her nieces and nephew. Patsy placed her arm through Annabel's, leading her up the curved, wooden staircase and along the corridor to Rupert's room. It contained a chest of drawers, a wardrobe, and a large scattering of toys. An array of teddy bears sat in a neat line along the bottom of the single bed, each in a different outfit or uniform, leaning against the mahogany footboard.

Moving the bears and stripping down to her petticoat, Annabel sunk into the mattress, pulled the blue eiderdown up to her chin, and fell almost instantly into a deep, exhausted slumber.

Annabel drifted in and out of sleep for an unknown amount of time. She took no heed of the time or date, waking only when she was too hungry or thirsty to sleep anymore and staying awake just long enough to satiate these human needs. Occasionally, she heard hushed voices floating up from downstairs or the laughter of Patsy's children in the garden.

The youngest of these children, Rupert, had taken to standing outside Annabel's door. His door really. Annabel would hear his light step creep up the stairs and then stop just outside the threshold. Sometimes, she would hear him whispering something, it sounded like a prayer for her.

"Aunt Anna," he breathed on one occasion. He was standing just inside the doorway this time, still clinging to the shiny handle. "Aunt Anna, are you awake?"

Annabel raised her head as high as she could, not much farther than the pillow, and tried to twitch her mouth towards a smile.

"Is Uncle Teddy really gone?" His dark eyes misted over all of a sudden, and a tear sprang out onto his face.

Not knowing what to do, Annabel held open her arms and the young boy folded himself inside her embrace, sobbing quietly on her shoulder.

"I love you, Aunt Anna. I wish Uncle Teddy and Gray were still here because I loved them too. E-everyone is dying."

Annabel put her hand on his copper hair. "Shh, it's all right, sweetheart. Just remember the good times you had with them. That will help."

Rupert raised his head, wiping his eyes roughly with his hands before he sat on the end of her bed. Once he was seated, he looked around him and bent back down to pick up two of the bears Annabel had removed from the bed. He handed one to Anna.

"Mummy says a cuddle always helps."

"Smart woman, your mother."

"Yes, she is. And so are you. You need to get happy again, Anna. I know Uncle Teddy is gone now, so you're allowed to be sad, but you could always stay in my room as long as you need to. Perhaps, when you feel better, we could go for a walk and get some flowers or buy a little cake from the bakery. I have some money in my piggy bank over there."

Annabel let a genuine smile form on her lips. "That would be lovely," she croaked, trying to hold back tears again.

"Oh dear, did Uncle Teddy like cake? Is that why you look sad?"

"No, darling. I'll be all right, eventually."

Rupert smiled and bent forwards again to plant a smacking kiss on Annabel's cheek.

"Thank you," Annabel whispered.

"What are you two planning?" Patsy laughed from the doorway.

"I was making Anna better, Mum," Rupert stated, puffing out his chest in pride.

"Were you, now? Well, I need to speak to her. So why don't you go help Dad downstairs?"

Rupert bounced to his feet and ran from the room, shooting a wink behind him aimed at Annabel. She smiled to let him know she had seen, and he disappeared down the corridor.

"I've found somewhere," Patsy declared, easing the door shut behind her with a click. "It's still within sight of the manor, but only from a distance. A two-bedroom cottage, pretty simple, at the edge of the forest. It's not too far from here either, so I can check on you every few days. Of course, I'll help you move in and stay with you for a while. You'll need a servant as well. I've looked around, it's all furnished, so it should be fine until we can find something nicer."

Grasping Patsy's meaning Annabel crawled her lazy fingers over the covers, squeezing her friend's hand. "Thank you," she croaked.

That same day she had her trunk put into the back of Patsy's car. She made a special effort to eat a proper lunch downstairs with Victor, Patsy, and the children. Rupert sat beside her, offering her his favourite bits of food to make her feel better.

Clean and fed, she made her way to her new home with Patsy at her side the whole time.

The cottage was small, made from grey stone with wooden shutters on both windows. A path wound its way through the grass, scattered with daisies—which she stepped over carefully. Pushing open the squeaking door revealed a cosy living room with two well-worn, red arm chairs resting in front of an open fireplace. A stove sat next to the fire with a copper bathtub which could only be filled by hand on its other side, and a shabby rug spread over the hardwood floor beneath her feet.

Directly opposite the main door was another, slightly smaller door, leading into a bedroom with a metal framed bed. The covers were a soft material decorated in the repeated pattern of roses in full bloom. A wonky wardrobe and chest of drawers were also housed there. Within the other, smaller bedroom to the right of the living room sat a familiar ink-stained writing desk. The one Gray had sat at nearly every day of his life. His armchair, draped in Gray's beloved fur bed throw, sat in the corner. On a side table taken from Theodore's office, there were two portraits, one of Gray and one of Theodore standing in their uniform. Another empty frame stood expectantly next to them.

"Patsy, it's perfect." Annabel pulled her friend into a tight embrace, her eyes roaming over the bare stone walls. She had wanted to flee the ghosts of her past, but she realised now she had needed some small amount of comfort to remind her of all she had loved and lost. With shaking fingers, she slipped the photo of her laughing family into the empty frame, releasing a tear for the brilliant future both the men should have seen.

*

Out of the manor, Annabel cared nothing for material objects. She learnt to care for herself once more and found she didn't need a servant. Instead, she bought her own food from the local market, teaching herself to cook simple meals and to clean. She spent her days keeping the house tidy and the garden flourishing, ensuring she was always too busy to think for long. Dozen's of her son's pre-war sketches and a framed picture of Gray, Theodore, and herself hung above the mantel where a vase of flowers, freshly picked from her garden, sat. The large sum of money she had inherited from Theodore had been given to Genevieve almost immediately. Annabel kept only what she needed for basic survival.

Her mother had sent only one letter, imploring her to come back to the manor with all due haste or risk disinheritance. Annabel had not replied, thus it could be said she was now a fairly impoverished woman, although she was not without anything particularly. She owned her house and had money for wood, coal, and food. She needed nothing more.

Genevieve's wedding was announced the following month. It was, as everyone expected of her, a lavish affair. Genevieve looked stunning. Her dark hair contrasted beautifully against the shimmering white lace of her gown. Billy simply shone with pride as he escorted her down the aisle of a heavily decorated church. Andrew stood in full uniform, his golden buttons gleaming. His left arm was still of little use, but the scar across his forehead was now covered in thick, butterscotch curls. His Victoria Cross rested proudly on the breast of his jacket.

The entire day was spectacular, yet nothing gleamed as brightly as the couple themselves. Their teeth sparkled in a constant smile as they gazed at each other with such raw, intense love, it was joyous to behold. Genevieve clung to her new husband's hand during every photograph whilst he kissed her with all the tenderness of a gentle summer's breeze, looking upon her the way every girl dreams of.

Genevieve didn't keep all her fortune. Like Annabel, she kept only what she needed for a comfortable life without worry. She purchased a house beside the park and put aside a moderate income before donating the rest to the hospital where she still worked. Andrew, declared unfit to return to active service, worked for the war effort from home. The news came along soon after the newlyweds' honeymoon and was accompanied with great joy from all sides of the strange family. The result was a quiet celebratory tea at Annabel's cottage.

At some point in the evening, Annabel had spotted Genevieve enter what she referred to as Gray's room and slipped in behind her for comfort. The older woman placed a hand within the younger's, squeezing her fingers lightly.

"We have Gray's photo on our mantle too, next to Andrew's brother," Genevieve whispered. "Everyday something happens that I have to tell him about, but then I remember I can't. I still miss him so much."

Annabel tucked a stray lock of Jen's hair behind her ear and coaxed the young girl's head onto her shoulder. "So do I, sweetheart, every day."

Epilogue

England, 11th November 1918

At exactly eleven in the morning on the eleventh of November 1918, the long silenced church bells rang out across the countryside. The beautiful sound echoed down through the hills, filling everyone who heard them with elation.

The staff members of the manor high up on the hill gasped, running outside to get a better listen to the sweet music of victory. Cheering bounced off the countryside from everybody in town. Music from somewhere started playing whilst people were hugging and kissing each other unashamedly in their joy.

Annabel, in a state of shock, came out of her own humble home a few minutes later. Looking up at the hill, on top of which sat a gleaming white manor house, she sank down to her knees—too numb and empty to cry.

The entire world was celebrating the end of the bloodiest war in history—the Great War as it had become known—but Annabel felt no joy for it had resulted in the loss of everything she had held most dear. Her's was a sacrifice she had never consented to pay but was forced to endure regardless.

People cheered, oblivious or uncaring of the one woman's grief. Each person so wrapped up in the knowledge their loved

ones were now safe, that they could finally enjoy this long-await-
ed peace. They had all seen so many grief-stricken people already,
one more made no odds to them, so Annabel closed the door on
their merriment.

Troops arrived back in stages over the next few months, many
were injured and all were changed. They snuck back into society silently in stark contrast to their celebratory exit—drafted out
with cheers and song. Casualty lists were still being posted in the
paper every day. It was with a heavy heart that Annabel read the
name Charles H. Grimsby, killed on the bank of some French riv-
er exactly one week before the ghastly war had ended.

It was in the new year, as she sat wrapped in a thick woollen
shawl, a book entitled *The Collective War Poems and Sketches of Gray
Brogan* resting on her lap, she noticed a soldier walking up the
path. Her heart leapt thinking for an absurd moment her son had
come home. Remembering, she eased herself up into a standing
position and walked to the door.

Stepping out into the cool, fresh air, she saw Daniel.

His limp was more prominent than when she had last seen
him. His whole body lurched to the side with every step. Despite
the darkness that haunted his eyes, he smiled when he caught
sight of Annabel standing in the doorway. It was a weary smile,
full of relief. After a lifetime of suffering, he'd finally made it
home.

He reached up and removed his cap. His blond hair was peppered with grey. Annabel crept up to him as if in a trance, her
eyes locked on his. Stretching out her hand, she brushed her fingers lightly over his cheek as if testing to see if he was real. She
had imagined his face so many times over the past two and a half
years as she'd sat alone in the cottage. She closed her eyes to take

in the moment, feeling some small part of her heart stir into being once more. A single tear escaped Daniel's hazel eyes. Annabel leant forward and kissed it away, the salt clinging to her lips as her own tears began to fall. As they cried, they clung to each other tightly, both afraid to let go in case they should disappear forever.

Annabel and Daniel were mere shells of their former selves, having experienced so much suffering in the short time they had been on Earth. Their youth would never return, and their wounds would never heal, but they had known love like no other. Even in their darkest hours, they could always count on that.

Their love couldn't change the world. Their love couldn't save the people that had meant so much to them. This wasn't a fairy tale. However, after all the pain, they finally had each other.

In the end, that's all that mattered.

Acknowledgements

I couldn't put my preferred dedication at the front, through fear of ruining the ending, but I would like to dedicate this story to all the unknown heroes of the First World War, who took their own lives. There has never been an official statistic for those who lost their lives to suicide, they were always recorded 'Killed in Action' to spare their family, but they were no less brave than any other veteran. Their pain was just too much to bear.

The Great War saw a turning point in the way we perceive and deal with PTSD—or shell shock as it was known then. For some, this revolution was too late. Living in the fortunate generation we find ourselves in, I feel it is our sole duty on this planet to remember those brave heroes. With our modern understanding of mental illness, we should look upon those men not with anger but with pity. These men weren't born soldiers. They had been farmers, students, brothers, and fathers. Still, they had been prepared to lay down their lives for a cause they believed to be worth something, only to be confronted with a war far bigger than they had imagined.

It is for their sake we must not forget.

About the Author

REBECCA M. GIBSON has been captivated by personal accounts of the First World War for years. Having been inspired by letters and poems from this era, *Rubies Fall* was born. Wilfred Owen is her all-time favourite writer, could you tell? Rebecca currently lives and works in Cornwall, UK.

Find our more at www.rebeccamgibson.com